YE GODS!

The goddess sat on a throne. To her right and her left, half a dozen ladies of honor danced along, each shaking a sistrum and intoning a modified Coptic chant.

Egyptian gods and goddesses, meticulously costumed, hawked their wares as they wormed through the thickening crowd:

"Masque programs for the temple show! Get the story on real papie-ree-us! With picture writing in heer-ey-ah glyphics . . ."

By E. Hoffmann Price
Published by Ballantine Books:

OPERATION ISIS

E. Hoffmann Price

A Del Rey Book

BALLANTINE BOOKS ● NEW YORK

A Del Rey Book
Published by Ballantine Books

Library of Congress Catalog Card Number: 86-91376

ISBN 0-345-33805-7

Printed in Canada

First Edition: January 1987

Cover Art by David B. Mattingly

IN MEMORY OF WANDA AND 1932,
WHEN SHE SAID,
"Instead of hunting another job,
dream up stories for the magazines.
I'll do the typing and we'll make it."
And so we did.

Chapter 1

THE SPACEPORT OF Maritania, the only city of the Martian Mining, Manufacturing & Agricultural Project, was in the easternmost of the ever-expanding complex of interlocking domes that retained the synthetic atmosphere of the developed region and the water vapor exhaled by its lakes and meadows. Beyond the spaceport and well into the level area bulldozed in the midst of the red desert's wilderness of jagged outcroppings, the *Garuda Bird* towered above her landing struts. A kilometer-long enclosed escalator led from the vast waiting room and was connected by airlock to the cruiser's boarding port.

Freshly refitted, her gleaming molybdenum alloy shell not yet pitted by micrometeorites, the old *Garuda Bird* had been modernized for the tourist trade. She would be packed with homeward bound Terrestrials. Now that Mars was "in" as a vacation spot, every trendy North American was pushing his or her Kredit Kard to its limit. In one respect, however, these differed from the other trained seals. They were in home territory.

For the past decade or so the Martian colony had been internationally, albeit grudgingly, recognized as belonging to and being ruled by the Limited Democracy of North America, successor to the short-lived Parliamentary Imperium of North America. Whatever doubts had lingered in minds other than that of Roderick David Garvin, war hero, war criminal, exile, and eventually

1

Governor-General of Mars, were settled when his defense system made it a one-way trip for the invading Fourth World Flotilla, which set out to impose liberation and utopia on the rich imperialism that someone else had laboriously financed and developed.

In addition to the goddamn tourists, as the Maritanian population termed them, there were the military and civil service personnel setting out on leaves of absence. Destination: Paris; purpose: rest, recuperation, and cultural evolution, a pompous way of saying "drinking, whoring around, and getting away from Mars, that ruptured hemorrhoid of the Solar System." The fact of the matter was that although Maritania offered plenty of such evolution, the cultural impact was greater away from home.

In one of the odd little nooks that were a by-product of making use of every square centimeter of floor space in a complex of spherical curves of dome and girder, there was a couple emotionally as well as bodily apart from the crowd. Two uniformed security men gestured with lead-loaded batons to keep souvenir and refreshment peddlers from invading the alcove. Back to that isolated couple: At first glance, one would dismiss the man as another sandy-haired nondescript whose features, though not badly matched, had been assembled from the spare parts bin. He wore English tailored tweeds that had not been pressed since leaving the Maritanian haberdasher. For several minutes he had been listening to his companion without ever a gesture or interruption. He was oblivious of his surroundings. The acre of milling travelers, the blaring of the P.A. system, and the vast red desert beyond the transparent plastic walls were dreary old stuff. The woman with him had his undivided attention.

Any graduate girlwatcher standing within half a dozen meters would have said, "No goddamn wonder!"

Her long-legged slender figure, with an understatement of curves that paradoxically enhanced the subtle sensuousness of body, suggested Shanghai, except that the peach blossom brocade skirt was not slit up to or beyond the knee. Furthermore, the dark eyes were not *quite* Chinese, nor were the cheekbones sufficiently prominent to give more than a piquant accent.

The woman's nose lacked the nostril flare of so many eastern Asiatics; it was longer and with a hint of the aquiline.

Finally, the dainty feet and elegant ankles declared that she was a thoroughbred.

Without further appraisal, the hypothetical girl-watcher would decide, "Uighur Turki, and the type that the Son of Heaven gratefully accepted when he and one of the kings of Turkistan declared peace after a gentlemanly war: friendly exchange of gifts, which left those distinguished young ladies delighted and wondering what their home folk got that was one-half as precious as what the Emperor of China was receiving."

Wrong diagnosis but not loutish ignorance. The nondescript man wearing tweeds, had he been so inclined, would have explained, "Not that it's any of your frigging business, but Azadeh is my Number Two Wife. Aboriginal Martian. One of a prehistoric starfaring race. Their space cruisers are what won the battle of Kashgar. Quarter of a million years old and way ahead of our Johnny-come-lately science.

"Sure, they'll tell you that *that* is pure distilled horse turd! Scientists are a jealous pack, and I don't deny that the legends and myths are a contradictory confusion. So the Great American Slob calls them Gooks and feels witty."

Confucius might have tagged Azadeh "Superior Person." Chuang Tzu would have retorted, "Simply superior in herself. And I beg of you, Venerable Kung Fu Tzu, do not remind me that I often declare that all is relative."

It boiled down to something like this: Azadeh was as incapable of looking up to this one as she was unable to look down on that one. It was clear that as a partner she would be difficult, and as a subordinate fatally impossible. Whether friend, lover, or husband, her opposite number had to be her equal in substance and self-assurance.

This suggested that Azadeh's companion was not so commonplace. And, indeed, when at last he spoke, she did not interrupt. Though he paused for breath, or to ponder, or to look far beyond her as if gazing into time rather than space, she did not cut in with something totally unrelated to what he had been saying or, in the manner of the North American female, lash out with a rebuttal indicating that she had neither heard nor understood a word of what he had been saying.

Finally, she pointed to a spot outside the alcove and spoke. "You and Flora were standing over there. And when Dad came to pay his respects, it was pure sleight of hand the way you gave him your palmed note. Speaking our language, he told you he would be standing near me, with his back to the *Saturnienne*. That conspicuous Gook pattern on his jacket would be a marker, and when you were on the bridge, you could pick me from the crowd for a good-bye look."

They'd spoken those lines many a time since their reunion in 2086, and especially since two of his wives had taken their leave. But that was the way of goodbyes, of the minutes before takeoff: rehashing trivia and choking on the unspoken meaningful. Such as the radiogram from France in which Flora had announced the birth of their son.

It was the afterthought line that he had never forgotten and which he was sure that Azadeh recalled: FELIX, NOT FELICE. I'VE CAUGHT UP WITH YOUR AZADEH AT LAST.

The man sighed. "My life is a long road, with leavetakings for milestones. Too bad we can't take this trip together."

Fond whimsy. Futile words. Neither was taking a vacation from the other. When it had become a fixed custom for him to sit at his telescope watching Earthrise, no matter what hour of the Martian night that might take place, Azadeh had known that it was time to tell him that she was as homesick as he. And this was convincing. He knew well how, like the Americans of North America, the Gooks had accepted too many of the worst features of an alien culture and had been unable to assimilate sufficient of its better phases.

So Azadeh would go back to the unspoiled asteroid, and he would head for Terra, where he would meet Felix and the boy's mother, lovely Flora, the enchantress who loathed Martian life. And furlough would include a survey of North America and the exchange of reminiscences with the aging Warlords.

That neither had included mention of that radiogram in their leave-taking prelude made it clear that each was aware of the pressures that could and might make his journey a one-way trip and a permanent vacation.

During the six years in which she had believed herself to be a space widow, Flora's TV show, the *Sudzo Detergent* program, had made her wealthy, the darling of two and a half or three and a half continents. And but for her husband's return, she would have married the man who became Imperator of North America. Dangerous bait, that fascinating Flora, the Number One Wife.

But watching Earthrise demanded a remedy, and being a superior person, Azadeh did not wait for the answer. She gave it. However she hoped to be right, she was not afraid to be wrong.

She began to appreciate the feelings of those North Americans who, sent into a grim war, had been forbidden to fight and win. Outwitting both enemy-loving government and the enemy, they had destroyed both.

Tough going for an army.

And it wouldn't be much easier for one female Gook.

The hands of the clock had not been lagging. Two Simianoid security men in black uniform approached. Halting with military precision, each clicked lead-loaded baton to cap visor.

"Governor and Madame," one began. "We hope you have not been annoyed. There was a disturbance." He made a sweeping gesture. "Purely minor, but it took us away for a minute or two."

"No problem, Higgins. No one tried to move in on us."

"Governor, we hope you have a nice furlough."

"Thank you, Higgins. Thank you, Edgewood."

"And my thanks, too," Azadeh added.

The P.A. system announced that only passengers were allowed in the passage leading to the boarding port. Azadeh went with Roderick David Garvin, Space Admiral and Governor-General of Mars, a far from imposing fellow when not wearing full-dress uniform, side arms, orders, and decorations—unless he had that 11.2-millimeter handgun at his hip and the man he faced needed killing.

The tailor had worked on the tweed jacket until the shoulder-holstered gun did not warp the garment's drape. Having cut his teeth on a gun barrel and having learned at an early age that self-defense is the first law of nature, Garvin knew that in a dangerous era, only a fool goes abroad unarmed.

At the boarding exit they wormed out of the crowd and snuggled against the jamb.

"When do you think you'll be heading for the Asteroid?" he asked inanely, falling back on typical leave-taking talk.

"Not until after you phone and I know you won't be back till you've had your fill of old times and old friends, and they're bubbling out of your ears," Azadeh answered.

A final squeeze, a fanny pat, and, "See you when I get back."

Garvin was going Earth and Sunward some 65 million kilometers. Azadeh, headed in more or less the opposite direction, her course depending upon the position with respect to Mars of that only known inhabited asteroid, would have an outbound voyage of 113,750,000 kilometers—provided, of course, that bureaucrats had not yet managed to repeal Bode's law.

And according to the Warlords, Garvin cogitated as he looked astern to see the entirety of the Martian green area, the conniving sons of bitches are working on that.

Comparing the cultivated expanse with the remainder of the ruddy disc, he wondered whether his son would live long enough to see the complex of domes removed.

The consortium of scientists was working on an isotope of nitrogen, using solar or volcanic energy—or both—to produce the heavy form of the gas that made up eighty percent of Earth's atmosphere and which, with its greater atomic weight, would not readily escape as had the original Martian atmosphere.

Meanwhile, biologists might team up with the physicists and dream up an even heavier inert gas, one that would blanket the planet. When this stage was reached, the low escape velocity of Mars would be offset.

"All green against red," he mused. "Bit gaudy, but so is that painted desert in Arizona."

And now that he was on his way, a thought that he had skillfully kept buried surfaced: Loathing Mars and space may not be hereditary, but you can bet Flora's made a career of downgrading both. With a sigh, he grimaced. "Goddammit, a man can't be everywhere!"

Ignoring the licensed Kruise Konkubines who added so much to spacing, Garvin settled down to estimating roughly how many thermal installations would be needed to synthesize atmosphere in volume sufficient to make a significant accumulation.

And before he landed at the Paris airport, he had quit damning himself for not having pressured Flora to send Felix for a look at Mars. According to her letters and judging from the photos she had sent, the young devil did have a cussed and adventurous streak, and there might still be a chance.

Chapter 2

AMONG THE NORTH American survivors of the battle that routed Kuropatkin's Army of Liberation were two notables, each still listed as unaccounted for. One was Lani, Imperatrix of the short-lived North American Democratic Empire: When her imperial consort, mortally wounded, had told her to hide out until the American-born lovers of the foreign enemy were exterminated, she had done so.

The other survivor was the Honorable Neville Ingerman, Minister of Defense, whose forged order had set in motion a troop movement that had almost given victory to the invaders. But for the arrival of an airborne Canadian division, treachery would have succeeded. Despite the price—100,000 pazors in gold—put on his head by the Warlords of the Provisional Government, Ingerman had loyal friends who had gotten him out of North America and to an island of the Lesser Antilles.

The tiny paradise of Sainte Véronique had never been surveyed; it was little more than a menace to navigation. Except for a girdle of alluvial plain, the island was a jungle-clad, steep volcanic structure. Until the War of Liberation, in which not a shot had been fired, it had gone unheeded and unknown except, of course, to the Coalition of Nations.

Once liberated, Sainte Véronique was welcomed as a member of the Marxist-dominated Coalition. The new nation had one vote, as did North America, which was outvoted by a majority of banana republics and the cannibal kingdoms of Africa.

Seeing themselves outvoted, the Warlords, once they had liquidated the Liberals, quit financing the Coalition, thus pushing that organization to the verge of bankruptcy.

The capitol of this new nation was built of coquina, using coral from a neighboring nonvolcanic island. Komissar Igor Petrovakovitch, Life President of the Republic, was also architect and engineer. He began with Modern Vauban, then tunneled from the fortress-capitol to bombproofs in the base of the long-extinct volcano. Skillfully camouflaged antennae near the crater rim fed their input to a communications system that was versatile out of all proportion to the nation it served.

Except for the white Liberators, the population of Sainte Véronique were the descendants of black Haitian refugees from French tyranny. These people raised sugarcane from which they distilled rum. Their tobacco crop was cured through fermentation, to produce something like the perique of Louisiana's St. James Parish, used in many of the costlier pipe mixtures. The Haitian blacks spoke a patois of three centuries past, which no one but another refugee or a philological specialist would recognize as French.

Approximately two percent of the white population of Sainte Véronique sat in the lounge of the residential wing of what was at once capital, capitol, barracks, and factory. The others were at work in the technical wing. The lean tired one whose once wavy blond hair was now thinnish and white was Neville Ingerman. Things had reached a neat balance: The Warlords still had their hundred thousand pazors in gold, and Ingerman still had his head. He was gainfully employed as Technical Adviser on North America.

Ingerman's opposite number, Prime Minister and President of Sainte Véronique, was Comrade Komissar Petrovakovitch, a survivor of the battle General Kuropatkin had almost won. As he had been only a lieutenant on that fatal day, the komissar's black hair was still copious and lustrous. His tropical tan indicated good health. He had none of Ingerman's sallowness. With a square face, and a head shaped like a casaba melon, the blocky komissar, an uncrowned king, was well cast for his role.

"Don't try to give these islanders socialistic indoctrination," Ingerman was saying. "They know all about it from way back. Sure, there are a hundred of us, more or less, and we have our daily parade under arms, when the colors are lowered. The French had all that, but the natives massacred them one day."

The komissar tried to speak, but he was cut short. "Comrade Igor, I do not give a good goddamn what the book says. Or what the Marxist saints preach. We have a good thing here, and when something is working, do not fool around fixing it."

The komissar's dark eyes blackened, but since there were no auditors, he did not balk at the self-evident truth. "You have been a most helpful guest, Comrade Nee-ville. I concede your point." He grinned good-humoredly. "Neither do I, not in private, make a religion of consistency. But your muttering and mumbling about the missing Imperatrix has become an obsession!"

"Comrade Komissar, you are right! It is my obsession, in the same measure as your passion for indoctrinating these blacks. And it will be that way to the day of my death."

Igor nodded and gave him a fraternal pat on the shoulder. "While you were in office, you faced so many TV cameras that you had to send Comrade Offendorf to liquidate the Imperatrix. He was loyal to the death!"

"Goddammit, yes!" Ingerman's voice cracked. He gulped. "I sent him to that death."

"How many thousands went to their deaths when General Kuropatkin made the mistake of not suspecting that Alexander's Canadian friends were on the way? To make an omelet, one has to break eggs!"

"That's different. That was war. This was personal, a thing I cooked up and sold him. How that woman killed two men, stripped the corpses, dragged the bodies to the rimrock, and pushed them over the edge is still beyond me!"

Ingerman paused. "It must have been that son of a bitch Garvin!" he said, fiercely. "He wasn't acting out of social conscience. It was not even the warped conscience of Imperialism. It was pure hatred of everything we stand for. He vaporized our tank division at the battle of Kashgar and fused kilometer after kilometer of the Silk Road. And told the press that such instant destruction was the ultimate of humanitarianism, that not a man of that armored division had time to feel the atomization! A goddamn monster, do you understand?"

The komissar sighed. "Comarade Nee-ville, it would be more to the point if we learned what those freakish battle cruisers he led had. Imagine what we could do if only we knew!"

"You and your goddamn dialectical materialism! I'll get his hide if it takes till Judgment Day!"

"I appreciate and respect your zeal," the komissar cut in. He had to humor a slightly kinked but extremely valuable helper. "Garvin and his broad-tailed girl, one of Lani's close friends, helped her. Listen, Comrade! Garvin is by no means your age, but he is getting along. You've so often told me that the American mass is never interested in merit. That if Lani were young and beautiful, she would have their instant devotion! The Veiled Imperatrix, the so-called onetime glamour girl, is broad-tailed, waddling, sagging, and no longer the heroic siren who was with Alexander when he died and upset your grand work with his banzai charge."

"Wait till I show you what came in. Just got it from decoding."

The komissar jerked upright and snatched the paper from the hand that had it half drawn from a jacket pocket. He read:

Garvin proceeding France-ward. Signed, Diane.

"Who the devil is Diane?" he asked.

"Diane is a comrade working in the Basses Pyrénées section of our enterprise. She started in that deluxe whorehouse on Boulevard Rempart Lachepaillet. Never having a pimp, she saved enough to buy the two-story building pointing toward number forty-three, rue des Faures. Yes, this is Bayonne I'm speaking of, and the narrow ancient streets meet at crazy angles, flatiron shaped, hence I said 'pointing.' Between her attractiveness and her cutting rates she drew her customers from the parlor house to her apartment above the *épicérie* she operated during grocery store hours. Next she rented the store to an unattractive wench whose only charms were coffee, spices, bread, canned goods, and delicatessen stuff. For the past couple of years she has been live-in housekeeper for Flora Garvin and Rod Garvin's son, Felix."

The komissar's eyes went wide open. "You mean, the Governor-General of Mars?"

"That is the son of a bitch! Yes. And he is going to see his Number One Wife and meet the son he has never seen. Our comrades in the Basses Pyrénées have been watching her." He gave a wry grimace. "About the only way we can get around Maritania's security department."

"Mmmm ... a good many operators have disappeared," the komissar admitted. "And those who have returned come back with misinformation that's caused us a lot of trouble."

"You begin to see that I have more than an obsession?"

"A governor-general who did not ignore every principle of justice, legal procedure, human rights, and democracy would be a great benefit to the cause. You have a plan?"

"I have."

"How long have you known all this?"

"Ever since it started."

"And you're just now telling me!"

"Is it proper to assail the President of Sainte Véronique, a nation, with every scrap of gossip?"

To answer the rhetorical question, the komissar gulped fifty cubic centimeters of sugarcane vodka.

Ingerman reached for a hefty snort of dark, Haitian-style rum. "I thought you'd see it my way. *Masravia*!"

"And your health!" the komissar said without even wincing at Ingerman's inevitable mispronunciation. "Now tell me, Comrade Nee-ville, what all this amounts to."

"Details are not yet available. But we can be sure that Garvin will see his friends, the Warlords, and he'll visit Nameless Island to see Madame Broadtail, the late Dr. Brandon's girl. Count on them to see the Imperatrix wherever she is hiding."

Comrade Igor frowned. "Quite a few years ago, her death, with the publicity you and Harry Offendorf planned, would have been a triumph. You two would have been Red heroes. But now you should take no such risks. She's not a glamour figure."

"Quite right. But wherever she is, he would go privately, secretly. Without the publicity of a formal visit. Whatever her reasons for not having found a safe spot in Maritania, Garvin will humor her notions. Out of respect to Alexander and to her. You see, he'll be concerned about her security, and so he's likely to neglect his own. Concerned and careless."

"Very good," the komissar agreed. "But your work here with me is more important. You've told me that you are running out of time. So is Garvin. I cannot have you jeopardize your very real value to carry on with this personal vendetta. While he is getting acquainted with the son he has never seen, an accident could be arranged. Run down by a drunken driver, for instance."

"Logical , a good idea! But not in France. The guillotine is working again. The French Sûreté is a nasty outfit, and French legal procedure is different. A criminal resisting arrest and foolishly killing or even wounding a peace officer is never brought to trial. He is beaten and kicked to death, trampled to pulp at the police station.

"Comrade Igor, you do not understand the American system. Martial law is effective: execution before arrest. But once civil law gets a criminal—with the jury, of course, favoring the underdog—the penalty for a bit of

income tax fraud is more severe than for rape with torture and murder for trimmings. Over the years, my appearance has changed. The old-time "WANTED" posters
make that clear. And I have learned some tricks meanwhile. North America is the place to get rid of Garvin.
And that will finish the security that is keeping us out of
Maritania."

The komissar sighed. "Our counterfeit document and
money department will miss you. And your message
analyses. But if you succeed, I'll see that you get our
highest decoration."

"The Red Star of Sainte Véronique? If I wanted one,
I'd make a counterfeit better than the genuine. It's that
damned Garvin I am after."

Chapter 3

A FEW YEARS before falsifying his age to do a hitch of military service sooner than the law required, Felix Garvin had given his mother a bit of general information in words that evoked memories of his father:

"I'll show these Basque sons of bitches that they do not have a monopoly on flipping a ball against a backstop with a long wicker scoop like a pelican's beak!"

The Low Garvinese was English he had learned from a Hollander who, toward the end of his world hiking, cycling, and busing tour, stopped in Bayonne to visit relatives. Having added to his fluent English in North America, he shared those improvements on the language of Her Gracious Majesty, the Queen.

The ball game to which Felix had referred was pelota. With so many Basques in Bayonne, each taking pride in his national sport, Felix had been oversensitive. Being in no position to tell those fellows, "My dad can beat your dad," he'd had to prove his worth by performance. The game had finally hooked him.

And now, in an indirect way, his father's impending visit teamed up with his feud with the pelota sharks to give him a logical escape from another of Mommie's million unreasonable whims. Flora wanted him to sweat out the current *Sudzo* program.

"Sweet weeping Jesus!" Felix protested. "I do not have her shape, but I couldn't sing much worse than her best!"

"And that is exactly why I want you to tape the whole show. Right after that lousy imitation of my act, there is going to be a historic number. A playback of my very first *Sudzo* show."

Felix guessed that Flora wanted to tape the show to add long-ago memories to the sentimental richness of the family reunion. There was also another answer: Flora, as filmed a quarter of a century past, was expertly made up for facing the lights. She had the shape and the sparkle: nothing to do but transpose TV color to home lighting. What Flora did not know about makeup could be engraved on a pinhead, using a jackknife.

Felix had a very special date with Diane, the live-in housekeeper who was on vacation with pay until after the Governor-General quit Bayonne to head for North America. Before breaking out in a cold sweat, he got the answer from the hereditary built-in computer: "I've been working out for qualifying for a pelota match, my ass is dragging, and I couldn't stay awake for that show to start. But I'll help you connect the recorder."

"I can do that myself! I really wanted you to see some family history."

Felix retired to his quarters, the top floor of what had been carriage house and, later, garage and chauffeur's apartment, until women and children could cope with things automotive. A head taller than the Old Man, he resembled him in temperament and facial expression; two years of military service had given him an appearance of maturity somewhat beyond his age. However, there was a difference: Instead of the Governor-General's trick of leaving people wondering whether bawdy laughter or cold ferocity would take command, the son was never as explicit in either direction. His veneer of urbanity and the suggestion of "presence" must have been his mother's contribution from the Helflins, as exemplified by Flora's fifth cousin, the late Imperator.

Diane supervised the domestic help, managed the ménage, and could be considered the feminine equivalent of the Chinese "Number One Boy." Except to another woman, Diane looked a dozen years younger than she actually was, and in any event she was a long day's march from the barmaids near the barracks and the two or three whores who served a platoon or a company of recruits. She had class.

When the coast was clear, Diane, wearing nothing but woman under her dark robe, would edge into the young master's apartment, slip out of that garment, and into bed.

"For a good-nighter. We'll both sleep better," she had said the first time. "No lights. *Jamais!* Madame your mother might wonder, and I'd be looking for another spot."

He learned enough about Diane to develope fantasies and cravings and curiosities. What would she be like, dressed and with lights, and bit by bit, very deliberately, undressed, perhaps with his assistance. And then, pillow talk not whispered. And even waking up before dawn to fondle her before going home. Maybe not even going home for a few days or more ...

Felix left the walled villa by the tradesman's entrance. He walked briskly townward until, skirting St. Leon and the Parc des Sports, he came to the avenue that led to the Gate of Spain and into the walled city. Finding the pie-slice building facing 43 rue des Faures was no problem: Between pelota games at the sports park near the oak-shadowed spring of St. Leon, he had reconnoitered by daylight.

The ground-level *épicérie* was dark, as it should have been. Light leaked past the shades of the upper floor. The new duplicate key fitted smoothly, as Diane had assured him it would. Being sworn into the army had done much for Felix. Having a key to a woman's apartment was the thirty-third, though there really should be a thirty-fourth, degree in machismo.

Felix was not sure whether he ascended stairs or walked the most ethereal of air.

Out of deference to Diane's job and his mother's prissy notions, he would have to leave well before dawn. Naturally there would be a lot of talk about meeting the

father he had never seen. And then the door at the head
of the stairs confronted Felix.

Before he could fumble for the evasive bell button,
the bolt slid aside, a muted metallic whisper, the voice of
romance, of intrigue. The door opened on bewilderment
and total dismay. The pint-size, black-haired girl who
faced him—

Christ on a life raft!

The key had worked, but this was the wrong apartment.

The dainty package laughed softly, caught him with
both arms, and stood on tiptoe for a mouth-to-mouth
kiss.

"*Chéri*, don't look so blinking bewildered! *C'est moi!*"

Crepe de chine blouse gave hints of curves that,
though never before glimpsed, evoked tactile memories.

"Maybe it was the lighting. You just didn't look like
you at all!"

Taking his hand, Diane nudged him to the sofa, where
a floor lamp made an island of half brilliance; the remainder of the room was left in shadows accented by
glints of bronze, the twinkle of ceramics, the gilt of a
picture frame, and the glint of decanters and goblets on
the buffet.

"Your hairdo. And—" Felix was still embarrassed.
He must have gaped like the village idiot!

"It's more than the frivolous hairdo that a housekeeper simply does not wear!" Diane dipped into
shadows and produced a black dress and white blouse,
quite crisp, stiff, and impersonal,

"First time you've ever seen me wear anything but
this. Like the girl in the camera shop. And sensible
shoes. And makeup that simply is not makeup."

Diane flipped the horrible examples into the shadows
and stepped back a pace, giving him a good look at
dainty strap sandals, red reptile with high heels. These,
and the burnt orange brocade skirt of exactly the right
length, amazed him—he had never suspected that this or
any other woman could have such lovely legs and exquisite ankles.

"Of course I am someone else, and I love it! And you knew the difference between the dragon housekeeper, herding the staff around and browbeating tradespeople. Right now, you are not the young master and there is no one I address respectfully as 'madame'!"

By now, Felix was back to normal. Instead of being a juvenile moron, he had paid her a compliment. "You even smell different."

"Of course I do! Does a female major domo use perfume that competes with *madame la châtelaine*? Do sit down! You need a drink."

She poured Denis Mounier Fine Champagne cognac into medium-size warmed snifter goblets. Inhaling the fragrance of cognac, with occasional birdlike nips of the liqueur, has in spirit something in common with the stately Japanese tea ceremony; although there is nothing ritualistic in the enjoyment of good brandy, there is communion between drinkers and drink.

After pouring the cognac, she had seated herself in a chair facing Felix. Each regarded the other: This was so different from the "good-nighters" to which they had become accustomed. That they had taken so long to sip so little made it clear that each loved fine brandy and knew that the other did. And through cognac communion, they knew that moment after moment brandy was becoming less and less important.

Diane's deeply drawn breath and her leaning back and stretching from the waist rounded the crepe de chine blouse in curves akin to those of the glasses that were contoured like magnolia buds about to ripen into blossom. Exhaling, she twisted a little to set her glass on the kidney-shaped end table with its red marble top and saw-pierced brass guard rim.

The long moment ended when, instead of by legerdemain, it was dexterity of ankle and toes that got her feet free of red reptile and high heels. Suppleness of body made it beautiful when, with leg cocked over knee, she busied herself taking a reef in hosiery that he knew must be silk. When it gathered about the ankle, Felix was sure there were no such snags or runners as he would have started. When he had his chance to undress Diane in fact as he had so often in fancy, he would know how. That would be next time.

Having her between the sheets and by light borrowed from the adjoining room was luxury, but most of all was pillow talk, and not in whispers.

And time to refill the snifters.

Freedom from furtiveness! What the barracks boasters imagined they knew about women was becoming ever more pathetic.

In view of the Governor-General's history, there were questions; answering these and keeping the glasses replenished made it a marvelously busy evening for Felix.

". . . is he actually going to retire?"

And another fragment, between additions of another thirty cubic centimeters of Grande Fine: ". . . he'll be going to North America to see wartime comrades before it is too late?"

Like her guest, Diane was finding it a crowded evening.

Felix would ponder, frown thoughtfully, and come up with answers indicating that he had considered both sides of every question. His earnestness, his thoroughness, impressed Diane until, bit by bit, she realized that instead of clarifying anything, Felix ended by spreading a smoke screen of ambiguity. And since the dream girl had never met the Old Man, it was too soon for her to wonder whether thoroughness was in fact hereditary secretiveness, spontaneous and instinctive.

Felix did not know that Roderick David Garvin's fixed opinion—one of a great many, that is—was to the effect that "Women, especially wives, excepting of course Azadeh, make it their life's work to ask the god-double-damnedest questions."

Although Felix thus far had had no wives and only one mother, wherefore his generalizations were scarcely based on experience, the Garvin Doctrine was taking—had already taken—form.

"Now that your sister has completed her higher education, do you suppose that madame your mother would still find North America as revolting as Mars?"

For the first time, Felix had a forthright answer. "Honey, I am no mind reader. You might ask madame the Old Lady."

But to eliminate purely personal bias, he added that she should consult a good astrologer.

A medium dollop of Grande Fine went into each goblet. And Felix finally began to cogitate: *Diane is a girl-watcher's dream, a real* pièce de resistance ... *With the Old Man always having women on the brain, this Mademoiselle Hot Panites might get the idea of becoming the First Lady of Mars.*

Grande Fine Champagne grade of cognac is perhaps the most civilized, the most gracious of the many spirits that man has distilled. Accordingly, it is also one of the most insidious. Although a persistent clod can guzzle himself puking drunk, he or she who knows how attains the earlier stages of apotheosis, then restful sleep, and, eventually, happy resurrection.

When the clock of Cathedrale Ste. Marie trolled three, Diane was nearing nirvana. At the half hour, she sighed and stretched luxuriously. Although her words were French, they would have conveyed her meaning if she had addressed Felix in Old High Etruscan or Gujarati. *"Chéri, I have had it. And you have had your share."*

Instead of telling her that the evening was still young, he countered, "Of cognac or of you?"

"You devil! I'd love to have you stay for late breakfast, but not until Monsieur the Governor-General and Madame la Châtelaine are honeymooning, and she is too busy persuading him to stay in France and forgets to watch your hours."

Her voice was more convincing even than her logic.

"Might be a good idea, having a taxi meet me at the *épicérie* door. That way nobody would suspect I was leaving you."

He would be mistaken for a customer leaving the back door of the deluxe whorehouse that fronted on Boulevard Rempart de Lachepaillet. She was so pleased by his finesse that she did not follow his clear logic.

Diane sat up, swayed a little, fumbled, and found the robe that had gotten itself bemuddled with sheet, pillow, and evening paper. Abandoning her struggle with the garment, she gestured.

"In the living room alcove. That desk."

"I saw the phone."

"I meant the directory." Diane smiled drowsily, contentedly. She murmured something that might have been, "*A bientôt!*"

He drew the sheet and blanket to her chin.

Ever since early childhood, Felix had heard of those fabulous women who could drink a platoon of armor under the table. Clearly, this was not one of those wonder girls.

Steady as an adjutant on parade, the young master found desk and phone. He did not find the directory, which was obscured by several paperback books that Diane had not gotten around to having fitted with custom hardcovers, as she probably intended. They were classics.

Being sure that he'd find no taxi service phone numbers in Flaubert's *Tentation de St. Antoine*, nor in Bourget's *La psychologie de l'amour moderne*, nor the worn and stained *Guide fratique de Lyon*, he poked about in pigeonholes and shelf stacks of the desk's upper structure. The center drawer yielded nothing. Finally, starting over from a different angle, he got a glimpse of a color photo, used as if for a book marker, ten by fifteen centimeters, professional work, critically sharp, not the typical murky blurred blob. What had baited his curiosity was the space officer's uniform with kilometers of gold braid, hectares of medals, decorations, and orders, and epaulettes the size of wastebaskets.

That the man portrayed was Roderick David Garvin made it very much the son's business. That Flora had a much larger print in which the domes of Mars showed in the background was standard stuff. What piqued Felix was that Flora's copy, considerably larger, did not include the very good-looking old lady, an aristocrat wearing a formal gown with bodice of sequins all aglitter with highlights that danced as she breathed.

The Admiral's probably enjoying a standing ovation, and that two-teated brunette is proud of the old devil, he thought. *Must be Azadeh—my honorary stepmother, or my halfway aunt?*

With her makeup just right, Flora was more spectacular than Azadeh, and this left Felix wondering why Mommie had cropped an oversize blowup of that scene. Thanks to the enchantment built into every drop of cognac, the answer came to him: Though his mother was Number One Wife, she was not the First Lady of Mars.

But this particular picture was hardly unusual: There were Garvin fans all over the globe, and other groups who loved to hang Garvin in effigy and often did so.

Maybe, Felix surmised, *Diane just got this picture and hasn't had time to frame it. Or she's waiting to have him autograph it.* He frowned, then shook his head. *That's off the beam, too. Odd as balls on a bay mare! If she'd been a fan, she'd have asked all kinds of really damn fool questions.*

Then he found the phone directory and finally figured that he could be halfway home before anyone answered a phone, assuming that someone was on duty. At this hour there was little chance of an unpleasant encounter. It was too late for hopheads and trouble-hunting drunks. By now they had either gotten their fix or been knocked off in the attempt. Anyway, he had learned a promising kung fu trick. If the other fellow survived, as he probably would, he would not know his own name for the next two or three days.

Taking off his shoes, he tiptoed to the stairs.

Chapter 4

ARRIVING IN PARIS, Garvin went to the North American embassy to take care of some confidential paperwork. While waiting for the official mill to grind out papers to accord with his new identity—Pierre d'Artois of Buffalo, New York—he phoned Flora.

"I don't know how long this processing is going to take," he told his Number One Wife. "There's more than just a passport and identification accessories for the village police. I've got to get a wad of French currency and a permit to take as much of it away with me as I please."

"Sounds more and more cloak and sword, beginning with your radiogram from the Lunar Depot, of all places!"

"Before I forget it, be sure your housekeeper and staff are on vacation with pay."

"I took care of that when you radioed. But how about this new identity?"

"No problem. The Governor-General is delayed at the Lunar Depot. Pierre d'Artois is your distant cousin. He is likely to be checking out before Garvin arrives. Pierre is taking the Madrid Express with a stopover in Bayonne and then heading on into Spain—what are you laughing about?"

"I was thinking that if the embassy is bugged and someone is recording all this, he'll be caught in no time."

"How come?"

"He'll be perched in a high tree, screaming like an eagle!"

"Anyway, you didn't lose time putting the menials on furlough."

"Pierre! *Mon dieu*! I have nothing to wear. With household help, one is a slave round the clock. Honeymoon spirit and a wardrobe down to zero!"

"Whatever you've bought or made, throw it away or give it to the poor!"

"Are you crazy?"

"No, you are, darling. The stuff will be out of style before you get a chance to put any of it on."

Garvin was not going to fly to Bayonne. This first look at his native world was going to be from the surface. When the Sud Express, strictly deluxe and with only first-class coaches, pulled out of Gare d'Orsai, the brand new Pierre d'Artois felt like a high school punk on his way to pick up his first date.

Bordeaux, where Gallienus, Emperor of Rome, had built an amphitheater that was recently restored to look good as new, and the Landes—"Nothing but goddamn pine forest!"—he dismissed in favor of a magnificent prospect: Meeting the son he had never seen was a fine start, with Flora, a peak in any man's life, included as an extra dividend. She personified his history, from a cross between space tramp and freighter in Sinkiang to the man who had made Maritania a Terrestrial suburb. In all these things Flora had played a part, sharing the beginnings, and now she was about to sit with him and look back at it all. Each had spent a lot of time wondering whether the tempestuous marriage had been one of those major mistakes, despite the best of intentions on each side.

The answer was now quite clear: All that counted was the much good they had shared. And, furthermore, the letdowns and dark spots were part of the package, and so, a sharing.

His happy vision was interrupted at Dax, still lumber and turpentine country. There he learned that someone or something had fouled up in Paris.

"Monsieur, *c'est vrai! Vous avez raison*! Yes, this is the train deluxe. But she makes, what you call it, the bypass. She does not go to Bayonne. From here she goes to Pau, to Puyoo!"

"Gangway! Shove Pau and Puyoo, I'm getting off!"

"Monsieur, the refund—"

"Shove that, too! I've got a date in Bayonne."

Now that his luggage was sitting on the platform, the deluxe train resumed its way to Pau and other stations. Garvin's phrase book French, blended with profane Americanese cursing and swearing, diluted with *Instant Uighur Turki* and *Arabic While You Fly*, confused the stationmaster.

A cab driver picked up when Garvin and the stationmaster paused for a fresh start. "The train you thought you were boarding will not be stopping in Dax."

The stationmaster added, "The ticket is not for the Madrid Express. *Alors*, I cannot flag the train when it comes through."

"Death and damnation! Do I sit in this asshole of a village till the next train?"

Stationmaster and taxi man cogitated. "Monsieur," the latter said. "There is no problem. Let me explain."

The Good Samaritan was distressed when the belated traveler was not interested in sleeping with the very nice girl who worked at the bathhouse of the hot spring. There was further dismay when Garvin made clear that he was not interested in a room at the Hotel des Thermes, with or without a girl. When he explained that he had a date with a girl in Bayonne, the natives realized that he was entirely sane.

Having failed as pimp or hotel runner, the taxi man was happy when Garvin snapped at the first bid for the thirty-mile drive to Bayonne. But first, he had to eat.

Garvin phoned Flora to say that he was in Dax and might be a bit late. "Just leave the front door lights on—the driver might have problems. Well, I looked at a map, I'll see he doesn't get lost."

Then they ran out of *essence* and had to walk to a filling station.

There was time-out for a tire change.

Following the Adour downstream was confusing.

There were ambiguous road forks, especially deceptive by night. A number of times the driver, once he got a few kilometers beyond the corporate limits of Dax, took the wrong one and followed it to a dead end at some logging installation.

Garvin finally relaxed and found it amusing.

Reminiscence kept him company. When Lani and I started to shack up in Khatmandu, it took a split second of computer foulup to get us started on what was programmed as a one-way trip to Mars. Lucky they didn't fire up the computer in Dax or that girl and I would be spending the next six years in the mud bath at Hotel des Thermes . . . but you cannot beat the game . . . there was no computer that got me and Lani back to Terra just in time to keep Flora from becoming Imperatrix instead of Lani.

The events following Alexander's death in battle left Garvin conducting a silent, solo debate: Should Flora and Lani have cursed fate and Garvin, or given thanks?

North America revisited might give an answer.

Far too many hours after departing Dax they came to the confluence of the Adour and the Nive, and the St. Esprit Bridge, beyond which the spires of Ste. Marie's cathedral reached into moonlight. Triumphantly, the cabby pointed.

"*Voila*! Bayonne! Now what is it that one does?"

Having studied his *Guide to Southern France*, English edition, while waiting for the wrong train to leave Gare d'Orsai, Garvin gave the answer: "You don't have to wait for daylight to find the Lycée de Marracq. Cross both bridges, turn right and follow the river to Allées Paulmy to the Lycée, and from there it's easy. She'll have the lights on."

Although he arrived at four-nineteen in the morning instead of about five in the afternoon, Happy Hour began at once. He need feel no qualms about disturbing Felix, Flora assured him. "He has his own quarters, topside of the garage."

She had wasted no time when phone calls briefed her: The one from Paris started major shopping, and the one from Dax gave her time for last-minute frills of drink and delicacies. Starting with canned pheasant from the quaint, costly little shop on rue Pont Neuf, with Pommery Brut from her cellar, she later added a list terminating in cherry tomatoes stuffed with caviar, tropical palm hearts lined with Brie cheese, and quail eggs in piquante sauce. Before it was quite too late for messenger delivery service, she called for smoked albacore and aquavit, which would soon be chilled in the deep freeze. For good measure, there was a bottle of sherry that Monsieur Chevigny recommended: an unusually stern and manly Palo Cortado.

To relieve the tensions that built up during pauses devoted to clock-watching, there were changes of cosmetics. Flora was as fluttery as the time when, just qualified as a teenager, she had tried and failed to seduce her fifth cousin, Alexander Heflin, only to get even with him a couple of years later by marrying Garvin.

With Garvin's arrival, spontaneous detonation was forestalled, and the honeymoon began. Despite gropings, shattered glass, and spilling a goblet of Pommery Brut laced with Peychaud bitters and Armagnac, Garvin finally had his chance for a few coherent words.

"I'm your cousin, Pierre d'Artois from somewhere in New York, on my way to somewhere else, because I do not want to draw a flock of media vultures. They'd include too many enemies from the Third and the Fourth Worlds, and I have a few surviving in North America, too. There would be no real problem in my home territory if I had to liquidate a few, but in France it would cause complications and the very kind of publicity I am shying away from."

"Wait till I get my thermometer, darling."

"Thermometer?"

"To take your temperature. Shying from publicity, you know."

"Coming from the Sudzo Detergent Queen, that's got me worried."

There was a detour discussion of hot flashes and the special hormones he had brought, an improvement on the kind that might have accounted for Felix on that all too long ago farewell honeymoon.

"Now that that is settled," he said finally, "I'll get at this silly beard. The minute I landed at Lunar Depot, I made for a space platform to hide out until the start I got on a tourist flight would give it a chance to look convincing in a photograph.

"This is not cloak and sword," he summed up. "All I want is a quiet furlough. A chance to get acquainted with our son. To see Dennis Kerwin, Number One Warlord, semiretired but carrying on. Not many of the old-timers left, and there are a few new ones I want to see some more. Better liaison."

Flora's apotheosis dimmed, and for an instant she was mortal again. This lasted only for an instant, yet long enough for Garvin to brace himself against a question. Although no question ensued, he was sure that he would learn that Flora had plans. Garvin changed the subject abruptly.

"Speaking of sons, what with all the hoopla, questions, and doorbells, and car door slammings—you mean he slept through all that or is he just too tactful to break in on a honeymoon?"

"When you phoned from Paris, I told you I'd already given housekeeper and staff vacation with pay, to have a family reunion without big ears auditing complicated Garvin family gossip."

"Smart girl, always thinking of everything. But what's that got to do with that young son of . . . uh, ours?"

"You just stopped short of calling Felix a son of a bitch."

"In his mother's presence, that would have been tactless."

"Lot of the time I couldn't think of better words! Whoever said that raising a son was a tough job, she spoke gospel."

"Until her favorite daughter gets knocked up higher than a kite!"

Flora sighed, and looked far back into time. "You and I thought we were marrying to keep me from being an unwed mother, and it was a false alarm."

Garvin chuckled. "Life's funny! Lot of my mistakes turned out better than when I was right. The Holy Family would rather have had you give birth to a bastard than have me in the family."

"Well, yes, until you and Alexander got to know each other."

Garvin got back to their son. "So Felix is sleeping late."

"I told you that he moved into the chauffeur's living quarters in what used to be the stable and carriage house. And he could have heard all the noise." She braced herself resolutely. "The fact is, if he is not in bed with my jewel of a housekeeper, he is sound asleep after a busy night at her home."

"Mmmm ... Felix romancing. She—"

"Diane Allzaneau," Flora prompted.

"She must be young, beautiful, and a hot dish, or you'd not have gotten her out of the house well before I arrived."

"Oh, you bastard!"

"Something I have never called Felix."

"That's about the only thing you can't rightly call him. But wait till you two get acquainted!"

This was getting sticky. They were old marrieds again. Having moved out and away from Mars so that her natural daughter, whom he had adopted, could get the schooling and cultural advantages of France, Garvin felt under attack by Flora's voice and attitude.

"Fun's fun, dream girl. Brief me?"

"It was military service. He committed every known kind of perjury to get in before he reached the legal age. Told me that if I dared squawk, he would head for Morocco, hitchhiking outbound or homebound, if he ever wanted to return. He'd set out with that stinker of a young Dutchman, Droste. That's how Felix learned Americanese. Low Garvinese."

"Things are getting scrambled," Garvin objected.

"Linguistics, a young Hollander who has been in north Africa and North America, and so Felix is sleeping with Diane Allzaneau."

"You've never seen her or you'd be imitating him."

"This is getting confused," Garvin suggested reasonably.

"I arranged it so he'd not be wallowing with the sluts that the soldiers play around with. You're not supposed to know about it, and neither am I. If he ever suspected, he'd get stubborn and find some seaport floozie, but as long as he thinks he is putting something over, he'll keep Diane busy."

Flora was on the verge of tears. "Oh, that awful Army language, it's worse than yours." And now Flora was in tears. "When I got more than broad references to those barmaids, those cantina girls, I suggested that there were really nice girls in Bayonne, if you looked for them." Sobs choked her.

"Darling." He patted her shoulder. "He'll snap out—"

His effort was wasted. Flora's voice rose hysterically. "And what that young whelp said about women told me something about his lowlife experiences. So I figured if he started with Diane, his taste might improve and he might amount to something someday. Instead of becoming an outright whoremonger."

"Honey, that was perfect strategy." Already Garvin was sensing disaster: a honeymoon devoted to improving his son's tastes in and attitudes about women. He glanced at his watch. "Christ, look at the time! What do we get for breakfast? Corn beef hash, eggs once over, lightly, toast and jelly?"

Flora brightened. "Serve you right if that's what I fixed! I'm all set for crab meat custard, and crepes suzette, and..."

Garvin was convinced that Part Two of the Felix problem was all processed and ready to swamp him.

Chapter 5

SHORTLY AFTER THE cathedral clock bonged the fifth melodious note, Flora paused at the door of her son's quarters. Instead of knocking, she balanced on one foot and gave the panel a flat-footed kick—she needed both hands to hold a tray of snacks. Garvin Senior stood by with a basket of of bottles, glassware, mixers, and accessories. She had warned Felix by intercom that the Old Man would be over for cocktails. She got this answer:

"Aw, hell!" he'd replied. "I ought to be going over to the big house to—"

"To pay respects to your father," she cut in. "Always the formal, continental gentlemen."

With Old World savoir faire, Felix accepted his mother's restrained reproof. "I knew you two would be sitting up until all hours, and I didn't want to break into your sleep."

"With you two men of iron roaring like lions and getting drunker than hoot owls, how would I ever catch up on sleep?" Now she said, "Don't stand there gaping! Please take this tray."

Felix did so. The Old Man crossed the threshold and plopped the basket on what would be the study table when and if his son ever resumed school. Flora's departure left two strangers confronting each other.

Tightly spaced seconds followed the latch click of Flora's departure.

This was a new situation for Garvin. When he had met Azadeh's son, his firstborn, the boy had been six years old and, since his grandfather's death, head of the house. This was never in doubt, however his mother ruled him with an iron hand. Self-assured from birth, Toghrul Bek had accepted the newcomer as a foreigner to be accepted because his mother did so. Facing Felix, however, was dismayingly different.

This fellow, a bit over two meters tall, regarded Garvin with self-assurance of an utterly different flavor: a critical appraisal, as if about to break into song, "I Am the King of Siam, I am!" All in good will and without a trace of condescension. Purely good fellowship. Not a suggestion of a skipper's "*Welcome aboard!*" Nevertheless—"

The Old Man thrust out his hand. "Long time, no see!"

Felix took the hand, grinned, and wagged his head. "I should be saying, I've heard so much about you that it's almost as if I'd known you all my life."

Urbane, whimsical, Felix was clearly enjoying the oddity of the situation. "There's a lot the books don't cover," he added.

"Such as?"

"Well, if someone called me Jesus, I'd have to say, balls, mister, I am only his second begotten son."

"For someone your size and grown-upness, the books do not fit. I am Rod, not God, so I won't be calling you Jesus. Not even if we get to Latin America."

Felix reached for a bottle, and they drank to realistic nomenclature.

The place was stark as a noncom's room in barracks. A pair of foils and another of épées were in a wall rack; *cestas*, the pelican-beak-shaped wicker claws of the pelota player, kept them company.

Garvin eyed the array. "I'd say that pelota is the mankillingest of the lot." In pelota, the ball was smacked about at pistol-bullet velocity.

"Those Basque players have made that plenty clear to me! You ever play?"

"Wars and the world trying to decide whether I was going to be an air freighter or a space tramp kept me too busy, but I did see some pelota in Cuba and Mexico."

Thanks to the North American tourist trade, Felix had found a bottle of real bourbon, Old Grandmother— Barrel Proof, at Chevigny's liquor store on rue Pont Neuf. The Senior Garvin, utilizing spare time in Paris, had located a bottle of Hudson's Bay Company Demerara Rum, 151 proof. This he dug from the basket of things appropriate to a meeting of Men of Iron.

Since *Old Grandmother* was only 114 proof, Felix took a jolt of Demerara, downing it without a hitch.

"With stuff this strong," he declared, "I usually take a chaser. How about a dollop of that Palo Cortado sherry?"

Things were getting off to a good start. Garvin noticed no frilly shower cap in the bathroom, no opulent mules, no sexy robe accidentally displayed to advertise that Felix was a man of the world. That the boy had not decided on *Old Grandmother* as a chaser for the 151 proof rum and, instead, joined the old man in getting acquainted with that stern and rugged sherry added to the Old Man's favorable impression of his son. He'd have to tell Flora that as far as language was concerned, she was lucky that her only son had learned Americanese from a hitchhiking Dutch teenager and not from the Marine Corps.

"Lots of young fellows hate military service. How come you went out of your way to get in?"

"I get points for not pleading exemption because my birth as an American citizen was recorded at the embassy. With my papers, I can leave the country with no fooling around and being told the last minute that the bureaucrat in charge of getting exit papers cleared got AIDS while vacationing in Sardinia and is taking a sick leave till he is cured."

"Sardine hunting in Sardinia is a hazardous sport," the Old Man agreed. He did not raise any points such as heading for Indonesia the next time the young Dutch traveler paused on an outbound voyage; he likewise skipped the idea that after so much female supervision, any lad worth half an inflated pazor per pound would look for an escape hatch. For any boy more than ten or a dozen years old, his mother ceases being his best friend and becomes his most destructive enemy.

Since thought moves with nearly the velocity of light, only a second elapsed before Garvin added, "We cleaned house after the last war, but I'm still wondering if we'll ever be liberated from our bureaucracy."

There was a long pause. "How long are you going to be in town?" Felix asked abruptly.

"That depends on when the *Semiramis* shoves off for Savannah."

"Spaceman, and not flying?"

Garvin reached for the bottle of Old Grandmother and poured for each of them. "There is all the glamour crap about capers such as the time your mother, hating space, flew all the way to Maritania to wish me bon voyage on what the fat boys had arranged to be for a one-way cruise. But I did circle Saturn, and homebound, as skipper, I performed the first wedding ceremony in space. Married my technical adviser, Admiral Courtney, to Lani, who became a princess after he died and then Empress of North America.

"I discovered, by pure blundering luck, an inhabited asteroid."

Felix poured the Palo Cortado chaser and not the Demerara rum, as Garvin had been expecting. "Madame my mother told me about that till it bubbled out of my ears."

"I was afraid of that! Well, aside from such high spots, there is nothing drearier than spacing through millions of kilometers of nothing and nowhere. I am here to review my acquaintance with E-A-R-T-H, Earth, till I get good and fed up with it and remember the unfinished business on Mars."

"So it depends on the *Semiramis*?"

"It's a goddamn long swim, and I'm not the athlete I used to be." He raised his hand to check the forthcoming protest. "That was a sort of short answer. It's this way.

She is a tramp waiting for cargo till she's down to her Plimsoll line. But if that's done before I am ready to leave town, the skipper will hold the boat."

"I be good-goddamned! This Governor-General business seems to give you a lot of pull!"

"Wait a minute! I am incognito, remember? I'm only a shirttail relative."

Felix looked puzzled. After a moment of groping, he asked how a remote kinsman could make such an arrangement.

"Just a matter of paying demurrage," Garvin explained, "the way you do when you keep a freight car longer than the free time for loading or unloading. With my salary, allowances, legitimate perks and presents, and nowhere to go to spend it—simple, isn't it?"

Felix cogitated for a moment. "Excepting that pipsqueak of an Asteroid, there is nothing in the Solar System that needs governing once you get beyond Mars."

"You mean opportunities for advancement are limited?"

Felix was too serious about it to realize that the Old Man was needling him as if he were a collegian with a brand new degree whining about the slow promotion when he found out that he could not start as one of the board of directors.

"Rod, the whole business sounds like tough shit! First you were a war hero, but before you got your Parliamentary Medal of Honor, they discovered you were a war criminal, and if the Imperator hadn't flung in every bit of political pull he had, along with some he borrowed, you'd have been shot. Death sentence was commuted to exile, until things got so hot in the next war that to settle the risk of the Imperatrix being taken prisoner of war and held as a hostage, you came back on parole and convoyed her to Mars, where she'd be safe, and you became Governor-General, sort of her errand boy."

"Sounds like making it the hard way?"

"Well, it's this war criminal business."

"From the original democratic republic, and all through the Democratic Parliamentary Republic, and well into the Empire of North America, ever since the middle nineteen-forties, swarms of American-born Liberals voted Marxist-loving politicos into office. There was a president who thought that Marxism was the greatest discovery of the century, which from then on made the nation a sort of vassal of the Slivovitz group of nations. Then there was a politico who discovered Americans holding high spots in the state department who were Slivovitz agents. He hounded them into the open, nailed their hides on the barn door, and eventually became president of the Republic. Then the Liberals caught him off base, and he ended by resigning to avoid being impeached."

"Where do you come in?"

"During the Hitler war—since you've not gone to American schools, you may have had history, which was abolished as irrelevant in our country—we blasted German and Japanese cities, incinerated civilians by the thousands, and everyone applauded, but when we used napalm and similar grim stuff in southeast Asia, there was hell from coast to coast, student riots, all that muck. You must never be rough with a Marxist and never win a battle when you face Marxist troops. State religion, unofficial but working.

"I vaporized a division of Marxist armor invading Sinkiang. Hence the pyramids!"

Felix paused to digest that before going on to the next mystery. "The Empress you convoyed to Mars turned out to be a look-alike, and everyone still wonders what happened to the genuine one."

"There is a mishmash of contradictory details. Some of the facts are still top secret, or so we hope. This much is declassified, and I am allowed to tell you what lots of people already have heard.

"The Imitation Empress died, and I kept my promise to take her home and have her buried beside Alexander I, your mother's fifth cousin. She was a sincere woman, and I was a horse's arse, keeping that promise. There already had been leaks in security."

Felix leaned forward, all set, like a leopard about to

pounce. Before the feline snarl slipped from between
tightening lips, Garvin continued. "A Lunar Base patrol
signaled my cruiser to stand by for inspection."

"Whatja do?"

"My cruiser was one of the flotilla that killed a Marxist division of armor. She was disguised with sheet metal
that gave her a freighter silhouette."

"Then what?"

"The fool in command fired a warning shot across our
bow. I wagged my forefinger, and the officer on watch
cut loose with gunnery that had never been tested on
Terra. That illegal command to stand by got total destruction. Cruiser and crew left no debris in space. They
were vapor, waiting for a comet to join."

Felix exhaled a long-locked breath.

"The total disappearance of a patrol ship without a
general quarters call to Lunar Headquarters confirmed
the validity of the security leak," the Old Man said. "Son
of a bitch, a man can never win!"

"Dumb bastards learned that Garvin is poison."

"They always knew that, but they are dedicated."

The Old Man was doing nicely. The new problem was
to live up to the image developed over the years: the
skill, the cunning, the experience of twenty boys and a
third the energy of one. And then Garvin learned that he
was fatally vulnerable, that he had defenses he was not
able to use.

"You brought the Imitation Empress back home for
burial."

"Yes. Mission accomplished."

"And you didn't have time to detour to France and
see Mom and me."

However this had gnawed at Garvin, year after year,
this was the ultimate thrust. Facts at the time of happen-
ing had been Garvin's consolation. These, now history,
were old and toothless, as weary as he himself had become. Events could justify him. Explanations would be
futile.

Felix was on his feet. Glancing at his watch, he fixed
the Old Man with the eye of decision. "There is a get-to-

gether banquet in Biarritz. Pelota sharks and novices and professionals, and fans, and a tournament series. Mind telling Madame the Old Lady that I forgot to mention this appointment? Got to haul ass out, right now."

He extended his hand. "Maybe I'll lose out in the preliminaries and be back before you board the *Semiramis*."

It was an awkward but resolute dismissal. Garvin took the extended hand. "Tell your mother that on my way back to Maritania, I'll be stopping in Bayonne."

Chapter 6

GARVIN'S MEETING WITH Felix left him groping. Flora had not even grazed the subject with which that boy had nailed the Old Man, dead center. It was all too clear in retrospect how the Old Man's bypassing France after he had convoyed the pseudo-Imperatrix to her funeral had deeply wounded the youngster, leaving the almost grown man with an unhealed psychic injury. Flora apparently had taken an adult view and, after having digested rumors concerning the Imitation Empress, realized that Garvin's mission had not been as simple as surmise had made it. Furthermore, there had been circumstances sufficiently odd about the death of the retired Minister of Foreign Affairs, the Honorable Harry Offendorf, to indicate one of Garvin's off-the-record capers, which likely would have necessitated his immediate return to Maritania.

He decided not to mention the subject to Flora. The rule was: Don't fix it if it's working—and the honeymoon was. Having started with cocktails and dinner at four-nineteen in the morning, they breakfasted late. Parachuting to sea level occasionally, they eventually arrived at the conventional time for "Happy Hour." And while the chatelaine was busy with cosmetics and selecting a dress appropriate to her mood, Garvin prowled the shops of rue Pont Neuf. Some of his purchases went into the trunk of Flora's "darling" acacia yellow Guiletta Veloce. No woman has greater love than she who lets a

husband drive such a *gran turisimo* treasure. Others of
the goodies that Monsieur Chevigny sold were for delivery to the *Semiramis*, to be locked in the Garvin stateroom: a lot of cognac and several cases of Hungarian
Tokaija, not remotely akin to North American Tokay.

Two doors from Chevigny's on the river side was a
camera shop where Garvin bought a Swiss-made single
lens reflex Alfa, thirty-five millimeter, with a hand-fin-
ished optical system far superior to the best that German
or Japanese makers produced. He wondered at Flora's
sudden passion for photography, but instead of asking
questions such as why had she never bothered with pictures during their Martian years, he settled down to
scooping up the best.

Before he had finished studying the owner's manual
for a minicamera that cost about as much as a moder-
ately good compact car, Garvin learned that it was for
something they had totally overlooked. Before he could
ask where in Bayonne one could get a Chinese Pillow
Book, Flora explained: "We have not taken a honeymoon trip."

She shushed Garvin's quips about getting a sign
painter to put the French equivalent of "Just Married" on
the trunk and picking the his-and-hers shoes to hang on
the bumper. "We'll drive to Pau," Flora elaborated, "and
have someone take our pictures at the door of King
Henry IV palace. And then, in Lourdes, in front of the
Grotto, a picture."

"You going to be Bernadette Soubirous or the Holy
Mother?"

"You sacrilegious bastard! We'll face the camera."

"Mmm...turn our hind ends to the Grotto. Madame—"

"And it's not far," Flora continued, "looping about,
and homeward, to something you'd really love. Where
the first Armagnac brandy was distilled, in the thirteenth
century."

"Uh. That's near the town of Condom, in the Gers
Departement. That'd be educational. And then?"

"There's Domaine de la Mothe, where cognac brandy was first distilled in 1470. You'd love that, you old sot!"

"Starting with the unholy mother—then king, kondom, kognac. Grand honeymoon tour."

And it was, with a detour to Tarbes, the town founded by Tarbis, Queen of Ethiopia, who quit her realm when Moses would not marry her and, instead, herded the Children of Israel into the Promised Land.

Garvin was beginning to suspect that Flora was trying to sell him something, and at times it seemed that it would be very good indeed to leave space to the young and unwary and have Azadeh, and even Aljai, just for old time's sake, join him and Flora in this marvelous corner of France. His entire life, had it not been such a stern reality, would have been fantasy. For Azadeh and for Flora, at least, it must have been the same, in their feminine terms.

Retiring in France could be a pleasant opium dream, except that Azadeh, loathing North Americans, included all Terrestrians in her tabulation of the Damned and the Forgotten of the Goddess of Far Faring.

And here they were again, back in Bayonne; and here she was again, Flora shed of her seductive peignoir and glowing through one of the gowns she had herself designed. For many women, dresses do things. Flora was otherwise: She did things for the garments she designed. Whenever she flipped one over the foot of her bed, its magic was gone, for it no longer contained Flora.

Now they came to the balcony of their villa overlooking Lycée de Maracq, which had begun in the early 1700s as the home of an exiled Queen of Spain, and later, after having been gutted by fire, had been resurrected as a school where Felix might resume education. It was quite too early for dinner but never too late for the absinthe and Amer Picon wagon.

However much they had discussed their camera work and photos in general, there was not a word relating to the portrait of Garvin, a 15-by-28-centimeter news shot. Certainly it was not studio work. The girder structure supporting the domes was quite clear; besides, posing for formal likeness was never on his agenda.

What made the picture especially interesting was that the artwork that once had concealed the shoulder and upper arm of a woman now could be discerned, however faintly; it was enough to make one curious about her identity and why a larger photo had been cropped to exclude even a glimpse of her. The retouching dyes evidently had succumbed to Terrestrial air pollution. Garvin recalled the formal occasion: Only Azadeh, as First Lady of Mars, could have rated a seat beside him.

Clearly, this was no topic for honeymoon discussion. The photo was in Flora's bedroom, and her thoughts were her own business. It set Garvin to wondering whether his three wives had gotten along as harmoniously as he had fancied—and hoped.

Azadeh's son was half Garvin and half Gook.

Flora's son was half Garvin and half "Holy Family," which was hated or revered for the sake of Alexander the Imperator, who died in the battle that had routed the Socialist Liberators.

Long ago, a wisewoman had said to Garvin, "If your son turns out well, you have it made. Your daughter is another man's problem."

This was as true as history, which indicated clearly that many a war and many a campaign of assassination had been touched off by rival mothers, each maneuvering to advance her son.

The next Governor-General of Mars, whoever he might be, would control the present corps of selected scientists and the food Martian Eck & Ag would produce for an overpopulated world.

Old stuff, of course . . . and the cocktail moon was rising. Even Merlin, the Master Mage, had been charmed into giving a seductive enchantress the ultimate secret of power, the spell that not even he could resist.

Flora, the Enchantress, stretched luxuriously and picked from the silence what they had been saying of Pau and Lourdes and Armagnac Land, and cognac country. "You're in love with the town and the country for

kilometers around, the way I've been from the first sight
of it. Let's settle down and live for a little while before
we die. Plenty of room for Azadeh, or if she'd rather,
you could get her a spot not too far and not too close."

Instead of saying, "I told you twice, goddamn it, no!"
Garvin went Merlin-stupid and replied, "Terrestrians are
as revolting to her as Mars is to you."

He knew well that giving a reason against anything is
half acceptance or, at best, inviting long debate with de-
feat built in. He ignored the fact that he had survived
only because he fired from the hip and explained later.

Trusting her incantation, Flora continued as if she had
not heard what he had said. "You and Admiral Courtney
made Maritania a suburb of Megapolis Alpha. Taps
sounded for him on the Asteroid, and he was there when
you circled Saturn, and he mocked those who had put
you both into the Rehab Facility for psychological reno-
vation, as they called it. He needed a rest—and think of
the years that have given you no rest. You gave your life
to the Parliamentary Republic and to Alexander's Democratic Empire, and before Felix was even thought of, you
and Azadeh gave yourselves to the Warlords and their
Limited Democracy. Rod, we're all of us weary, and you
are so tired, you do not even realize how tired you are."

There was silence, and he sat as if listening to far-off
music.

Flora caught his hand. "Let's go to Biarritz and phone
Azadeh, and we'll give her a look at some of the big
blowups of our tour."

"We'll phone Azadeh," she repeated, "and then we'll
have dinner at Château Basque. It's not far from the
communication center for the fat boys who think they
have to keep in touch with Lunar stations and Maritania
and don't want to get too far from their fun and games."

And as the yellow Guiletta Veloce purred languidly
toward the sea and the Devil's Bridge, Flora murmured,
"If Azadeh moved in with us and found this part of Terra
pleasing, it would give our son, well, a chance to round
out the education Diane is giving him."

"Where does Azadeh come in? This gets a bit puzzling."

"When Felix sees you and me and Azadeh together, when you with all your fame and status could have your choice of all the young and beautiful of Terra, Mars, and the Asteroid, he'll begin to suspect that the opinion of women he learned during army service is—well, as silly as it is nasty."

"Sweet Jesus, woman! It does not take a committee of experts. Just life and the course of living—"

"Rod Garvin, if you had been a woman as long as I have, you'd know that Felix was speaking for ninety percent of the male population from ages ten to a hundred! With all his possibilities, you'd not want him to set out in life as a thoroughbred clod!"

Chapter 7

WHEN AZADEH FACED Garvin and Flora from the videophone screen, the women did most of the talking until he backed away from the transmission receptor to display the large color blowups, a few of which were thirty-four by forty-six centimeters, card mounted. At times he got in a few words, such as, "If you could only see this in 3-D, or better yet, the real thing."

Azadeh, never forgetting that she still was Number Two Wife, maintained animated attention, offered intelligent comment when it was in order, and all the while remained amiably passive until Flora had made all her points. All, that is, except the one she had used at the very last to make Garvin the trained seal. Either she had forgotten, or she saw no great use in mentioning that Felix would benefit. Finally there came the pause that Azadeh recognized as invitation to comment on the entirety. Her career of making Sudzo internationally famous had left her accustomed to acquiescence. Flora's business manager had never been able to make a meaningful comparison between Sudzo royalties and the payments made by manufacturers of duplicates of the panties laundered in the course of the show: Several contingents were quite evenly divided between pink, with forget-me-nots in an unforgettable area or blue with roses appropriately positioned.

"This leaves me quite off balance!" And Azadeh looked and sounded, for her, a bit fluttery, which left

46

Garvin groping and a shade off balance. He recalled phoning from the Asteroid to tell her that the riffraff crew of the *Saturnienne* had caused so much trouble for the natives that he was about to destroy the cruiser and all records, to protect the people of that cozy little planetoid against the treasure-hungry rabble that would follow if the *Saturnienne* and her crew ever returned to Terra. Far from telling him that she had given birth to their son, Toghrul Bek, Azadeh agreed that he was quite right in thus protecting her kinfolk, regardless of his and her personal loss.

And then Garvin sensed that for Azadeh this was nothing that required iron in the soul, such as had the time when Flora, convinced that she was in fact not a space widow, had gone to Mars to confront Azadeh with more than a bluff:

"You were working in communications when the *Saturnienne* radioed from the Asteroid that she had landed for minor repairs. Rod gave a glowing account of the planetoid's unusual density, which kept it from losing its atmosphere. And no more transmissions of the cruiser's logbook. And gaps in the talks you had with the natives. You had to translate when Rod's skimpy knowledge of the language failed.

"Then that tremendous flash that was reported by the Martian observatory as a nova. In the asteroid belt. And then the report was denied. They declared there never had been any such report. But I have some facts: The flash was a nuclear blast, and the spectrum indicated that the shell of the *Saturnienne* had been atomized.

"So there is a plan to cruise the asteroid belt and fire nuclear shells at high-density, high-albedo planetoids. A way to find the heavy ores, platinum-iridium, that make the extreme density. And your kinfolk will be destroyed. Along with members of the crew who weren't caught in the explosion.

"So you'd better tell us what you have been holding out when you censored the reports you translated into English."

Garvin recalled that long-ago pillow talk when, after

six years, he and Azadeh were reunited in Maritania. And he had never forgotten her words: "Better have them decently destroyed by nuclear bombing than be invaded by North Americans. Your people, many of them, say, 'Better red than dead.' We say 'Better dead than swamped by you barbarians.'"

No threat had made Azadeh waver.

But that sales talk?

"Now that you two are together again, and I can take off to see my cousins, and everyone's homesickness is cured..."

The words were not iron, nor was the music of her voice.

"...and when you two have had a comfortable fill of France and North America, and I've learned that I've been craving something that never existed..."

Garvin was scraping bottom: *Well, she's not fumbling it the way I did*...And that thought bounced to hit him between the eyes, as if he were a bumbling pelota player knocked out by his own ball: He had been hoping that Azadeh would pull him out of ensorcellment. *Move over, Merlin, make room for a fellow horse's arse....*

Azadeh paused for a moment of beatific glowing. "We'll decide whether to meet in Bayonne or in Maritania, Flora, darling, after each of us is fed up with what was craved so long. After my quickie wartime glimpse of Terra, a longer look might make me fall in love with the place and the people. So just let's keep in touch, and it was sweet of you to call me."

She cut the connection.

Simple as pouring bran out of a boot.

Genghis Khan became emperor of all mankind, but he could never have managed the twelve-girl whorehouse that made number thirty-four rue Lachepaillet, the finest street of Grande Bayonne, justly popular in song and story. And this thought started the sprouting of new wings for the Governor-General.

Garvin recalled that small-town girl who quit school at the sixth grade and within a couple of years became First Lady in charge of 124 female chocolate-dippers in a village candy factory. She retired forty years later, sane, sparkling, and in good health.

There are jobs that are not a man's work.

When they came to the darling little Guiletta Veloce, Flora handed him the keys. "Skip the Devil's Bridge and that restaurant. I've had it."

Whether this was letdown after victory or falling apart after staking all that she had, leaving her helpless in the hands of destiny, was an open question but one that needed no answer. There were times, Garvin thought, when the right woman was more helpful than a division of armor. Two such women, however, could at times complicate matters slightly.

Back at the villa, Flora remained sufficiently herself to slip into the ultimate of sleeping gowns, but that garment did not offset her weariness. It could not keep her awake.

Garvin was good as new. Azadeh had transferred something across a gap of some 65 million kilometers. He looked at his watch. He counted on his fingers. Then, after a bit of mental arithmetic, he made for the library, where he seated himself at the escritoire. Even allowing for the time difference between Bayonne and "The City That Nobody Wanted," the approaches to which Alexander I had defended to his death, it was a gruesome hour for a phone call.

Nevertheless, he put through a call to five-star General Dennis Kerwin, Emeritus Chairman of the Consortium of Warlords, the rulers of the Limited Democracy of North America. He was going to have a few things decided before the Flora-versus-Azadeh contest took total command.

Getting Kerwin out of bed before reveille would be good for the Warlord's soul, and it would be a first for Garvin.

"What the hell's on your feeble mind?" Kerwin grumbled. "Do you have to make it a night problem to tell me you are in Bayonne, shacking up with thirty three and one-third percent of your wives?"

"You're off base! She is fifty percent of my wives.

And I didn't have to do it this way, but she does talk in her sleep, and this way I'll not be interrupted. They have been debating whether I should retire in Maritania, where I can keep an eye on the Water and Air Synthesis Project—WASP, we call it—or retire in Bayonne."

"You, retire? Goddammit, Rod, I'm still semiactive and doing as much as three of you young punks on supposedly active duty!"

"General, if you ever had two wives simultaneously and they started wistful wailing—"

"All right, *all right*! What is all this crap?"

Garvin explained.

"So," Kerwin finally said. "Now you're reduced to only two wives and you're getting old and dependent! And to make it worse, you have a teenage son who uses a four-letter word when referring to women. Tell him to learn Arabic or Latin—also, that there is a three-letter word for it in French! Simpler is you just kick his goddamn prat till his nose bleeds, and then when you have got his attention—"

"When you get to the lecture on child psychology, give me a chance to tell you I am weary and worn out. I have not been sitting on my arse, swirling mint juleps and every so often telling an aide de camp, 'Archie, take the son of a bitch away and have him shot, and don't bother me with trivialities.'"

"Rod Garvin, I wish you had my job!"

"How about you taking my job and see how you like preparing Martian meadows to feed an overpopulated Earth that should have started mandatory and universal abortion four generations ago."

Garvin was glad but not amazed when Kerwin finally said, "I've got to have some rest before breakfast and golf with—oh, hell, I can't even think of his name, but he is important!"

"And I'm not waiting for either. I am hauling out before Flora wakes up and starts all over!"

"See me at my headquarters, and we'll negotiate a few details. Unless you go wild with perks and allowances, it's all yours, but there is one important proviso.

There is a special task that no one but you can accomplish. Do not mention names."

"I can just about guess what it is going to be."

"Make it and write your own ticket."

"One thing I'll need. Got a pencil handy?"

"Have got. Well, my memory is tricky."

"So is mine," Garvin said, and gave him a code number. "Get that to Barstow, in the Mad Scientist Section, Biological Department. Maritania. Top-secret it, ship immediately. If no cruiser is scheduled for departure within three days, get one going, an express run."

That did it.

"Over and out."

Garvin wrote a few lines for Flora:

"Darling, my life has been a series of leave-takings. My retirement is subject to my undertaking one task. Confidential but not hazardous. Should not require much over a year. *Don't* pressure Azadeh. Make no promises. You and I have had another one of our Nights of Truth. Everything has been so clear for so long that I could not see it. And this time there will be no reason for not stopping in Bayonne.

Old custom had prevailed: One suitcase awaited, packed for immediate departure with handgun and other basic necessities. Whatever else he might need he would do without or get from the ship's slop chest.

Garvin set out afoot. It was less than two kilometers to the city hall and the two rivers.

Bayonne remained an enchanted city, even though Flora's siren voice was not with him to make it so. Perhaps after a couple of years of WASP he would feel like retiring, until Azadeh loathed Bayonne or elsewhere. And she might love that which had been prized ever since the first Roman legion made its palisaded camp not far from the spring of St. Leon and Parc des Sports. Presently, crossing Pont de Mayou, he paused to salute the statue of Cardinal Lavigerie on the redoubt. Once on the right bank of the Adour, he made it downstream to the docks until he came to the *Semiramis*, berthed and perhaps waiting for him to pay up the demurrage she had been accumulating.

He was greeted at the gangplank by the man on watch. "Monsieur, a long and hefty young fellow who paid for transportation to Savannah is aboard. He says he is your son. If this is a fraud, we'll put him ashore."

Garvin then knew that his blundering methods paid off better than had Merlin's wisdom. He fished one of those multicolored, hectare-size Banque de France notes of impressive denomination from his wallet and folded the man's fingers about it. "Tell the skipper right away that I apologize for disturbing him at this gruesome hour. Tell him that if he shoves off as soon as reasonably possible, it would be as profitable to him as to me.

"While you are disturbing monsieur the skipper, let me talk to that young man immediately. If he is not who he claims to be, I'll boot him over the side myself.

"If anyone, such as a hysterical woman or the police, comes with inquiries, please assure them that neither Monsieur d'Artois nor his son is aboard. His mother does not know that he is taking this cruise with me. Before we go down the river, she may realize that he is not at home where he should be. Such might make her emotional, irresponsible."

"Monsieur d'Artois, remain tranquil."

"I am, but she often is not."

"That is understood. I, too, am married."

"And something else: Chevigny et Cie, on rue Pont Neuf, I ordered three cases of cognac and four of Istavan Palugyay Tokaija."

"The king of wines and the wine of kings! It is in your stateroom. To prevent accidental breakage, we did not put it in the hold."

Garvin went to his stateroom. Hungarian wines varied, but Tokaija ruled a kingdom all its own. Among the rarities that had blessed Garvin's shopping was at least one that Lani, the undercover Imperatrix of North America, might never have tasted.

Chapter 8

THERE ARE TIMES when the vast Pacific is a mis-named monster and the semivast Atlantic is congenial going; such was the latter as the Garvins, father and son, found it, after steaming southwest out of Lisbon, making for Funchal for another pickup and discharge of cargo. After four days of wallowing her way, all the while listing crazily to starboard, the *Semiramis* reached her destination.

"Funchal looks different from sea level," the Old Man remarked. "Never realized how steep the landscape is. All on edge, in fact."

After swooping up through three kilometers of sea-water, volcanic peaks rose another thirteen or fourteen hundred meters to flirt with wispy white clouds. Despite hot winds from Africa, patches of snow crowned the higher summits of black lava. Funchal, a crescent-shaped city, clambered up the slopes in terrace after terrace of white stuccoed buildings. Streets were so steep that many were impracticable for wheeled vehicles.

Felix handed the binoculars back to the Old Man. "I'll be a son of a *bitch*! Oxen pulling sleds up those crazy grades! Take a look!"

"Age of science hasn't skipped this island," Garvin Senior answered. "Radio masts and, I imagine, cables to Paris and to Plymouth, happily cabling away. Anglican church, over yonder." He brandished the glasses. "Brit-

53

ishers still like to winter here. And they still feel they
own the place. Used to run it."

"Uh . . . grabbed it after a war?"

"No war. They drank their way into power."

"Horse shit, Rod! Those tall ones you've been telling
me ever since we left Bayonne were fun, but this is going
too far."

"Goddammit, I meant what I said. For a century or so
they bought all the Madeira wine, which made the natives wealthy and made the British right, even when they
were wrong."

Later, when the *Semiramis* was made fast, Garvin
said, "Ever since you told me about looking for the
phone directory and finding that picture when Dream
Girl Diane went to dreamland, I have been cogitating a
lot."

"You mean, you and that good looking k-ku—uh,
woman in Maritania?"

"Son, you are improving. You didn't even refer to the
First Lady of Mars as a well-stacked broad. Anyway,
when you wondered how Diane got that old photo, I've
been asking myself *why* she wanted it. Your guess—"

"When I said she must have been a space fan, I
wasn't sure of what I was thinking. I'm still not."

"You have that devious duplicitous touch that has
made me so many nonfans. Just for a change, why not
share some of the thoughts you've been hoarding."

"Do they shoot spies in France or lop their heads
off?"

"Couple centuries ago, Mata Hari faced a firing
squad. And after the Hitler war, there was a lot of informal liquidation, pretty much the way we still take care of
spies in Maritania. How'd you get notions like that?"

"Questions she asked and things she did not ask."

"I ought to phone your mother," Garvin said abruptly.

"You telling her I'm aboard?"

"What I tell her depends on what she tells me. On the
face of things, Diane knew that Roderick David Garvin
was on the way from Mars. Time of arrival, indefinite.
Inspection tour of Lunar Installations.

"If Diane knew I was traveling as Pierre d'Artois, it would be awkward. If she thinks Pierre d'Artois, a distant cousin, dropped in to say hello and then moved on, while I had not yet arrived, that would change things.

"What I tell your mother depends on what she told Diane when the household staff got a furlough."

"You mean my being on this trip with you might kick up some trouble? Foul things up?"

"Could be. And again, could be a great advantage."

"For Christ's sweet sake, Rod, do you ever say yes or no outright and finally? I mean really settle a question, for keeps?"

Garvin pondered for a moment. "Well, yes, come to think of it, I did. This was when I was having a confidential talk with the undercover Empress of North America. The Honorable Harry Offendorf—high-ranking government Liberal and, of course, a Marxist sympathizer—had found her hideout. He had seen through her incognito and he intended to talk her back into public life for someone else to assassinate before she ever met her public. So I told Harry that for him to know her identity and hideout was embarrassing to her Imperial Highness and fatal to him."

"What happened then?"

"She and Madame Broadtail found her a new sanctuary. And someone found Harry Offendorf's bones in a ravine a thousand meters below the cabin he had barged into."

"Is that all of the story?"

"You like crisp and concise and definite statements, or questions? If you meet Madame Broadtail, she might tell you the story, with lots of words. She settled Harry's gun guard with one jab of a hypodermic. To protect a couple of helpless women, I had to finish Harry.

"Now that *that* is settled, let's get back to business. You get a tourist guide to find some good wineries. Buy up four or five cases of good stuff. Cama de Lobos and Sercial—some of each. By the time you are back, I will likely know what to tell you."

The first thing the Garvins learned once they were

ashore was that no one was answering the phone at
Flora's villa. The second was that the loggerhead turtle
soup was lousy, compared with what one could get in the
West Indies and New Orleans; and the third, that they
were lucky to get any turtle soup at all. More and more
loggerheads were being exported to Caribbean islands to
make mock green turtle soup for gourmet tourists who
didn't know the difference.

With lunch disposed of, Felix realized that getting experience in buying wine would be more profitable than
waiting for his mother to come back from shopping—or
whatever.

"She is probably pacing the poop deck, figuratively
speaking," Garvin suggested. "Building up blood pressure and cursing God, you and me. But apron strings
have to be cut, and talk does not work as well as scis-
sors. You run along and shop, and leave the suffering to
her and me."

With Felix on his way, the elder Garvin found a cool
spot to sit where both telephone and McKesson's very
dark stout were within a few meters of each other.

Finally Flora answered the phone. She was so distressed that she forgot to reproach him for tiptoeing
away and leaving a note. "I just know Felix eloped with
that bitch!" Her voice was a decibel and half an octave
short of hysteria. "Oh, I could skin her alive! And him,
too, that stinker!"

"Honey, you think of the damnedest darkest things."

"I phoned her and phoned and phoned, and no answer. Rod, what really happened when you two sat down
to get acquainted and comfortably drunk, and he walked
out to go to a pelota tournament that was totally imaginary? For one thing, I know he was fed up with your
high and mighty Governor-General arrogance. And he
was fed up with my trying to tone down his awful language. Rod, we're both to blame, and of course he'd run
away with that slut!"

"Did you report this to *la Service de Sûreté*?"

"I didn't dare! There was your incognito, and then

there would be a scandal, your son running away with a wench like that! And he did his military service before he was of age for it, so I don't know whether he's a minor or what."

"Who have you talked to?"

"With all your cloak and sword history, I didn't dare do anything but clam up and worry myself half crazy."

"Then keep it so, unless you want to be an instant widow."

"Where are you?"

"In Funchal."

"*Funchal*?"

"In the Madeira Islands."

"What on earth are you doing there?"

"Kicking about the lousy turtle soup."

"Oh, you *bastard*! Can't you ever be serious? Haven't you even a guess as to where Felix might be?"

"I haven't phoned the North American embassy yet. You're the first one I've called."

"And what's the embassy got to do with this mess?"

"The ambassador will ask the prefect of police or whoever runs the Sûreté's really big business. Find out if it's a crime for someone his age to elope to Spain, for instance, with an old bag her age. Whether you are still his legal guardian, or whether you are just the person who does his worrying for him and saves him the trouble."

Sounding so constructive, Garvin's guesswork checked the flood of questions as well as incipient hysteria. This gave Garvin a whack at playing his cards. "When did you get that long-haired etiquette book to teach Felix a few nice words when referring to women?"

"What's that got to do with where he is?"

"A great deal or nothing whatever. You can bet that the fact that you are my Number One Wife was not top secret for more than fifteen seconds after you moved to Bayonne. Every household employee, every visitor except the most casual local, would be checked by Sûreté

Générale or whoever watches out for governor-generals' wives."

"As if I were a criminal?"

"Oh, for Christ's sweet sake! No. To protect you against kidnapping, terrorism, extortion. In North America, for instance, you'd be snatched as a hostage to get the release of some Marxist bastard Denny Kerwin figures to rate a firing squad. Which is why I have them finished in Maritania without any hooraw."

This convinced Flora that her husband was not the imbecile North American tradition makes all male humans, once married.

Garvin got the embassy with little delay. "I do not want to talk to the First Secretary or whoever else keeps the nuisances from His Excellency. If he is in bed with some really fashionable lady, I'll call back. And tell him this—" Garvin recited a few code words and numbers. "I want to tell him a thing or two on security. I cannot sit on my tail indefinitely. If I am not here two hours from now, I'll be aboard the *Semiramis*, Malagasy registered."

Garvin stretched four McKesson's extra stout as if they were grand fine champagne. Before his hind teeth were afloat, the call back came through.

"Two days after the date you mentioned, Sûreté raided the upstairs apartment of the pie-shaped building facing number forty-three rue des Faures," His Excellency stated. "Judging from closets, dresser, bathroom cabinet, and other signs, she left without luggage. One operator states that she was seen with market basket and wearing a housedress, making for rue Pont Neuf. There was no photograph of you and the First Lady of Maritania. Sûreté made an amazingly detailed inventory of the contents of the apartment.

"The Mrs. Garvin of Bayonne has been under protective surveillance ever since your Martian Defense System made a Fourth World Invasion Flotilla a one-way cruise.

"What the bloody hell is your next move?"

"Your Excellency, soon as I know, I'll phone you.

Right now I have to tell my Number One Wife that I still do not know where our son is."

This was a true statement. Garvin had not the foggiest idea which of Madeira's many *bodegas* was overcharging Felix. But no matter: As long as the wine was good, all was well.

Chapter 9

DIANE ALLZANEAU, Flora Garvin's jewel of a housekeeper, had no trouble getting out of France one jump ahead of the Sûreté Générale. After her routine flight from Spain to the Dominican Republic, where she assembled a wardrobe, she set out from Santo Domingo for a bit of island-hopping until she came to one of the Caribbean spots large enough for an ICBM site and landing fields for troop and supply carriers. There she switched to a motor launch and made for Sainte Véronique: from minination to micronation.

A series of cosmetic and costume changes along the way had turned Diane into a peasant, a quadroon whose facial bone structure indicated an aristocratic ancestor. A billowing skirt, a field hand's indigo blouse, and flat-soled shoes combined to disguise the fact that the nation's visitor never had been one of the machete-swinging sugarcane cutters of any plantation, nor had her mother or her grandmother.

Four black stevedores, each balancing a suitcase on his head, booted dogs, chickens, or naked brats out of the way as they headed toward the fortress. The massive doors swung wide to admit Diane to the coquina heart of Sainte Véronique.

Two hours later, and after a change of dress and complexion, Diane sat with Neville Ingerman, whose treason had almost succeeded in giving victory to the Marxist Liberators. The idealistic renegade and Comrade Komis-

sar Igor Petrovakovitch were listening intently to their
visitor's summing up. Diane's being the first eyewitness
and active participant in what had happened in Bayonne
made her sufficiently important to be admitted to the
austere study of the President of the Democratic Republic of Sainte Véronique.

"... I'd been so accustomed to the local cops that
when madame started preparing for the Governor-General's arrival, I noticed it right away when strangers took
their place. The change warned me, and it gave me another advantage: The newcomers were not familiar with
my comings and goings. I had no trouble selling madame
the idea of giving me and the household staff a leave of
absence. Give the honeymooners total privacy. She
loved the idea and made it vacation with pay, and that
helped."

"In what respect?" the komissar asked.

"Instead of my going to bed with her son at the villa,
in what used to be the coachman's apartment, he'd come
to see me in my place, over the shop. That distracted
surveillance.

"Anyway, when there were new faces, I suspected
they were of the Sûreté."

"Just as any but the stone blind would suspect that it
was not a farm girl who came to my headquarters," the
Komissar cut in. "Flat shoes and makeup helped, but not
much."

Diane's mental response was, *Si les cons peuvent
commander une armée, ce cochon la serait général en
chef*! What she said was, "Comrade Komissar, four
porters were not designed as a disguise. I did my best to
show respect to the capital of a nation."

"So you got out of France instead of finding local
cover and remaining in observation?" the komissar
asked.

In theory, and in other circumstances, his comment
would have been valid. Diane devoted an instant to wondering whether he might not have read her mental estimate of him. "I got out," she retorted, "in the French
equivalent of what I wore when I arrived at your head-

quarters. A market basket, mind you. And all around, so frowzy that surveillance may have mistaken me for household help. And if they had recognized me, this was their chance to diddle with the locks, for a quick look next time. Naturally, I left the door unlocked, just in case they did make first moves for future entry.

"You understand, Comrade Komissar—create the illusion of hurry, with a quick return in mind?"

The komissar did not comment.

"As it turned out," Diane resumed, "I had more luck than sense. When I crossed the border at Hendaye and got to our nearest headquarters, I learned that if I had waited a few hours longer, I would now be in jail in Paris." She radiated charm. "Something, or someone, touched off—" She shrugged. "Who knows what? There seems to have been no need for further observation. My apartment had been raided, turned inside out. Madame Garvin told police, told newspaper people, told everyone that her son had eloped with me. Basses Pryénées department swarms with security officers of all sizes and grades."

"Where is the young man?"

Diane sighed and explained the arrangement Flora had made. "But when he came to my apartment for the night, instead of my slipping into his apartment for a good-nighter, all furtive and sneaking so his mother would not know, about all I learned was that the brat of a boy can speak more words and give less information than any politician playing both sides of the fence at once. Some three or four nights he would be away at a pelota tournament. Then madame went hysterically wild, and, too late, we learned he had left on the *Semiramis*, tramp steamer, Malagasy register, someday to discharge cargo in Savannah."

"And the boy told you nothing?"

"He told me a smooth mess that boiled down to zero."

Neville Ingerman finally got in a word. "Do you suppose that young devil turned you in?"

"I'd not put it past him."

Diane noted that this admission pleased the komissar. And in any event, she was not going to mention that she had had, in her apartment, a photograph of the Governor-General and the First Lady of Mars. Combining two ingredients as treacherous as Felix and grand fine champagne cognac had been an error.

"Comrade Neville," she said. "Is it not about time for you to make it clear to the komissar that you gave me a free hand in this project, carte blanche? Discretionary, is it not so? I am really here by your order, because my judgment told me that you would order thus."

Ingerman gave Petrovakovitch a long look. "Comrade Komissar, I think Diane has a point. When she radioed from Spain and told us that Garvin and his son had left on the *Semiramis* for Savannah, you agreed that my plan was sound."

"In general, yes, of course. But the details?"

"Such as?" Diane cut in. "Please clarify. We need every bit of understanding. There are many blind spots."

"You, first of all! With a slight change of complexion, high heels, and a different dress, you would have the image of the First Lady of Mars, with maybe a security guard to make it convincing. You speak English, but with a French flavor. What good can you do in North America?" The komissar smiled and wagged his head. "In some situations, being conspicuous is essential, or at least an advantage. This is not one of such."

"Monsieur le Commissaire," she retorted in French. "Comrade Neville and I are taking the risks. You, president of this nation, are not. We have only one chance, and if we succeed, our escape will be more a matter of luck than of good planning."

Not to be outdone by Diane's sarcasm, the komissar also switched to French. "Make it clear, if you please, how you, a foreigner, could help one who has the experience and viewpoint of a once prominent official high in the North American government."

Diane had come prepared. She dipped into her handbag and took out the photo that Felix had found so interesting. "This latest picture of the Governor-General and

First Lady of Mars, his Number Two Wife, was taken maybe twenty years ago. Unlike some officials, he avoided photographers whenever possible. It is said by the very few who knew him well that when he is not wearing his uniform, orders, and decorations, he is a commonplace fellow as far as appearance is concerned."

"It is not clear to this day," Ingerman put in, "how he killed Harry Offendorf and his armed escort, and without firing a shot. There was no disturbance heard at the retreat center."

"Comrade Nee-ville, we know he is dangerous game." His gesture and glance were equivalent to demanding, "So what is this glamour girl good for?"

Diane smiled. And she looked quite amused when Ingerman retorted, "He is a notorious fool for women."

"Comrade Nee-ville," the komissar reproved gently. "None of those women ever kept him from killing wiser men."

The ensuing pause gave Diane her chance: "Almost certainly, more than homesickness or a craving for visits with Terrestrian friends brings Garvin to North America. His previous trip to Terra was nicely timed. The two comrades who came to liquidate the Imperatrix, the real one, left their bones in a ravine, and the Imperatrix found a new refuge.

"Limited Democracy does not have the glamour that the return of Lani would have, as empress. So—"

"Please, we know all that! Do come to the point!"

"Garvin is twenty years older, and so is she. Makeup and good lighting would build her up. But the only way to find him before it is too late is to watch Nameless Island, which he would surely visit. That would identify the Garvin-today, and then, his son. Having seen a good deal of that young man, I'd recognize him and follow him until we find his father. You begin to see where I fit into this and no one else does?"

There was no rebuttal.

Chapter 10

THE SEMIRAMIS NO longer listed to starboard as she headed across the Atlantic at twelve knots. Cargo stowed or cargo discharged at Funchal had got her on an even keel. She had begun as a cattle boat and had done well until condemned as unfit for transporting animals; however, the SPCA lost when a war qualified her as a troop ship. Later, promoted to freighter, year after year, and despite thump and pound of bearings, she made Charleston, South Carolina.

"Floyd of London insured her," Garvin said to his son, "so you can bet most of her crew consists of criminals."

That left Felix gaping.

The Old Man explained as they walked toward the embarcadero. "If you are born to be hanged, you'll never drown." He halted abruptly. "That reminds me. Over yonder, you come to the battery. Cannon in the park. Whether Confederate or Union, I don't know, but there is a bronze plaque with an inspiring inscription."

"That historical crap!"

"Pipe down, Felix! It *is* inspiring. Pirates were getting to be a pest all along this coast several centuries ago. And the Caribbean was almost as dangerous as any large American city was in more recent times, before martial law discouraged crime."

"So what?"

"There was a drive to hunt and round up the pirates.

Like they used to have jackrabbit drives out in the Old West, all the settlers turning out, making a cordon, driving the critters into a dead-end gulley and clubbing them to death. Except this pirate drive was done with sailing ships. With no bleeding hearts, no psychiatrists, no shyster courts that loved criminals, Charleston's bag was twenty-six pirate captains. The whole lot was hanged one afternoon as the tide was ebbing. Perfectly timed. Last man quit kicking when the low water mark was clear, and that was where the double bakers' dozen was buried. That ended piracy on the high seas. Congressmen and, later, members of parliament learned safer ways to rob the public.

"When you are fully inspired by America when it was really American, keep bearing to the right till you get to the hotel. There's a good bar there, and I'll meet you soon as I get through phoning."

"That lard-ass ambassador again?"

"With all your bad guesses, you are your mother's son all over again! I am calling the lady who slapped the greatest scientist of the twenty-first century till he was nearly cross-eyed."

"What for? Trying to feel her up?"

Garvin sighed. "Makes sense, but wrong question. She had just demonstrated that she had an unusual mind and quick wit, so he said, 'Madame, next time I am in one of the big cities I am buying you a broadtail jacket. With your shape—' That was when Mona cut him short."

Felix frowned. "I don't get it."

"What Doc Brandon meant was a super deluxe fur from a karakul or broadtail sheep from Central Asia, and this country girl thought he was quipping about the way she was built.

"It is about time I briefed you. My phone talk with the ambassador, while we were in Funchal, left me feeling that your dream girl in Bayonne, the one who was supposed to teach you how to talk like a gentleman, is actually a Marxist spy put on the job to watch your mother and make such moves as I finally did make, except for details, of course. The Sûreté told the ambassador that special agents had raided her apartment. But she had left in a hurry. Maybe she realized you might have found that picture of me and the present First Lady of Mars while she—I mean your girl—was having grand fine champagne dreams, or it could have been the way you answered those questions that sounded odd to you."

"I sure fouled that up, and king-size!"

Garvin shook his head. "I'd say it was intuition plus professional experience. Could have been something you did not say or your disappearing instead of coming back for more. Well, Sûreté did not get the girl, but they did grab a microwave—not much power, but enough to reach across the border and into Spain.

"So I am going to talk to Madame Broadtail, also known as Mona Smith. She is the trustee of the Avery Jarvis Brandon Foundation. Nameless Island is about twenty kilometers off shore and maybe a hundred south of Savannah. If your ex-dream girl and people who seem to dislike me are planning to follow me around while I am executing a mission, you and I are going to head for Nameless Island as the first move in throwing them off the track.

"I'll have Mona send some of her Burmese and Malay forestry crew to Savannah, towing a raft of teak logs to the usual dock. You and I will slip aboard the towing tug and get to the island. Mona has a good communications system—Doc Brandon developed it during the war before the last one, for keeping in touch with your mother's fifth cousin, the Imperator who died leading a banzai charge.

"Lani, the Imperatrix, was supposed to go to Mars so the invading Liberators would not nab her as a hostage. She pretended to go with that scheme, but she sent me and a look-alike to fool Alexander, the public, and the enemy. She stayed here; she wore an Amazon uniform and looked so frowzy, no one ever suspected she was the Imperatrix. So she joined him at army headquarters, and when Alexander died, she found a hideout.

"Our government has always been riddled with high

officials who became Marxist stooges and sold the nation out to the enemy whenever there was a chance. One of them figured out where Lani was hiding and went to bait her into a one-way trip. Which it was—for them, not for her. And low-minded bastards sometimes suspect I killed the punk and the minister of something or other, when they found two male skeletons and identified them. No matter what I am actually here for, I'll be suspected of looking for Lani.

"Anyway, here is a chance to learn about teak-logging."

Felix looked disgusted. "Nothing but a bunch of goddamn lumberjacks!"

"Son, never mind the brass plaque and the twenty-six pirates. Just make for that bar and get into an optimistic mood. Show them your faked I.D. card, and they'll serve you all the liquor you can hold. Just don't get mixed up with too many strange women."

Felix brightened at the prospect of outwitting the uncouth and uncivilized customs of North America. In his native France he had seen too many five-year-olds trudging home with a loaf of real bread a meter long and a liter of *vin rouge* for the family supper.

Father and son parted, each on his own mission.

Chapter 11

ALTHOUGH COMRADE IGOR, boss of Sainte Véroni-que, objected to Neville Ingerman's quitting his job to undertake a personal vendetta, the komissar kept communications busy. He radioed Funchal and learned that the *Semiramis* had set out for Charleston, South Carolina. Using data from one of Ingerman's many departments, Comrade Igor estimated when she would reach her destination. Although Diane worked very well in the face of opposition, she felt better when he told her and Comrade Neville that his calculations had missed by only four hours and eighteen minutes.

Although Ingerman was quite sure that his and Diane's quarters were not bugged, their pillow talk was in French, which the komissar fumbled sadly whenever he tried to impersonate a citizen of the world.

"You mangle our language in a different way," Diane assured him. "He's become accustomed to the patois the black slaves learned three centuries ago. Like the Cajun exiles who came to Louisiana. A person speaking real French would suspect their talk of being Choctaw."

So, after noting the komissar's pride in his prediction, Ingerman said to Diane in French: "The old bastard loves to brag. And for all his downgrading of our ideas, my bet is that he is hooked."

Diane agreed. "If he really is not interested behind his grumbling, we'd better pretend we are discouraged and slacking off. Meanwhile, see what you can stir up. Such as commandeering that speedboat. To make sure we get to Savannah well ahead of that old tub. So we can make our arrangements. You've been away so long."

"I've kept in touch, sort of. Especially with the comrades in the Savannah area," he assured her. "*Chérie*, so often your logic gets under his skin. In spite of all his doctrine, he can't listen to a mere woman very long without finding fault in what she says—and, later, using the idea as his own thought. Just keep a nice balance."

Neither made any pretense of being in love with the other. Each was a realist in many respects.

Diane had not spent much time in Madame Pudding's elegant parlor house at thirty-four rue Lachepaillet in Bayonne; she had gotten an "ambulant" license and selected her clients instead of parading her goods and being selected. That, plus not supporting a pimp, had advanced Diane to *entrepreneuse*, an independent business woman.

Realism had carried her further: Diane's definition of "idealist," which included "intellectual," was a simpleton with a keen mind and the inability to see people and their world as they are, and so, one who is devoid of experience. Such a person imagines that he is the first of all mankind to sense that the world is less than perfect, and from there he moves on to the ultimate silliness of believing that he is the first of mankind's uncounted generations who has the answer.

In her slightly French-flavored Americanese, she summed up intellectuals, idealists, students, and too many of their teachers: "What you call it, ze congenital horse's ass. By birth. The indoctrination, it only assists nature."

And Marxism consisted of two strata. Diane had picked hers, and Neville Ingerman, a likable fellow, had his; each could help the other get a foothold on the upper terrace.

Although far from genius, Ingerman had done exceedingly well as a zealot and a traitor whose betraying an army had kicked back, after near success, and he was distinguishing himself as works manager of Sainte Véronique. Whatever komissar was sent to that tiny island to be lifetime president had only to compose anticapitalistic manifestos, stir up student riots, and attend conferences of the Coalition of Nations, where he would vote against North America and its few friends. Comrade Neville Ingerman, too zealous to stick to pure ideology, was a superb executive, as once he had been a Minister of War for the North American Empire. Under his supervision, the Department of Printing and Engraving was the most expert in the entire Marxist Imperium, producing counterfeit passports, seals, documents, and currency that only the most rigorous technology could expose as phony.

Several minor nations had gone bankrupt, defaulting on their loans that Free World bankers had begged them to accept. In due course, the legitimate governments of those non-Marxist nations would invite Marxist troops to restore order, and the fumblers whose technology was primitive and whose farmers produced far less than they had before the revolution would gain another vassal.

Ingerman was valuable.

Largely by tricks of semantics, Ingerman turned ideological gibberish, the sort of stuff that would earn a million as a cure for insomnia, into convincing slogans. Ingerman himself was no master of such language. He simply found and set to work those masters who could do what he knew was needed, and without ever offending any komissar on political education. Ingerman's talent approached genius: He saw the gullibility of others and remained unaware of his own. Quite simply, since he knew nothing of any of the crafts and arts that he supervised, he had only to pick subordinates who knew. He never told a subordinate how to do what was required. He simply stated what had to be done.

If the result fell short, the subordinate was fired. And replaced by another.

Thus far, he had not suspected that Diane saw through him.

"Comrade Komissar," Diane said. "If Comrade Nee-ville fell dead this minute, no one would miss him except you and me."

"Uh—huh—what?"

Before the komissar quit sputtering, Diane took the floor. "Madame Pudding," she declared, "weighed at least one hundred kilos. She was not as tall as she was broad. Rust-red hair; the face of a bull bitch; though there were two dainty features, the feet and ankles, which were arranged for number three shoes. Looks, shape, or voice, none could have gotten her a job in the cheapest house in town, between the two rivers, I mean, in Bayonne. Hustling the streets or playing the cafés, no. I do not suggest that she was a virgin, but I have wondered what hero, what compassionate one, deflowered her.

"A fact never needs an explanation. The fact is that she had an instinct for picking girls who would draw a crowd of steady customers. Why question or quibble about Comrade Nee-ville's broad plans?"

Once the talk got away from ideology, the komissar had a lot of common sense. He leveled his dark glance on Ingerman. "Comrade Nee-ville, what do you say to all of this?"

"Comrade Igor, must you always have butter on your *kasha*?"

"Goddammit, *yes*!" The komissar chuckled. "Even if the butter usually is rancid. And I'd be happy if you told me what is really behind all this rhetoric."

"It's all history," Ingerman countered.

"Our Liberation Army was a gross error. You did your best to correct the mistake. When I finally got the story of how you faced the council of generals the Imperator called to his trailer to hear you and how they would have shot you then and there if he had not interfered—"

Ingerman exhaled a sigh that must have come from his ankles. "That was ticklish. Still gives me creeps."

"Under cover of the disturbance, and during a short distraction, you had a chance to be alone in the Imperator's office and had presence of mind enough to grab an order form, pocket it, get off the battlefront, and come back, impersonating a wounded aide-de-camp heroically delivering a forged order—Neville, it almost worked. You are a Red Hero. Let well enough alone!

"With their stupid security, their silliness with that 'freedom of information' business, we were stealing what little technology we could not buy. And they were selling us all the wheat we wanted, with some to sell for a profit.

"So, all you want now is to assassinate a national hero, which that goddamn Garvin is. Assassination is only a specialized mode of warfare, but liquidating him would stir up a wave of nationalism. The Warlords would tighten up on security and put an embargo on wheat. And quit buying chromite from us when they could get it cheaper from capitalistic South Africa. You remember Calabasas Cay?"

"I damn well ought to. Harry Offendorf and I were questioning Garvin about that, and then one of you idiots got a Liberation Army going."

"Our error," the komissar conceded. "Off the record, of course, it was a gross mistake. All we'd lost was an island with nothing but a landing strip—and, of course, a crew making soundings off Nameless Island.

"Your Liberals nearly had Garvin condemned as a war criminal, but the Imperialists got him off with exile to Mars. Only they made him Governor-General, and he came back and murdered Harry Offendorf. Most of the Liberals were hunted down and killed, and Garvin became an Imperial Hero."

"*Merde, alors!*" Ingerman exclaimed. "North America is doing too nicely, and the farmers would squawk as usual if anyone tried to embargo wheat. The public is fed up with war heroes, anyway."

The komissar had an answer. "Garvin's second in command, call him Vice-Governor-General of Mars, could send a flotilla to obliterate a dozen islands like ours, and who would avenge us? And damn little good a postmortem avenging would do me. It's taken us a long time to get intellectuals to protest and to pack the schools with another wave of Marxist instructors."

When the komissar paused for breath, the unusually silent woman made the most of her chance. "Comrade Igor, this is not a problem in theory and political science. Allow me to remind you that we deal with people and facts. Such as, that this Garvin is a tired old man, debating whether Number Two Wife can be talked into living in France, or Number One Wife persuaded to return to Mars.

"We all know that religion is the opium of the people. But in India there is a mixture called *panj*, which is a weird way of saying five, *cinque, cinco, fünf*."

"Don't forget *khamsa!*" Comrade Igor reminded her, but his mockery was good-humored; he was interested. "Is this a bartender's guide you cite?"

Diane's smile was appreciative. Ingerman welcomed the rescue party; though air conditioning controlled the temperature, he mopped imaginary sweat from his forehead.

"Opium," Diane resumed. "And hashish, dissolved in arrak, flavored with rosewater and honey. In Hindustan and thereabout, Indians and Moslems loaded with *panj* do not go to sleep. The massacres—racial, religious, or on general principles—are spectacular.

"North America is a religious country. Puritans, who simply could not say, yes, yes, aye, aye, sir, observe all the silly formalities, and believe as they pleased, had to leave their country and nearly perish in New England. Then, Mennonites. Dunkards. Mormons and cults of all sorts, even suicide clubs.

"The North American complex is religious. It has a passion for worshiping someone or something. They even worship warlords, but never for long. Because so many who came to North America did so to avoid military service in their native lands. A nation of draft-dodgers. In the new free country, they avoided all military service and took pride in pacifism triumphant. But once the army killed most of the Indians and herded the survivors to reservations to die of drink and malnu-

trition, there were no conscientious objections to farming the lands from which the savages had been driven.
Piously, they continued scorning the military and profit-
ing from the killings that wicked and godless soldiers had
done.

"North America has to worship, and they'll worship
almost anything but the military, which has so often
saved their hides! The real danger is the hidden Imperatrix. Devoted widow of the glamour Imperator, who,
after all, was a damned militarist. North America has
been a matriarchy this past century or more. If the Imperatrix ever comes from cover, at the right time, of
course, you are in trouble. Fatal trouble."

"That old bag? She's as old as Garvin, maybe older."

"Messieurs Comrades! You have a rogue's gallery of
notables from all over the worlds, and from many years
back." Diane sighed. "I would never suggest that these
news film clips and press negatives help terrorists and
assassins, but there's no harm at all in studying whatever
we have."

When this was done, they had seen Garvin, skipper of
the *Saturnienne*, marrying Lani and Admiral Courtney,
the first marriage in space; Alexander and Lani, who was
veiled out of deference to the North American Empire's
fundamentalist Moslem allies, who soon repented of ally-
ing themselves with infidel dogs who ate pork and drank
wine in public instead of guzzling brandy in private. Finally, there was Eileen, the look-alike, the Imitation Imperatrix, broadcasting from Mars, getting away with the
imposture until odd incidents relating to her illness,
death, and Terrestrial funeral led the Slivovitz Government to suspect that Lani had never gone to Mars. Despite Garvin's rigorous security corps, which never
arrested a well-established suspect but quietly killed
him, there was the once-in-a-great-while operator who
risked the dangerous Martian assignment and returned to
report.

"As for that 'broad-beamed old bag,'" Diane elaborated, "you may have been fooled by 'Madame Broadtail', a close friend of the Imperatrix." She put her

hands at her waist, paused a moment, then traced the curvature of her hips, at least far enough to give meaning to her words. "I'm not as young as I look, but I could never be a look-alike for the lady who is boss of Doc Brandon's Nameless Island. The darling who probably knows what happened to the five comrades who were making soundings offshore of the island."

Giving her derriere an affectionate pat, as one of her most precious possessions rated, Diane continued. "No matter how broad-beamed that Imperatrix is, imperial robes would take care of that, and so would the veil, which she'd probably wear in memory of Alexander and to live up to tradition. She could probably risk being barefaced—well, at dramatic times—to bedazzle the public. With proper lighting and perspective, she'd have a grand camera image. Madame Pudding would have picked her, instantly, as prima donna of number thirty-four. She could play the house virgin."

"Wait a minute! A virgin in a whorehouse?"

"Of course, Comrade Nee-ville! You idealists are so naive! The permanent virgin is standard in a good many parlor houses. The same chassis, of course, but a different paint job, a different gown, a new chastity belt, and the Limited Democracy will worship her—they'll be the same compulsive worshipers they've always been." She paused a moment to look beyond the two men and far out of the austere room. "Such devotees..." she murmured. "In Guyana, a century ago, a thousand North Americans committed suicide when the cult leader told them to."

When Ingerman had finished explaining this to the komissar, Diane broke the silence that followed. "Veiled Imperatrix," she said in a soft, dreamy voice. "The ultimate sex object and the goddess of a matriarchy composed of mother-worshipers."

Diane, however languid she appeared, was watching the komissar intently. Then a perfectly penciled eyebrow rose to form a Gothic arch, and the other flattened ever so slightly; her whimsical grimace was seconded by the sparkle of her voice. "On the other hand, Comrade

Igor, you may be right. The Divine Imperatrix is your ally. Imagine not a thousand but a whole nation committing suicide in a frenzy of adoration."

For a moment she held her breath and hoped that the komissar was not too terribly liberal-minded. She wondered how long her faked spontaneity would be convincing.

An intolerable pair of seconds finally ended, and Comrade Igor chuckled. "That would be butter on my kasha! If you set out swimming, you'd miss Garvin and never find Lani. With our new speedboat, you'd get to Savannah way ahead of him."

Chapter 12

WHEN FINALLY THEY reached their living quarters in Savannah, not far from the riverfront yet not too conspicuously near the area devoted to warehouses, flophouses, and ship chandlers, Diane looked about her. "No wonder Igor didn't want you to leave!" she said to Ingerman.

For a moment he faced her with a frown of perplexity. "Honey, I don't get it."

"All the preparation. I've not seen even one cockroach, and they tell me they have miniature polo in Savannah, riverfront rats riding the giant cockroaches. I mean, the entire trip, everything—your department's doings, and you've quit the job."

He shrugged. "A good assistant, and then the assistant to the assistant. Neither knows a damn thing more than I did, and that's little enough. Simply a matter of picking specialists in a lot of things that no one man could possibly know." He grinned and wagged his head. "Like your Madame Pudding, remember? When you told him about her, that was the start of my getting free."

Though far from a novice, Diane was ever more amazed by the precise meshing of the spy system's intricate gear train. Far offshore, a fishing boat met the speedster from Sainte Véronique. The latter appeared to be no more than a gentleman's sporting craft; there was nothing about its looks that suggested engines that could drive it at sixty or seventy knots, or maneuverability to outwit bombers, or armor that would withstand light-arms fire. After the transfer of passengers and luggage, each craft put about for its takeoff site. Diane and her companion did not make for a secluded cove or a landing in darkness. Their destination was bubbling with week-enders pursuing happiness, a recreation area where arrivals and departures by land or water made a masking confusion.

Wearing and carrying fishing gear, they made for a shore lodge. Before dawn, a camper took them toward Savannah and their operating headquarters, whose freedom from cockroaches amazed and delighted Diane. The commonplace "shotgun" cottage was jammed, but not too closely, among others of its kind, and furnished to accord with its companions, which were neither badly run-down nor well kept.

En route, Ingerman had stopped to make arrangements with a telephone answering service, and when they had moved into their home, the telephone and its extension caught Diane's eye and aroused her interest. "A bit deluxe for the neighborhood, isn't it?"

"By no means. Bedroom, bath, or kitchen, wherever it's best for you to be, you can listen and tape what goes on, cut in or stay out, according to my word signal. Before we can establish ourselves here in our dye complexions, we'd better get busy with our paint remover."

Reminiscence made Diane almost laugh aloud. "When you explained your plan for not being recognized in spite of having faced so many newsreel cameras, Comrade Igor looked the way Moses must have when the Good Lord handed him the tables of the Law! It was such a simple approach, too! But that's what sold him." That last bit was craft rather than modesty, though she readily gave Ingerman credit. "It'd never have occurred to me, either."

She paused. "Bedroom mirror is awfully old and cloudy," she commented, "but let's have a good-bye look at our old selves. And we ought to have a picture of us."

She turned to her suitcase.

"What the hell!" Ingerman exclaimed. "What for? To send back to Bayonne?"

"I'll tell you when the photos are taken."

She dipped out a secondhand Alfa single lens reflex, set the self-timer, and gestured. "Stand over there. Bit more to the right. Hold it! And don't move or you'll crowd me out."

Ingerman didn't know whether to be puzzled or amused. He did neither. Instead, he was a convincing honeymooner, and being quite careful not to ham it up, Diane was a lady of color, as the saying still goes in the Antilles, who has finally snared a white man for keeps.

After fifteen seconds of timer buzzing, the shutter clicked.

"Try another, just for luck."

The camera spewed out Instakolor prints: Since these separated from the basic negative, duplicates could be obtained ad lib. They looked at the prints, regarded each other, and decided that the pictures were better than standing in front of an inferior mirror. Not until Diane was three strides down the long hallway that led past two bedrooms and the bath before opening into the kitchen and dinette did Ingerman remember and he raised his voice: "Wait a second! Goddammit, *spere poco!*" His mangled gleanings of Spanish amused him. "What's all this about?"

Over her shoulder, she laughed. "If you guess before I come from the shower, you get an extra dividend tonight."

"Oh, all right! I was afraid you'd say I'd get a weekend, all-expense flight to Honolulu."

The bouquet of dye remover and the splash of the shower told that a work of art was on its way down the drain: a quadroon glamour lady such as every old-time New Orleans planter had to have as a matter of fun, status, and relaxation from an arranged marriage. Diane's makeup had been patterned after actual photos of quadroon girls whose white ancestry came from French gentlemen from Martinique. When it came to counterfeiting, the Democratic Republic of Sainte Vér-onique was meticulous.

Ingerman, though just as realistic, was devoid of glamour; reddish-purplish nose and cheekbones some-what less lavender and not quite as ruddy duplicated perfectly the side effects of treatment and prevention of one of a dozen tropical diseases that touched the natives lightly, if at all, but severely harassed the white intruder. Although not grotesque, the skillful fakery made Inger-man conspicuous. It had gotten him discreet but re-peated glances at the telephone service during the short while it had taken to make arrangements on the way to the cabin.

To be conspicuous was desirable—and intentional. His best disguise would be the removal of the dye.

Diane paused on her way from bath to bedroom. "Made your guess?"

He ignored the question. "Plug that phone in while you're dressing. The quicker I get rid of my disguise, the better. We won't be going out for dinner, not this eve-ning. I'm expecting a call."

The Ingerman who emerged from the shower had so long ago won his battles with tropical ailments that the Caribbean tan combined with the barely perceptible but persistent leaden-gray tint. His once lustrous blondish-ruddy hair had been sun-blasted to a neutral drab. His cheeks were taut, though he was by no means ema-ciated. The grayish eyes were tired, sharp yet weary. This was not the zealot, the long-ago Minister of Defense who, coming to Alexander Imperator's battlefield head-quarters to present a brief for negotiated peace with the Liberator Army, had narrowly missed being shot by an enraged three-star general.

It was not Ingerman's words that had so infuriated the hard-pressed field commander, subordinate only to the Imperator; it was the boyish idealism, sincerity blended with ignorance, confronting the commanders of outnum-bered divisions dedicated to destroy an equally dedi-cated enemy.

It was suicidal sincerity, and ignorance such as would be fatal anywhere but on a privileged, sheltered college

campus. Despite the death so narrowly avoided, the
zealous boy had responded with daring, almost causing
the destruction of his nation's army.

That boy no longer existed.

Exile and brooding had not changed the bone structure, yet the face was not the one that so many press
videotapes had recorded.

"Got the answer?" Diane challenged when he stepped
into the living room wearing seersucker slacks and a *camisa de chino* gaudy with hibiscus blossoms.

"Simple. We're going to lose those pictures when we
leave, and the housecleaners will find them, and they'll
have instructions as to whom they should show them to.
Might lose them in the cab that takes us away? An in-
structed driver would know what to do."

"Oh, you son of a *bitch*!" Diane was learning Americanese. "Well, that place we passed on the way, it's not
far. What's a Brunswick stew? Something the aborigines
concoct?"

"Early Georgian, and I bet they'll send it over, along
with some fried pies and barbecued pork ribs and what-
not. No air conditioning, but the umbrella trees out front
will keep us from being gawked at and keep us cool."

"I hope the mosquito spray works!"

"*Chérie*, don't borrow trouble. That spray is just in
case the electronic bug-killer conks. You should have
been out here when all they had was burning charcoal
and a few thunks of olibanum to stir up a smoke screen
that mosquitoes seemed to like."

When the food arrived, Ingerman had the messenger
take it into the small, well-lighted dining room, which
was an extension of the kitchen.

"We're strangers here," he said to the motorcycle
messenger, "and I couldn't understand everything the
girl at the phone said, so I told her to use her judgment
and send some real food. And trying to understand her
talk, I forgot to ask what'd be good to drink with it."

The amiable man chuckled. "She's from Mississippi,
and so is the cook, and they just can't talk English. Lot
of folks forget the drinks, so I tote Coke and cold beer,

just in case. Just a slight extra charge for my toting license."

Ingerman gave him a grin and a wink. "Bet that toting license costs about as much as you make in pay."

"Sure does help," the messenger agreed, and hustled out to get beer. He liked a customer with a sense of humor; it was a real change. And as Diane emptied the containers onto platters and into serving dishes, he unreeled Georgian hospitality.

"These here—" He pointed to the finger-slender, pale jade-green peppers. "You don't eat these. You bust them a bit, and you squeeze a few drops of the juice on these here collards. A Yankee tried eating one afore anybody could warn him, and it was pretty near twenty minutes that he couldn't speak a word. He just sat there choking and coughing."

By the time he had given Diane the ingredients of Brunswick stew, he had noticed that she was a white woman and that Ingerman was a peaked old fellow, no ruddy nose or cheekbones or other tropical stigmata.

They ignored the collards and the deadly peppers.

"This fried pie—" Diane thrust her specimen aside. "I could forgive them for filling it with stewed dried peaches, but that crust!"

"Further west you go, the worse they get. Now, in Texas—"

The phone rang. Ingerman grabbed the instrument and gestured to Diane. "I am Mr. Inglewood," he said. "What is my first name?"

"Miguel," the caller answered.

"Who are you?" he paused. "Please spell it . . . Ah, Miguel Rodriguez. Of course! From where? Yes, yes, of course, the Philippines—but what province, what town? Ah, the *boondocks*. Very well. I'll hear your message."

And this is what Ingerman and Diane heard:

"One of my friends working for a news service radioed the *Semiramis*. She will berth at Pier Nineteen, maybe as early as four in the morning. It depends on the tide and the pilot. No one goes ashore until cleared by customs and medical officer. But no one called Garvin is aboard."

Ingerman cursed. Diane smiled cryptically and said nothing. Here was where she would begin paying her way.

The caller resumed. "Only passengers aboard are Pierre d'Artois and his son."

"No problem," Diane cut in. "Let him carry on."

"She is right," Ingerman told Miguel Rodriguez. "Now get this carefully. Right away, find a ship chandler's loft or a sailmaker's. One that we can look from and see the gangplank of the *Semiramis*. If no windows, we can bore peep holes.

"Or some seaman's flophouse, or any friendly house with a window in the roof. Yes, a dormer. No need to bore holes.

"Is that clear? So far?"

It certainly was.

Ingerman resumed. "The hock shops—I said *hock* not *hook* —along the waterfront are open all night when things are busy. Get three binoculars. Get good ones. Go ahead and let them rob you, but get the best you can. Yes, I said, *three*. Yes, goddammit, Mike! You will be with us. Now get this last bit. When you call back to tell me all is fixed up, phone the answering service. I'll give you the number. Be sure you get my name right: Norman Inglewood." He spelled it out. "When you have done that, phone me at this number. I want to check up on that answering service just to make sure."

All was clear, and Miguel set out to execute the orders.

"Why pick a foreigner from way over there?" Diane asked when Ingerman hung up. "I know he must be reliable, but—"

"In the first place, his great-grandfather was a big man in the Hukbalahap movement in Mindanao, the big southern island of the Philippines, and his grandfather is back there doing a good job stirring up trouble for the government."

"Hukbalahap—who or what is that?"

"A Marxist revolutionary group. Yes, during the Hitler war. As usual, the upper bracket of the American state department gulped the line, with hooks attached, that the Huks were not, and never had been, Marxists, and never would be. Just the way they did later, when they knew that Mao was an agrarian reformer, and Castro was the same, and neither of them Marxists, of course not! And we had the press and the universities and students becoming believers. Naturally, the intellectuals are the quickest to see the truth. It takes the stupid lower levels so much longer."

"Where is the *boondocks*?"

"Oh, *that*? That's code which in Americanese means 'back of beyond,' out in the sticks. I haven't the foggiest idea where the word originated, but it's become standard Americanese."

"How fascinating." Diane sighed. "But that extra dividend. We'll be waiting for a phone call. How about a rain check?"

Chapter 13

EIGHTEEN MILES UP the river, the *Semiramis* found her berth at Pier Nineteen, in Savannah, a historic and tree-shaded city on nine square miles of plateau, about sixteen feet above sea level. Garvin and son were on deck, standing by the heaped cases of liquor they had brought as gifts for Madame Broadtail and for General Kerwin, Number One Warlord.

The Old Man wore the tourist gear he had packed for Savannah's climate: mesh shoes, white slacks, a tropical-weight gray jacket, and a Bangkok hat. Felix wore what he had bought from the ship's slop chest. He did not look like a tourist, and he did not give a damn. Garvin Senior had handed him binoculars to remedy faulty costuming.

Although there was virtually no danger of the ship's sinking at Pier Nineteen, Garvin lost no time getting wines and cognac through customs. That done, the Garvins got two taxis to carry cargo and passengers to a warehouse not far upstream. On arrival, the Old Man sorted the cases and divided them into two lots, getting a separate receipt for each. One of these he gave to Felix.

"In case I get sudden orders when I phone General Kerwin from Nameless Island, I'll send him this receipt and he can have my greetings to him and the Warlords picked up. Your receipt is for what we are taking to the island for Madame Broadtail's special cellar."

Dismissing the taxis, they walked upstream.

"We're going to locate that tug or launch, whatever you want to call it. Let the skipper know we are in town so we won't get sliced in half by mistake. Which reminds me, when I mentioned Nameless Island and teak, you went totally negative, like I'd said a dirty word. Dismissed the business as 'nothing but a bunch of goddamn lumberjacks.' How come the grudge?"

"From what I saw around Dax, where you nearly got hauled to Pau by mistake, there was nothing but hot springs, pines, and turpentine, and dumb bastards cutting down trees."

"No real problem, Felix. Madame Broadtail manages to get along, and I figure you can do the same, somehow."

Having business along the riverfront, Garvin arranged to live aboard the *Semiramis* instead of going to a hotel. She would be in port long enough, unloading and stowing cargo. Furthermore, he and Felix would be far less conspicuous there than in downtown quarters.

Ever since Alexander's first war, Garvin had known where the teak rafts from Nameless Island were dismantled and the logs put ashore; but too many years had elapsed, and a night operation was ticklish at the best. Accordingly, reconnaissance was in order.

As they tramped along, dodging hand trucks, forklifts, and trailer rigs, Felix saw nothing as interesting as what the riverfront of Bayonne offered. For diverse reasons, the elder Garvin considered it bad medicine to have Felix go inland with him, and not one of those reasons was a reflection on the youngster's character or substance. Although teenagers were somewhat less than human, the better specimens often attained humanity. Felix had good prospects, but the project just around the corner was not one that could be explained. It depended upon instant improvisation, as had the noiseless killing of an idealistic traitor.

Finally Garvin snapped out of ambulant reverie and spoke aloud. "Now I've got it! She's just around the bend."

"What's your landmark?"

"Isn't any. It is smelling and hearing."

"Nothing but noise and stink," Felix countered.

"Stand still, sniff, and listen."

Felix did so. "Someone is thumping away, and it is not bearings," he announced presently. He waited a long moment. "Now I get it. Spices. Kind of odd. Like the Lascars on the forward deck of a tub in Bayonne, grinding curry for their rice. How come you noticed it before I did?"

"I've been exposed to odd smells three times as long as you have. And I have not smoked since I was younger than you are."

Felix chuckled. "Those French cigarettes. Like copper smelter fumes. So I quit. How come you knocked it off?"

"By not smoking, I could smell a tobacco user from way off unless the wind was wrong. Couple of times, that warning gave me a chance to get into shadow, with my gun ready. Son of a bitch never had a chance."

Felix grinned. "Taught him a lesson. Smoking is bad for the health."

Within a moment or two they saw what they had heard and scented: the *Tiburón*, the shark, and aptly named, as spies learned.

"Stand fast," the Old Man said. "Use your glasses."

It was the same old tug, still with the black paint job she had had that night when her crew towed from Nameless Island a spy boat that had been making soundings off the island. Whether the micronation, Sainte Véronique, had planned a submarine base or a landing field or both was never clearly determined, if only because Alexander's second and final war broke out before Security could investigate.

Whether the tug was waiting for a broker to accept or reject the raft of logs, each about twenty meters long, only the skipper and Madame Broadtail could say. The only certainty was that the teak was well seasoned, else it would not float.

The skipper, standing by watching crewmen polishing brass and tidying up, was not an old hand; the sight of his resolute face and air of command left Garvin feeling old and sad. U Po Mya and Maung Gauk, who used to supervise operations, must have died.

He wondered how the years had treated Madame Broadtail. Not being disturbed by ancient memories, Felix had not noticed deckhands: His attention was caught by one of the girls, sitting cross-legged on the teak deck just forward of the companionway leading below. Tawny and good-looking, she was evidently a Filipina, wearing a piña fiber blouse whose sleeves, reaching less than halfway to the elbow, flared like magnolia blossoms fully opened. She was vigorously pounding spices in a mortar, and the activity was doing wonderful things to her anatomy.

Another girl, with breast scarf, bare midriff, and an enticing wraparound skirt, was busily stirring something in a copper pot supported by the bricks of a jackleg brazier devised to protect the deck.

Felix finally lowered the binoculars. "The old fellow shining brass. Is he a Malay?" he asked.

"Not bad reckoning, but he's Burmese."

"How about those brunettes stirring up curry?"

"The one with the flaring short sleeves is probably from Luzon—" Garvin snatched the glasses. "Tagalog, and very likely a mestiza, half Spanish. The other is Burmese, and you'll never get a look at what's inside that funny skirt unless she's in an amiable mood and unwraps it. Same goes for the mestiza. Quite a few Asiatic women are broad-minded when dealing with an American, but that doesn't mean they are quick and easy as instant noodles. Now we'll knock off the girl-watching and haul out. I am in my native country, which also is enemy territory for me, in places and sometimes. Rather not be too conspicuous."

Felix took back the binoculars.

"Notice carefully where this is," the Old Man resumed. "I have arranged with Madame Broadtail to have the crew let us sneak aboard and stow away in the *Tiburón*. Offhand, I do not see any reason or chance of our being separated, but if I have to dive for cover, don't follow me. Watch your step and hightail for the tug."

Felix frowned. "You mean, if things get sticky, I should run out on you?"

"Forget some of the traditional definitions of chicken-shit. I am not trying to protect you from danger. For all I can tell, right this minute you may be a sort of reserve. I'll know when I have talked to General Kerwin at First Army headquarters. Whatever he tells you, it is okay, and don't screw things up by demonstrating when you have not a dime's worth of facts."

Chapter 14

AFTER A TAXI tour that included the high spots of Savannah's landmarks and quite a few of the historic sites, Garvin spoke to his son. "Now that you have girl-watching off your mind, we ought to get us a solid meal to keep that Brunswick stew and the other snacks company. Unless the place has changed for the worse since I was here, well before you were born, it's a good second to Antoine's in New Orleans. Not an imitation, just good in its own right, and quiet enough for talk without shouting. We can catch up with a two-way briefing while we have a chance."

Although the tables were somewhat more closely spaced and the voices slightly higher than what one might find in New Orleans, Armand's was uncrowded, low-keyed, and congenial.

Once dinner was ordered, the talk got down to serious matters.

"Rod," Felix began. "If it is top secret or just none of my business, you won't lose much time letting me know. So far, I don't know whether I am afoot or on horse, and you've made it plain that I'm going to be on my own. With not much notice. Almost any time after we get to Nameless Island. What are we scared of?"

"Your question shows that you assume *we* are scared. I am reckoning in terms of giving my, our if you please, opposite numbers some good reasons for developing battlefield diarrhea. Sound off. Now would be good, and when I start answering, you can avoid getting a mouthful of paper bag instead of pompano with sauce and stuff."

"We are going to stow away aboard the *Tiburón* and stay out of sight till the Number One Warlord has had a talk with you and given you an okay. What are you aiming to do when you get to where you are going, and where are you going, if that's not top secret?"

Garvin watched as Felix got the pompano filet clear of the parchment bag in which it had been baked, then replied. "I am heading west. Whether with a camper truck or a mule team, I don't know yet. Destination, one of the trade routes from the far west. During the wars, the Navajos and other Amerindians revived native arts. In Arkansas, for instance, wildcat diamond mining and handcrafts were revived. There were similar capers in New Mexico, especially north of Albuquerque.

"The people have not stuck to their back-to-primitive days, but some of the revived crafts have caught on, and no matter how much they go back to TV, their pioneer ways—or Amerindian ways—have not been dumped.

"I am going to one of the caravan centers along the route, where I can watch who is going west, and who is going east, and what is bartered for what. Lot of people love bartering and haggling about trades instead of thinking in cash, though the government currency is sounder than it has been for a century or more. I'll make a show of some cover activity so I'll not be too conspicuous. Got to trade a bit or pretend to.

"I've picked a settlement. A spot I heard rumors about quite a few years back. First talk of it was when I came back to arrange the funeral of the look-alike who doubled for the original Imperatrix. Alexander tried to get Lani to Mars and safety, but she outwitted him. Well, I went into that before, but incidental to my getting the body of the Imitation Empress to a grave beside Alexander's, I heard about a colony of settlers that lived Egyptian-style. There were the Alleluia Stompers and the Testifiers, two fundamentalist fanatic Christian sects who always hated each other's guts until they had these abominable imitation Egyptians to hate. So they had enough hatred in common to forget their hating each other.

"More North American craziness, that is what I called it, but when I got back to Mars and my post and duties, I kept hearing rumors about that cult of imitation Egyptians. And about a Britisher who, they say, claims he is a reincarnation of the late Sir E. A. Wallis Budge, a pioneer in Egyptology and a great scholar."

Garvin turned to the waiter. "Dig up a Duff Gordon's nutty amontillado or something else of that sort." Then he resumed his explanation.

"That settlement seems to be growing. Not a landslide, but steady growth. Off the record, Limited Democracy cleaned out the horse's-arse social programs that were driving the nation bankrupt, but something the standard American has to have is lost. No one unhappy but—something lacking. Which is dangerous. It takes more than the hunt and kill that got traitors out of upper-level government."

"What the hell's the matter with the Warlords?"

Garvin shook his head. "They are doing a good job, but this country is made up of immigrants quitting their homelands either because of religion or to evade military service. Sometimes it is both. The way the conscientious objectors who would never kill another human being waited until the army killed off the Indians or herded them to reservations, after which the C.O.'s exploited the rich farmlands of the middle west. And felt pious as all hell."

Felix refilled the glasses.

"So," Garvin summed up, "we are a nation that kisses the military arse when there is a dangerous emergency, like when Alexander fought his final war. But once the situation is cooled off and stable, the grateful nation remembers its principles and makes the military eat shit with a wooden spoon. And like it."

"That started yet?"

Garvin shrugged. "General Kerwin may brief me on that, but as a guess, I'd say it is beginning to begin."

Felix frowned. "This Egypt business?"

"Well, the place is sort of at the crossroads, and it may indicate a new trend in believers and beliefs. Used to be Hindus that had a monopoly. Everyone looking for a guru. And then about a century ago, some idiot talked nine hundred Americans into drinking cyanide and killing themselves. They obediently did so. Our public buys anything if it is insane enough."

"So this Egypt thing is crazy?"

"The fellow who claims to be the reincarnation of Sir E. A. Wallis Budge may be a foxy promoter." Garvin cocked his head, grimaced, and an eyelid drooped, emphasizing the glint of eyes shifting from gray-green to a glint of falcon-hazel.

"So I spent the past four or five years studying Coptic. That is the original Egyptian language, supposedly extinct since the middle seventeen hundreds. But the couple of million Christian Copts in Egypt have been using computers to compare classical Greek and modern Greek from sculptures which also had inscriptions in hieroglyphic and hieratic and demotic Coptic. Comparing this with the Christian Coptic church liturgies, and with computers to speed up mass comparisons, underground Copts have been reconstructing the not-so-lost language."

Felix pushed aside the remains of his *caneton glacé aux cerises*. "You mean those colony people talk Egyptian?"

Garvin grinned. "They probably can't even talk good Americanese. Or maybe a few of them can, but not many. But don't you worry about *that*! You might find a spot there."

"Me?"

"Uh huh. By pretending you are handicapped. Well, not really half-witted, but not awfully bright. And you could mingle with the natives and tune in on their chitchat when they chatter in Americanese, or real English for that matter.

"Finding out whether this is old Egyptian culture reshaped to fit North America or an outright fraud to hook chumps. See what I mean? Find out what makes this appealing. What there is that makes the colony grow. And no government grants."

When the Nesselrode pudding arrived, Felix was eating valiantly; and the Old Man, as he toyed with the dessert, was still sounding off about the social insights they could gain: That this cult was considered a dangerous rival by both Alleluia Stompers and the Testifiers signified that it must have a powerful appeal.

Felix listened intently until he ran out of Nesselrode pudding. The Old Man did not try to catch up with him.

"How does it sound to you?" Garvin asked.

"Tell you the truth," Felix responded after pausing to weigh his words, "it is mighty interesting. But when you set me right when I squawked about what dumb bastards lumberjacks were, you spoke an afterthought that has kept nagging at me."

Garvin scooped up some more dessert. "Such as?"

"Well, it might have been when you told me about how Doc Brandon got scientific and sent for a couple of elephants to see which was the best, animals or tractors, for snaking teak logs down the crazy slopes of that island. Didn't mean much to me till I remembered elephants have lives as long as their memories, and even if they were prewar, they'd be young and vigorous and working.

"I'd rather learn a few things about driving elephants, logging teak, and learning conversational Burmese."

Garvin kept a straight face. This was just right. Don't spoil it. "So, you mean Sir Ernest Albert Wallis Budge and the ancient culture do not fascinate you? It is a rare opportunity."

"It's got its points," Felix conceded. "Only, nothing there but a bunch of damned Egyptians."

Garvin gravely considered his son's decision. "I see you've been thinking things out."

Madame Broadtail could not have put two better shaped girls aboard the Tiburón, *he thought. Even if they'd not been grinding spices or stirring stew, he'd still have developed a burning urge to learn all about teak and elephants.*

But what he said aloud was another story: "I have to brief you on something that's bothered me all day. I grew a beard and borrowed a name. I called Nameless Island from Charleston and asked Mona to send the teak-towing boat to town. Good reason for everything I did, but I've cooked up a no-win mess."

Felix yawned. "How come?"

"Unless she sent the *Tiburón* soon enough, we'd be dallying around town, which would be bad, this being enemy territory for me. Getting here ahead of time and running up demurrage is a perfect way of calling me to mind. Madame Broadtail and I are suspected of knowing why a high official's bones were found at the foot of a thousand-meter drop, instead of the bones of the hide-out Imperatrix."

"Madame Broadtail been worrying much?"

"She's got nothing to brood about. Nameless Island had proved a death trap for snoopers. You and I are not an island.

"Now hear this. This is no drill. Get a long sleep and a leisurely breakfast, prowl the riverfront as if looking for me or just gawking around, girl-watching. Do not, re-peat, not, sneak aboard the *Tiburón*. Very likely we are already under observation, so I am going to act as if I were conspicuously drunk." He slipped Felix a nine-millimeter compact automatic pistol. "You probably won't need this, but I am doing a disappearing act while you are ad libbing."

"Where you going from here?"

"Let you know when I find out. Here's the charade."

Samples of his son's improvisations in the matter of lumberjacks, teak-logging, and Egyptian culture assured Garvin that he could depend on Felix.

Having outlined the routine, Garvin relaxed and fum-bled when he poured a refill of Avery's Dessert Sherry; the too-big splash proved that the wine was rich and dark. Although his voice was somewhat louder, the in-crease in decibels was not a breach of decorum. His conversational gestures were somewhat more sweeping than his son's Gallic hand-talk but not really too much more.

And then the tallest waiter in the house stepped into the dining room. On a tray, held well over his head, was a silver bowl containing New Orleans-style coffee, spiced with cinnamon sticks, cloves, zest of orange and lemon, and other additives. Armand's satanic coffee was famous. However, it was the brandy float that made the waiter's stately approach conspicuous: Tall blue flames of the blazing liquor came near to touching the ceiling. A carnival parade in a cemetery could hardly have been more conspicuous. That the Garvins were oblivious of what approached them, as if they never drank coffee unless it were ablaze, did not detract from the production.

The waiter set the tray on the table. The flame subsided in the way of a geyser nearing the end of its cycle. His timing had been perfect. He ladled the postprandial drinks into porcelain goblets.

At the waiter's second stride from the table, the Old Man reached for his drink.

"Good luck," Felix exclaimed, hoisting his own. "But don't say down the hatch till it's cool enough!"

The Old Man reached, fumbled and ran afoul of a sherry glass. Trying to keep it from rolling to the floor, he almost pitched from his chair. His recovery was a work of art: Only a drunk or an acrobat could have made it. Then he stumbled, but when the fascinated diners were sure he would be clawing the floor, he recovered his balance and stood for a moment, swaying but secure.

Felix pounced to his feet in time to detain the waiter who had turned to assist. "Don't you embarrass him, you hear me? Just pretend nothing has happened, he knows where he's going. You humiliate him, and he won't ever come back."

Though weaving erratically, Garvin never grazed a table or inconvenienced a guest. Felix resumed his seat and, as fascinated as the other diners, watched skill improve upon nature.

When the uneasy waiter saw Garvin turn in the direction of a door marked "Men," he sighed and watched a busboy set the table in order.

"Maybe I could assist?" His gesture made his intention plain.

Felix shook his head. "You just let him alone or you'll hurt his feelings. And if he doesn't come out, he probably puked all over himself or the floor. If so, he'd take off his shirt and mop up and sneak out the back door to the alley. He remembered this place from when he was a real drinking man, and he's embarrassed. Anyway, he just ate too much." Felix took a hearty gulp of his café diabolique, which by now was not too hot to drink. He slipped a folded bill into the waiter's hand. "You might bring me the check or send the other man with it. If there's anything else I want while I am waiting for the Old Man, I'll sound off."

A busboy beckoned. The waiter stepped over to listen, then returned to report to Felix. "There was no mishap in either toilet room. No one saw him leave."

Felix shrugged. "Probably felt queasy like. Walking it off, getting fresh air. By the time I finish this bowl of Creole Fire, he may be back, straight up and sparkling." He glanced at his watch. "If he's not back in the next half hour, he's likely to be home. If getting a cab this hour is a problem, send for one and tell him to start his meter ticking till I figure I ought to get going."

Chapter 15

AFTER A GOOD night's sleep and a hefty breakfast, Felix headed upstream to the nearest telephone booth, where he poked his card into the slot and played the numbers tune that should get him the most confidential connection. That he got an almost instant answer suggested that a call had been expected. However, the dialogues all the way from Funchal had made him wary, and he played it accordingly.

"Avery Jarvis Brandon Foundation? May I speak—"

A woman's voice cut him short. "I'm sure I know who you are. Do not mention names. May I have a word with your father?"

"He left before breakfast. You are out of luck. I am calling from a pay station."

"He phoned me three or four hours ago. What cargo are you bringing me?"

"Brandy and myself. Cut out the crap and let me talk to the boss."

"Relax. This is Madame Broadtail" The woman's voice was low-pitched, an octave below the scream of the standard American female. For an old bag, she sounded sexy. "I'll mention one name. When will you be sleeping with Diane?"

"If the answer is never again, I won't commit hara-kiri."

"Now that we're pretty sure about identifications, I'll brief you: When you board the tug, ask for U Po Sin or the mate, Maung Than. They speak English, sort of. I phoned them a clearance for you, just in case. Anyone looking for your father is making himself an endangered species. You are likely to be under professional observation, maybe already are. Be conspicuous about going aboard with your liquor, and from there play it by ear."

That ended the talk. For all its terseness, the dialogue had been educational.

"*Tiburón*," Felix mused aloud. "That ought to be her name. Madame Shark, that smooth-talking old bag. Broad ass, nudging thirty-five or forty and dangerous as a basket of rattlesnakes or cobras."

None of that imagination-based description fitted the brunettes aboard the *Tiburón*, and with such samples the island ladies would offer Diane's memory some competition now that antique hags were the subjects of cogitation.

The more he pondered on his rejection of Egyptian culture, the more Felix realized that he had been quite right. From all that he had ever heard of ancient Egypt, he had arrived at the reasonable conclusion that the ancient natives of the Nile valley spent so much time thinking of the hereafter that they never had a chance to live, so much emphasis on the future that they never had a present. Mummies were apparently the keynote of their culture.

Mummy cases, and sarcophagi, and *The Book of the Dead*.

"No wonder the Alleluia Stompers and the Testifiers hate the guts of those Egyptian cultists. Got so much in common, making a career of getting ready to be mummies or just to be saved."

Back aboard the *Semiramis*, Felix lost no time packing up. During his several days in Funchal he had bought luggage and a couple of outfits to wear until he learned what the American milieu required. Although Savannah's latitude was the same as Funchal's, the former city was handicapped by the great earthquake that had raised Nameless Island high above sea level and, incidentally, deflected the Gulf Stream. So here he was, ashore again and learning things about the climate.

With three pieces of luggage to carry and heat that made him break out in a sweat, he needed a porter, a taxi, or one of those horse-drawn *calesas* for tourists from up north. He cast an impatient glance upstream and downstream, then cocked his head to squint down an alley. He was on the verge of cursing God, going to hell, of course, and into a better climate.

"Mister, if it is a porter you look for, here I am."

The speaker had a light handtruck of tubular aluminum. He rose from a bench set against the gnarled trunk of an umbrella tree whose dense bluish-green foliage cast an inviting shade. The young man wore white slacks and a gaudy *camisa de chino*, and showed not a drop of sweat on his tawny skin.

Arabs, Greeks, and those indefinite people they called Levantines—these were old stuff to Felix. There was no place on earth where you didn't find a Chinaman, but he was sure that this was not one, though the cut of the jib was Asiatic. His complexion was somewhat like that of the Burmese girls aboard the *Tiburón* and somewhat like that of the one with magnolia-blossom sleeves, the one whose piña cloth blouse jiggled delightfully when she stirred stuff in a pot.

Too good to be true.

"With that dinky little chain store shopping thing?" Felix asked, looking askance.

"No problem, sir. It won't bust. Neither will I." The man displayed white teeth gleaming like tombstones by moonlight. "Where do I take your stuff?"

If this deal is rigged, Felix thought, *he knows more about me than I know about him. Instead of giving him the yo-heave-ho, I'll spread bait.* "You looking for work?" he asked.

"Sure am."

The Mexican huaraches were new and umblemished. Despite the boyish sparkle, the man was probably half again as old as Felix.

"On the way to the *Tiburón*, we'll pick up two or three cases of liquor. Can do?" Felix asked.

The porter got the luggage on the truck. Then Felix checked him. "I have an idea. I'm going to a teak grove. It is off the coast on an island."

"Teak?"

Felix nodded. "You act alive. No lard ass. I don't know what kind of outfit I'll work for. If you can make it as Number One Boy, you have a job. If you don't like it, draw your pay and get out. Nobody is going to stop you."

He paused long enough for a question. Since there was none, he made note of the fact and posed one of his own. "When we get a look at the spot and know what things are like, we'll talk about your pay. Not that it makes any difference, but are you Burmese or Cambodian?"

"Not that it makes any difference, but I am from the Philippines. I am Miguel Rodriguez."

"I am Felix Garvin. You speak English I can understand. The guys I'll work with, nobody can understand them. Uh . . . you said Philippines. What part?"

"Way up in the boondocks."

"Boondocks" was a new one on Felix, but he was not about to ask for a translation. "You speak real American-ese," he said. "How come?"

"I was so young when I come to this country."

When luggage and liquor were stowed in the cabin of the tug, Miguel said, "Sir, it would not be right to keep this truck. I must take it back."

"You've got plenty of time." Felix handed him fifty pazors.

"A down payment. I'll start you with what the loggers get."

U Po Sin, the skipper, took it for granted that a gentleman would have a servant. Felix's image would have been improved even more by the addition of two or three concubines. But he had to make do.

Chapter 16

ONCE MIGUEL HAD Felix's gear stowed in Nameless Island's guest house, Mona singsonged instructions in Burmese, then U Po Sin addressed the Number One Boy. "You come this way, we have one nice place for you."

Miguel's glance shifted to the boss. Felix answered the unspoken question. "We're guests. Go along with hospitality."

"Will do." The servant followed the mayor of the native village.

Mona gestured. "Before you get a tour of the island, let's go into the billiards room and I'll get us some drinks."

"That reminds me of stuff I picked up in Savannah. Be back in no time."

He returned from his room with a thirty-millileter flagon of Pale Hands and three bottles of cognac. Although he made good time, Mona had absinthe drips set out. Felix gaped. "I figured this'd be quicker and handier. How'd they get dripped so fast?"

She explained the ready-mix routine, one of high technology's more important advances. They compromised, agreeing to dispose of the drips and then switch to cognac.

"And before I forget it, here's some perfume I picked up in Funchal. Unless the label is faked, it's made in France."

"Pale Hands! They would have a sequel to Shalimar! Thank you, and Flora certainly raised you right."

"She had a housekeeper that helped a lot. An old bag, thirty anyway, but not bad-looking."

Mona reminded her guest of Benjamin Franklin's verdict on the error of judging a book by its cover rather than its contents. With that bit of ancient wisdom digested, they got a start on the second round of drips when Felix cut into the chitchat. "Before I forget it, what does 'boondocks' mean?"

"Where'd you hear that?"

"Is it something dirty?"

Mona laughed. "If Doc Brandon were sitting with us, he'd shout *yes* so loud you could hear him on the mainland."

"I might've known better. Sorry."

"You missed the point. With his informal speechways, the idea that any word, per se, was dirty—well, he always said it depended on who said it. What do you know about Doc?"

"Mom often gave him free time, and so did my Old Man, during the boat ride."

"Well, back in nineteen sixteen-seventeen, when he was about your age, he was soldiering in the Philippines, and he learned that and a lot of other words. Like *bagsak* and *bugao*. They were new in soldiers' talk. Well, nobody said *boon*docks, and *boonies* would have been too ridiculous to imagine, an invention by the Johnny-come-latelies. It was bun-tocs. From the Bontoc Igorotes, way up in the mountains, headhunters. It got to mean out-back-of-nowhere, and when soldiers came back with malaria and strange talk, they'd call chicksale, two-holer country 'out in the *bundox*.'

"In the German-Japanese war, the troops who got into the Philippines didn't have the opportunity to build up traditions and learn to butcher languages.

"How come this interest in elementary Tagalog? The Old Man told me an eyeful of Burmese girl gave you a burning passion for teak forestry."

He sketched his encounter with Miguel. "You'd

warned me about security," he concluded, "and maybe it was coincidence and maybe it was rigged, this business of a porter standing by, right when I wanted one. 'Boondocks' was a new one."

"You were suspicious, but you gave him a job."

"I gave him a job *because* I was halfway suspicious. Keep him around, learn more about him, maybe find out who put him on the job. If he'd said Manila, or Zamboanga, or Cavite, he might have been running the risk of my asking something about the town. Like I had been there. When he said, 'the boondocks,' I got the idea he was covering up, not naming a town."

Mona's eyes were more intense than ever, and her voice became soft as she repeated, as if to herself, the substance of what Felix had recited. For some moments he had the feeling that he was sitting alone in a deserted billiards room with no company other than a stand of samurai armor. When her presence verged on the uncanny, she flowed smoothly out of her chair and to her feet.

Mona made for the phone. She spoke one of the Asiatic languages, listened, and spoke again. Then she turned to Felix. "We'll find out more about Miguel. There is a girl from the Philippines, awfully good-looking. Lived pretty much around the islands. No use sitting here. I have a bar and kitchenette in the Foundation headquarters building. We'll wait there for a call back. This is bound to take time."

Although being marooned on an undesert island with Mona presented nothing Felix had not encountered in Bayonne, he was kept busy revising his concepts of bar, cuisine, and old bags. Bringing cognac and Pale Hands to the Brandon Foundation's number one trustee was like pouring a bottle of Vichy into the Pacific Ocean.

Mona was fascinated when he told her of Bayonne's classic liqueur, around each flask of which was a tissue-paper poop sheet entirely in Basque, with more trebled consonants then a Welsh wizard used to spell out an enchantment. He was by now so much at home that he did not feel foolish when Mona asked whether he would take the yellow Izzara or the green, which was 110 proof. His answer—"Both."—established public relations, being in the spirit of Nameless Island.

It was not long until Felix could not decide whether Pale Hands smelled good or tasted good. Undoubtedly the correct answer was, "Both."

In due course Felix decided that there were matters he should not discuss with Mom's former housekeeper if he ever again met her.

When he became aware of a persistent drumming *thump-tap-tap-thump*, he realized that he had heard much of it while he slept and that waking up had taken an unusually long time. Eventually, he decided that the sound was coming from the Burmese village. Time began to kick up capers; it was standing still, as Doc Brandon's antique clock seemed to be demonstrating.

One bell . . . interminable lapse . . . one bell . . . a period of unconsciousness, and again one bell.

This had become irritating.

"Get up and kick the silly bastard," he muttered. Instead, he fell asleep.

He knew he did, because then something woke him:

Bong . . . bong.

Two o'clock.

There was nothing wrong. What had puzzled Felix was hearing twelve-thirty . . . one . . . one-thirty . . .

What spoiled everything was that scream. When at last it reached a higher peak of agony, there came mutterings, murmurings, then blessed relief from that cry. But relief was followed by the impossible: a cry that made the earlier ones sound like sighs of contentment.

Regardless of Pale Hands, he was not in bed with Mona. This he learned when he clawed upholstery, twisted about, and clawed the deck.

He got almost to his feet and stumbled.

The scream came again. Each time he knew that it could not tear him to shreds, but each time it did until no shreds remained. Now the prolonging of the intervals became more excruciating than the measured beat had been.

Felix was about to cry out, when the phone rang. Mona answered, then cradled the instrument. Lights came to life, and she drew a Nile green robe about her. Idiosyncrasies of air and water currents made for sweltering days, with ninety-eight percent humidity, but night hours could be chilly.

"Feeling better?" she asked.

He was on his feet before she could give him a hand. He was in the sitting room. Without stumbling, he got into the adjoining room, which gave him vistas of bar and kitchen and bedroom and shower.

"I feel like a horse's ass, passing out."

"Think nothing of it. I have a peculiar metabolism. Digest liquor so fast, it never really hits bottom. You must be Roderick David Garvin's genuine personally begotten son."

That made him feel better. "What was that awful screaming?" he asked.

"Miguel confessed. Like he'd had an emetic."

Felix blinked and chewed air.

"He's never been in the Philippines," she continued. "Never heard of Bontocs. He is working for someone whose name is Norman Inglewood. My guess is that's something picked at random from the phone book.

"His job: watch the Garvins, find out where they go when they leave the *Semiramis*. Old man and boy go to Customs House. Then back to boat. Miguel pretended he was a porter. Old man is missing. And from there on—"

Felix cursed bitterly. "He got conscientious about taking his truck back to where he had borrowed it. I bet he phoned he had got a job and a ride to your island."

Mona smiled cryptically. That the smile was for him, instead of about him, was comforting. She had her phases of being the sweetest woman he had ever met, and then there was her total indifference to those excruciating screams. No doubt at all that whatever happened on Nameless Island was with her advice and consent. The main difference between Mona and a falcon or tiger was that the victims of the two last named were quickly terminated.

"If Miguel had not phoned, Norman Inglewood would not know where you are," she said.

"That's what I mean!"

Mona glowed as if proud of him. "We would not know that he existed. We would not have his phone number." For a moment he saw the warm feminine radiance; then the eyes changed, and when she spoke it was with a different voice. "You just about shuddered yourself into fits when you woke up and heard, quote, 'some of those diabolical Asiatic tortures.'"

Felix choked, got red to the ears, and agreed.

"Nobody touched him. Not even that beautiful mestiza from the Philippines. Those drums do give one cold horrors when they are played right. And we have a sound track. We used to have a Chinese woman here. Battered old hag. Used to earn enormous sums of money wailing at funerals.

"If the widow was unable to turn out a heartbreaking awful wail, Chinese style, she'd lose face. So this old woman was in demand. Chinese custom changed, and she retired. But while she could still hit a peak performance of ultimate agony, Doc made a sound track. There were two or three selections.

"Miguel thought the agonizing screams were someone getting the processing he was going to get. So he told all he knew."

"What'll we do with him?"

Mona shrugged. "You probably mean behead him, or slug him and feed him to the sharks?" When she saw him groping for the answer, she said, "Too late for more sleep. How about early breakfast and a siesta, and then we'll know."

A spicy crawfish bisque with rice and stuffed crawfish to give it substance laid the foundation both for a rest and to get a fresh start on a sticky situation.

"You've as good as guessed that the Old Man lost no time phoning to tell me that your sudden interest in teak-logging made his business in a settlement called Egypt too dull to consider," Mona said.

"He tried to talk me into going."

"Knowing that that would keep you far away from there. He said that if I couldn't keep you on the island, there probably would be enough Burmese or Malay girls to have a chance. Said you were naturally stubborn and contrary. I said you took after your father, and he laughed and said it worked. Our early workout for breakfast shows he was right."

Felix bristled. "Trying to protect me."

"Don't be so touchy! How about protecting himself and safeguarding whatever he is trying to accomplish? Alone, he got off the ship, and whoever—let's call him Inglewood for short—missed him and had to depend on Miguel. So, you'd be a handicap. Just like Miguel turned out to be a handicap to Inglewood."

Since it was still too early to do anything about Miguel, Mona briefed Felix, somewhat, on Egypt and the missing Imperatrix. Finally she phoned General Kerwin, using scrambled frequency microwave. She plugged in an extension.

"When I get the old Warlord, listen in, and if you think of anything new, tell us before you forget."

By this time, Felix was not surprised by the short time it took, with the right number and the proper wavelength, to get Dennis Kerwin.

"Morning, Denny. Did I wake you up?"

"Mona, well, for Christ's sweet sake! What's on your mind?"

She told him.

Felix's newest surprise was that this general, at least, was not the snarling, roaring, barking, growling stuffed-shirt stinker that American writers and journalists had to make any officer above the rank of captain.

Kerwin listened to Mona's account, then spoke. "Hold the line while I try the number the prisoner gave you. I hope you've not beheaded him or fed him to the sharks."

The Foundation's confidential message room remained silent until the Warlord called back.

"It's the number of an answering service," he said. "They would be pleased to accept a message for Mr. Inglewood. I said, 'Interesting arrangements have been made. We will phone when further details are available.' Naturally, I did not give any name or call back." He paused. "Felix Garvin," he said then. "Cognac and Madeira have arrived. Your father has not.

"Once you and Mona arrange a convincing escape for your prisoner—I suggest you wait two or three days until we can arrange a few stakeouts—we will meet you at a mainland rendezvous, time and place to be arranged later. Transportation with security escort will bring you to my headquarters. Thus far, well done. Very well, indeed!"

A few words from Mona closed the talk.

Felix finally broke the long and reflective pause that followed. "This beheading business. Was he kidding?"

"He was not. And there once was an incident: Five heads rolled. I had not ordered it, and probably it was the best solution. So I gave the perpetrators a severe talking to, without hurting anyone's feelings, and then I staged the fanciest pwe they had ever seen. It lasted five days." She was silent a moment. "That beautiful mestiza, Catalina, is going to fall in love with Miguel and help him escape, and about the time they get to Savannah, she will drop that *bugao* like a hot rock."

"What's a *bugao*?"

"It is a bad word in Tagalog. She is going to be busy falling in love with Miguel, and if security nabs him in Savannah, he'll wish he were dead, and it may not take long."

Felix reflected for a moment. "Once Dad gets the Imperatrix back into the spotlight and retires in Bayonne, are you ever going to quit the island?"

Mona shook her head. "Doc Brandon was the greatest, and I am the last of his girls. My place is right here. No disrespect to you or to your father, but that is how it is."

Felix got to his feet. "Madame Broadtail, now that I have no cause for moral scruples and about a hundred and seventy years to get in training—"

Mona cut in. "Probably be four or five days before the Warlord sends an armored personnel carrier for you, so we'll have time for a tour of the island."

Chapter 17

GARVIN SAT IN the enormous study of General Kerwin's year-round residence well outside The City That No One Wanted. Not yet retired, Kerwin served as chairman of a consortium of warlords on semiactive duty. They were the group that pulled the strings that made a puppet prime minister do what was required to keep a Limited Democracy working effectively without becoming a despotism based on votes bought with taxpayers' money. In effect, this was comparable to the Consortium of which the late Imperator had been chairman during the final years of the former Parliamentary Republic.

What made Garvin feel as old and weary as the elder statesman looked was Kerwin's aide-de-camp, a tall, thin-faced colonel, lean and redheaded. His previous talk with Oscar Emberg had been about eighteen years before, when the latter had been a buck private guarding an extremely high velocity rifle, the Alexander Mark I, a self-propelled 105-millimeter weapon one of whose caissons of propellant charges also contained the embalmed body of Ersatz Imperatrix Eileen.

"Oscar, I see that Captain Wilson promoted you to private first class, as I suggested."

"Admiral, he said that it was not every day that a military career began to prosper because a sentry neither shot the spy nor the dog. A grand officer, B.G., and going up."

Garvin chuckled. "Was he referring to your career or his?"

"Both, I hope."

An orderly came in with three mint juleps.

"Rod," Kerwin said. "Instead of sour mash, these are mixed with the cognac you sent, with your compliments."

"I was afraid my son would swill it, hence my precaution. But I never heard of a julep with brandy."

"Until the damn Yankees ruined things, gentlemen of the South always preferred cognac or Armagnac—and could afford it." He pointed. "And the first one today is dedicated to our deceased comrade."

From the study, they looked over the mists billowing several hundred meters below and saw a massive red granite boulder, raw, ragged, and unshaped except for a mirror-burnished rectangle about forty by sixty centimeters.

The Senior Warlord handed Garvin binoculars. "Read the inscription."

Garvin did so.

ALEXANDER IMPERATOR
EILEEN VICE-IMPERATRIX

They raised their glasses and drank.

"So the facts leaked out," Garvin said. "A grand girl, a great lady. Sincere. Too serious, worried herself to death. But why no dates?"

"Before he pulled the switch," Kerwin answered, "he told me a few things. Some never got on the air. One that was scrubbed went about like this: 'Enemies at home and abroad—and the former outnumber the latter—have so long cursed the day I was born that they need no reminder. And survivors will remember the day of my death.'"

Garvin took a moment or two for digesting that one. At last he spoke. "Not chiseling that epitaph on the rock will speed up the tapering off of old-time hatreds."

"Take a close look at that rock, a bit left of the polished rectangle."

Garvin squinted again. "Eyes aren't what they used to be . . . now I get it! I'd swear the rock had a bullet metal splash."

"Eyes are okay, Rod. Zealous Liberal announced to a crowd what he was going to do. And after a rally-protest, made good by pissing on the grave. Sharpshooter drilled him twice before he fell."

"That was violating the guy's civil rights. Freedom of expression is not restricted to spoken or written words."

Emberg was doing his best to keep a straight face.

Garvin regarded the colonel's Distinguished Rifleman's badge, a rating so much higher than Expert that few were ever issued. His glance rose to Emberg's eyes. "Looks like one shot missed."

"Sir, that is the splash of two shots, penetrating the target one on the heels of the other. We found two ejected cartridges, and we studied the granite with high-powered optics."

Garvin turned to the Warlord. "Denny, if you ever find out who did the shooting, see that he gets his Distinguished badge."

Kerwin snorted. "He got a court-martial for wasting government ammunition. One shot sufficed. But he did get his badge."

"According to history books," Garvin observed, "the flag of the Republic fared far worse than Alexander's grave, and a patriotic public sided with the demonstrators and applauded. Speaking of old grudges and hatreds and activists, I see that Lani's name is not on the rock of ages. Well, not yet. Any rumors?"

"About the time our counterattack was massacring the enemy, I told her to get going and stay hidden till things quieted down. So far, no change."

Garvin frowned. "That's old habit, Denny. Last time we discussed Lani, you made a point of knowing nothing. If you had studied as much history as I have in the course of governing Mars, you'd know that for nearly a

century after 1917 there were rumors about surviving
members of the Russian czar's murdered family."

"I remember our talk. Times have changed. Industrial
potential is being realized in the less backward areas.
Foreign commerce, reviving fairly well. There still are
enemies of Limited Democracy, not enough to constitute
a quorum. Not open opposition but the organized foot-
dragging and disguised sabotage and manufactured ob-
stacles.

"Well, goddammit, yes! There have been rumors
about Harry Offendorf's disappearance, along with his
chauffeur or whatever. Investigators finally found bones
in a ravine. The thousand-meter drop had not damaged
any teeth. Dental work identified that nice, harmless
Liberal.

"What started the investigation was a Benson limou-
sine, a rental, abandoned at the Ecumenical Coed Christian Retreat. The abbot said a Mr. Higgenbotham and a
Mr. Wolfe came to visit one of the Retreat's customers,
Sister Zenia. The visitors were last seen heading for her
cabin, well in the woods at the fringe of the plateau.

"Tea had been served. No sign of struggle. Also, not a
goddamn fingerprint in the shack. The weirdest thing is
the massive bureaucracy. Massive in spite of...um...
attrition, it has not spent a billion pazors making a study.
Whenever the fat boys run out of drinking and whoring
money, they tie the government into running-bowline
knots until a hundred million is spent on some 'study' or
for 'consultants.'"

"Manure!" Garvin flared up. "Nothing odd about that.
The retreat is one of a chain, sort of. In wild country, for
people who do not want to be bothered during troubled
times. As long as it is Christian, it has to be dealt with
cautiously.

"Harry was incognito and in wild country. He rented
an impressive car to look official-important. That son of
a bitch of an Ingerman had faced so many news cameras,
he was too well known, but Offendorf wasn't news-
famous. Whoever Sister Zenia was, Harry and his helper

had plans for her. Plans you can bet they intended she would never discuss with the media.

"Something went wrong. Hence the pyramids. Two male skeletons, and I'd bet Sister Zenia still has meat on her bones."

Kerwin frowned. Colonel Emberg sat like a graven image that tried not to look like one.

"One recluse pushed two men over the edge?" the Warlord asked.

"She could have been a dangerous woman who happened to have an equally dangerous friend or two. If things had happened as planned, Mr. Higgenbotham and Mr. Wolfe and nobody else would ever know where Zenia went."

"But now," Kerwin cut in, "she knows what happened to Harry. You have as good as told me Zenia was and is Lani Imperatrix."

"I've told you nothing. No one of Offendorf's status would bother with small game. No other woman in North America was important enough to rate his personal attention: Although retired, he was important enough to be convincing when he approached an empress in hideout with a supposedly nationally urgent deal." Garvin sighed. "If it only had been that bastard of a Neville Ingerman who almost sold an army to the Slivovitz slobs."

"Ingerman must have left the country. He did face too many media cameras," Kerwin conceded. "Too many ex-soldiers and loyal citizens would love to hang him by his toes and flog him to death, and he'd be happy they were too impatient to stake him out over an anthill in Arizona."

"That's gospel." Garvin drew a deep breath. "Me, I am making a survey, incognito, with a mule-team wagon, trader outfit. To find out about the real state of the nation. With respect to updating the program of Martian Eck and Ag."

"Rod, skip all this crap. You know where Lani is."

Garvin grinned. "When you invited my Flora, my Number One Wife, to be glamour Imperatrix, I suspected Limited Democracy needed opium dream-essence to sugarcoat military dictatorship. I think so now more than ever. Give me a free hand and maybe I can talk her out of her genuine loyalty to Alexander's memory, her notions on noblesse oblige that make her balk at leaving until the Imperium is restored—or she dies, hoping for its comeback."

"You sold me a bill of goods."

"I have to have a free hand. I want a cruiser landed in an open space behind a ridge near where she is. I need a crop-dusting thing cooked up by the agricultural crowd. It will have to be a navy-type smoke screen so dense, the cruiser can land without being noticed by ground observers.

"I will not, repeat, goddammit, not risk surface travel in any direction, and I have to have space-patrol cover for the cruiser during landing and taking off.

"The public has to have something to worship. For lack of better, a lot of them picked Karl Marx and all other sorts of socialist horse shit. The Stompers and the Testifiers have made peace, and they are getting stronger and stronger."

Kerwin frowned. "Those silly bastards just climbed down out of the trees. So what and why?"

"It is the congenital American passion for worshiping someone or something. Look at those stupid assholes in Guyana back in the 1980s. The cult leader told them to commit suicide, and damn near a thousand did so."

"Rod, you should be a historian."

"Students declared history was irrelevant. Their elders worshiped the brats and agreed instead of booting their behinds until their noses bled. Ask Oscar about the Stompers!"

Chapter 18

THAT IT WAS long past suppertime was not what kept Miguel Rodriguez craning his neck and peering between the bars past that *chingado* of a Burmese guard who continued to curse and threaten him for being the funkiller who was keeping him, the man with the Mark I assault carbine, from the fiesta in the village. It being tactless to curse the Mistress of Nameless Island, who pampered and coddled the late "Doc" Brandon's protégés and encouraged the beheading of anti-Brandon snoopers, Miguel was the one who got the hate ration.

Although few of the Burmese spoke more than scraps of English, the guard had wagged his head and beamed happily when the Lady had given him his orders.

"Can do," he declared, and added something that probably meant something like "I place my head beneath your Golden Feet."

What Mona had said in clear English was: "If this son of a bitch tries to escape, give him the whole clip."

The Mark I accepted a clip that held forty cartridges.

Mona had paused long enough to say to Miguel, "Mike, as long as you behave, you have nothing to worry about."

Miguel had no intention of being "shot while attempting to escape." What's more, the cage itself made the very idea of escaping ridiculous: It had once confined the late Avery Jarvis "Doc" Brandon's masterpiece of ge-

netic engineering, the re-creation of a saber-toothed
tiger, the long-extinct Machaerodus, *Smilodon californicus,* whose bones in the asphalt pits near Los Angeles
were all that remained of those deadly Felidae.

What did worry the prisoner was that the blond bitch
who ruled the island might have caught his only friend,
the lovely Catalina, in the act of snitching food for him
from the Foundation's white-collar section. Catalina and
others of the kitchen force had always looked forward to
serving in the galley of the *Tiburón* when she towed a
raft of teak logs to Savannah. It was on the homebound
trip that Miguel and Catalina had become acquainted,
before either suspected that he would soon need a friend
—and need one badly.

Maybe she had not been caught in the act of cooking a
Tagalog delicacy for him; perhaps she had been put to
work fixing snacks for the fiesta. Those Burmese
bugaos!

"Don't worry," Catalina had told Miguel the first night
she had sneaked special food to him along with the
guard's ration. "Yes, she suspects you. But not like she
did the fellows who were running a boat without lights,
measuring how deep is the water off the island. Her
friend, that Garvin, he used a special gun that sees in the
dark. The bullet made an explosion when it hit something that stop the boat, and the men think it is a mine
which they hit with the propeller.

"She send help for the strangers. Towed their boat.
Then, when they got their feet on land, the visitors they
got the heads chopped off. Very sudden. She acts that
way.

"But you—you worry about the guard. He is to make
sure you do not give a present to someone in the village,
someone with a key for the lock on the chain."

She indicated the chain that secured the door, which
was of steel bars as heavy as those of the cage.

Although Catalina had made no promises on the boat
ride from Savannah and there had been no chance for
serious lovemaking on the crowded tug, Miguel had

every reason to believe that the beautiful young lady from the Philippines was quite fond of him. And that she might leave the island with him once he quit his job as Felix Garvin's Number One Boy.

With a happier background experience, Miguel would have enjoyed the drumming, the Chinese fiddles, the moaning flutes, and the interludes when the golden mellow gamelan took over and all this was tied into a pentatonic rhythm by the *tock-tock-tock* of red-lacquered "fish-heads," hardwood rattles that accented the drums.

The single-stringed fiddles, fascinatingly sweet and well bowed, gave him chills: Their sound evoked memories of that torture by suggestion, that funeral wailing which had so horrified him. Moment by dragging moment, the village merriment made him ever more depressed. During a lull in the chanting and music, night sounds nagged Miguel.

The voice of the bamboo stirring in the wind, the snap of a breaking twig, or the crackle that sounded like a dry teak leaf being stepped on made him start and glance about into the darkness.

The cage itself was revolting. As an old barn has the scent of horses many years after it has sheltered only tractors, so it was with the home of a saber-toothed tiger: The major difference was that while equine bouquet is acceptable to many humans and loathsome to very few, if any, feline scent would rate in the opposite way, especially that of the mighty Machaerodus, *Smilodon californicus*, in every sense, the most fearsome of the Felidae.

Although he had become used to the scent, it depressed him more than he realized. Degrading . . . an animal's cage.

And then with moonrise the night became beautiful. Sea breeze purified the air and brought him a whiff of Seven Bells: not that ancient classic of Luzon gin but a luscious Asiatic scent. Catalina was near. She emerged from deep shadow and into the light, balancing a *pinga* pole on her shoulder, a basket fore, another aft, in the old Chinese mode of carrying. This one-time taxi dancer from a barrio near the American naval station at Subic was lovely, but there was something odd about her gait. And her skirt did not sway and ripple as she paced. A prisoner caged soon notices things he would never observe if he were free.

Ignoring the prisoner, Catalina unshipped the baskets and handed one to the guard. She said something in Burmese. He brightened, seated himself on a stump, and set his assault carbine between the uprights of the bamboo and palm-thatched shelter that kept him out of the sun's glare. As he dug into his meal, the spicy odor set Miguel to wondering what she had brought for him, if the watchman got such savory fare.

Pulling up a camp chair, Catalina took the cover from the prisoner's basket.

"There was so much extra work," she explained. "That fiesta. So I kept you waiting." She lowered her voice to a whisper. "Eat real slowly. Of course you are hungry, but do like I say."

There was a bowl of rice, another of curry sauce in which were morsels of chicken, and a third with cubes of broiled mutton making little islands in a sea of hot *satay* sauce. Each bowl passed between the bars of the gate, with a few millimeters to spare.

Miguel was too hungry, too happy to wonder why or if he imagined hearing a faint metallic tinkle. Certainly it could not have been Catalina's coral ear pendants.

The bamboo chopsticks and the porcelain Chinese-style soup spoon were useless for an escape attempt. He had been wondering when to bring up the subject of hacksaw blades.

"Take your time, don't hurry," she whispered.

From the basket she dug a little bowl of tamarind chutney and a saucer of tiny fish in a molasses-flavored syrup. Once he had the extra delicacies set on the concrete slab, Catalina retreated to her chair. Something was cooking. Keyed up by anxiety, Miguel's sharpened senses told him that she was tense, all on edge. Her low voice told him that much, but no more.

Slices of mango . . .

The delicacies began to choke Miguel. If that *chingado* had sensed her excitement . . .

Finally Miguel risked a glance at his guard. The man had quit eating. So had Miguel. Then the watcher's bowl clattered to the coquina paving of the narrow roadway. The fellow sagged and collapsed. He rolled over, a sodden heap. He was within grabbing distance of his carbine, but he might as well have been a kilometer away.

Catalina was at the tiger cage. "Now you see why I said eat slow."

She hitched her skirt up to her waist. By moonlight Miguel might have noticed the pretties she had bought while shopping in Savannah. The moonlight was quite bright enough, but what startled and fascinated the prisoner was the web girdle she wore and the implement suspended from it. When she unsnapped the concealed cargo, he knew why he had heard faint metallic tinklings.

The implement was a bolt cutter. She slipped it between the bars.

"Cut the chain. I'm too weak."

He had the strength. When a link gave way and the chain with intact padlock surrendered, the gate creaked open, and Miguel stepped into the moonlight.

"Bring the cutter!" Her voice was choked, a gasping, a quaver. She caught his hand, as though to yank him toward the stand of bamboo across the way and the path leading into it. "At the boat—we need the cutter."

And then Miguel caught the full force of the charade. He could not doubt Catalina's honesty, but that blond bitch and her trickery, that unconscious sentry who might be wide awake, waiting to snatch the carbine and its clip of forty rounds . . . He stood fast.

"Run for it! While you can," he ordered.

She obeyed the voice of command. A flurry of skirts and she was swallowed by bamboo darkness. Her inarticulate cry did not hurry him. If this were a trap, there would be others, if not the sentry, to cut him down.

He made an obscene gesture and deliberately strode toward the pathway.

When rustling bamboo enveloped him and he was busy with an armful of Catalina and hampered by a bolt cutter, he knew that this had not been a trap. And it did not take long to get to the pier, cut loose a pirogue, and paddle toward the mainland.

Chapter 19

LONG BEFORE HE reached the turnout on the high ridge from which he got his first view of Egypt Township, Garvin was glad that he had taken General Kerwin's advice:

"Things are not as primitive as they were when you brought Eileen up from Pensacola for her funeral. Take a truck with a trailer for a motorcycle for scouting around the whole area. Go as a representative of the Brandon Foundation, making a survey."

There was no doubt that the army had become over-motorized and was right in reviving jackass batteries and mule-drawn equipment for service in nasty terrain and climate. Garvin, however, felt far more at home with a First Army truck and a motorcycle, both done over with a civilian paint job.

The ridge ran southwesterly and overlooked the river that emerged from a hilly stretch on his right. Two dams fed irrigation canals. Windmills on the river's right bank were ready to pump when the water level was low. Through his binoculars Garvin sized up a settlement shaded by poplars, sycamores, and cottonwoods. Flat-roofed buildings, some apparently of adobe, others of concrete construction-blocks, marked the heart of the colony. He wondered whether the verdant tract was the classical six miles by six miles or whether purists had made it a 9.654-kilometer square or an even ten kay-ems each way.

"Tractors grinding away," he noted, "and trucks, campers, and mule teams heading east and west..." Swinging again to his right, Garvin saw what looked like papyrus: stalks, each with a fanlike crest, rising a couple of meters out of the river's lagoons and swaying in the breeze.

After a moment of wondering at such attention to local color, Garvin centered on the view of what must be Main Street, across the bridge. The female denizens wore jeans of diverse lengths or gingham housedresses; whether shoes, sandals, or bare feet depended on individual taste. In two respects, however, the women were uniform: All had black hair in tight curls, not quite shoulder length; and however much or little skin she exposed, each owed her complexion to the tan that an infusion of black walnut hulls would give.

For a woman hiding out, this was the ideal spot.

Some carried shopping baskets. Others were heading for the fields with lunch boxes no doubt holding second breakfasts for the workers. There seemed nothing in this cult that made work a blasphemy and crime against nature and nothing in this religion that demanded retirement to gracious living at age thirty-five. And thus far, Garvin had not seen anyone wrapped up like a mummy looking for a vacant sarcophagus.

Driving well into town, he learned that accommodations were available at the Isis-Osiris Inn. After a quick look-see, Garvin found stark simplicity and no cockroaches in sight. Impressed by this blessing, he returned to the desk. There was off-street parking, storage for personal property at the owner's risk, and no charge for space.

"When I am caught up with chow and sleep," he told the clerk, "I'd like to make an appointment with Sir E. A. Wallis Budge or his reincarnation. Or whoever is running this town." Garvin presented his Pierre d'Artois identity papers, along with his credentials as an agent of the Avery Jarvis Brandon Foundation. "This is business, not an application for cult membership."

"I am sorry, sir, about that ridiculous rumor! We've never been able to squelch it!"

"Anyway, this is Egypt, judging from the papyrus in the lagoon and the way the women wear their hair and the name of this hotel?"

"There is an Egypt in Texas, one in Kentucky, another in Arkansas, but this is the best of the lot. The entire township belongs to Mr. Bertram Turner."

"He owns the works?"

"Thirty-six sections, each a mile square."

"Please tell Mr. Turner that I want to make a deal with him for renting a house. Tomorrow, midafternoon, or when it is convenient for him."

After rest and a snack, Garvin set out to meet the town. He took his audio-video recorder to make a foundation for the question and answer session with Bertram Turner.

There was little traffic and no sidewalks. Well ahead of him and across the street was a sign:

EGYPTIAN WEEKLY BULLETIN

&

JOB PRINTING

This looked like a good start until he noticed the queue reaching halfway down the block.

A male brat, reading Garvin's scowl, shouted from the line and beckoned. "For a pazor, I'll getcha one!"

Garvin crossed the street and gave him a coin.

"That's for service. Got to have another for the paper."

The boy got another.

"Something big happened?" Garvin asked. "All this lineup?"

"Ain't nothing happened. This is the first paper in three weeks."

The whir of machinery and an open window attracted Garvin's attention. He gestured. "I'll be in there."

Garvin stepped to the entrance of the job printing department. The operator had nothing to do but watch the final run of a three-color and black offset job. Noting the foreigner's interest, he beckoned, and Garvin stepped in.

"Hieroglyphics! I'll be damned! *Coming Forth by Day.*"

"You read picture writing?" the printer asked.

"No way! But there's the start of the next strip coming up. Ani the Scribe and his wife."

"That's what Mr. Turner told me."

"Looks like awfully good registry. How do you do it with this continuous feed?"

The man picked a scroll from a cabinet and handed it to Garvin, then offered a glass. "Electronic, constant correction."

Garvin looked. "Perfect registry, and on papyrus."

"We grow our own in a lagoon up the river. Run the crude paper between compression rollers and make it smooth."

"Says on the margin, '*Made in Egypt.*' You mean you get tourist business out here?"

The operator grinned and spat tobacco juice. "These go to the original Egypt, for tourists from all over the world. And we've got a line of scarabs. Stamp them out of a mix of porphyry dust and fire them up for a fine glaze."

Garvin bought three, and went to get his bulletin. His next stop was at the city limits. There he paused at the temple long enough for a look down the avenue of sphinxes, at the entrance, with an obelisk at each side; an open court; and, beyond that, a court whose roof was supported by columns.

Dismissing this as tourist bait, he circled the town and the varied agricultural zones that skirted it. A little before midafternoon, Garvin was approaching Egypt House, whose white stuccoed front presented, in fresco, friezes, and panels of red, ruddy brown, and ocher, with touches of green and blue and black: gods, pharaohs, prisoners of war, festive groups, and dancers. From human to divine, from fancy to fact, Egypt paraded.

An Egyptianesque woman admitted Garvin. Her ice-blue eyes and the freckles that were perceptible through

her conventional Isis complexion dye suggested that she
was a born rehead. If such were the fact, there was more
than cultism in the makeup: Were she demoted to field-
work, her face and throat, if left unprotected, would
soon be as seamed and wrinkled as sun-cured rawhide
and eventually develop skin cancer. Since Garvin was a
foreigner with audio-video gear and harness, she gestured and conducted him to a comfortable library devoid
of the Nilotic.

A large antique Feraghan rug welcomed visitors. The
field was deep red, solemn, stately, without a trace of
either scarlet or crimson. The repeat pattern was Herati.

There were massive leather chairs. Facing the fireplace was a leather sofa. On the floor before it lay a
Tekke Turkoman rug, of a clear *transparent* garnet red
with a main border of silk. But for the moment, what
caught and held Garvin's attention was the bald head of
the man who sat facing the hearth: a lordly dome with a
fringe of black hair.

And then the Lord Proprietor and Garvin were facing
each other.

"Mr. D'Artois, I'm sure. They told me you've been
busy recording the sights of Egypt and questions and
answers vis à vis the denizens. Sorry neither Sir Ernest
nor his reincarnated self is here to greet you."

Bertram Turner spoke the kind of English that any
literate North American could understand. Voice and
manner told Garvin that he was welcome.

Not quite a head taller than his visitor, Turner was
deep chested and broad of shoulders. Although by no
means square, the tanned face was neither narrow nor
angular. The ears sat close to the head. The brown eyes
were flecked with hazel. Trying to decide whether he
was an elderly thirty or a boyish fifty would have been
silly and pointless.

Garvin unslung the AV gear. "After you've told me
about Egypt, we can record the negotiations. When my
client has played it back, we'll meet again for you to
answer her questions. I have not the foggiest idea of how
she—Mona Smith, the director of the Foundation—in-

tends to use my survey. I made it clear that I would not undertake this work unless you cleared the material. Until credit arrangements are made, I'll be on a cash basis."

Turner raised a peremptory hand. "It was the late Dr. Brandon whose Nameless Island suggested my buying this apparently useless land. Let's see your show!"

When a field of electric-blue flowers filled the screen, Garvin's comment sounded from the speaker: "Damn if it isn't flax."

"Quite right," Turner said. "Linseed oil for ships' stores, oil cake—though fabric and lace are our main line. In spite of modern machinery, handcraft still prevails with linen. For export, of course. Too valuable for us to wear. Except for the annual Osiris-Isis Passion Play." He sighed and grimaced a burlesque of woe. "A newspaper man had to call our masque 'the Egyptian Oberammergau.' And when a Stomper or Testifier who could read got hold of the paper, we had two sets of enemies. Each decided we were blasphemous, sacrilegious bastards. A journalist came for another interview. I assured him that our pageant had been established seven thousand years before the Christian plagiarism—poor imitation!—had warped the original myth all out of shape. They waxed exceedingly wroth."

"I damn well imagine," Garvin agreed. "But Osiris, Isis, and Horus were the first trinity, and regardless of her apparently...um...irregular domestic arrangements, she was the first of a flock of Virgin Mothers. At times you do seem to be tactless."

Turner shrugged. "My most conspicuous social error got me these thirty-six square miles of township."

Garvin made a ninety-degree bow, with mock ceremoniousness. "Sir, welcome to the club! I'd like to stay here long enough to master your formula. A minor error on my part got me exiled to Mars."

Turner regarded his visitor, admiration blended with awe. "Would it be impertinent of me to ask for particulars?"

"Not a bit, provided that you give me your formula."

"This was wretched land. The people who sold it thought I was an idiot. I set a group of disgruntled Mennonites to work on it. Odd characters, the world's masters of agriculture. But as the Isis cult developed, they suspected us of worshiping graven images and bailed out. In high dudgeon. Rugged nonconformists themselves, but they objected to us. Except a few renegades who succumbed to higher salaries and continued supervising this development."

"Sir Ernest—uh, Sir Bertram—Goddammit. The formula! The suspense is bemuddling me!"

"Now I remember! You mentioned a club. I belonged to one of the better ones. The bylaws strictly forbade a member's bringing his wife to the club except for the Annual Ladies' Night Dinner. Possibly I had been drinking more than necessary, and doubtless she had. In any event, the Committee called my attention to the bylaws.

"My demurrer was immediate and truthful. Since the lady was not my wife, I was not in violation. Fact is, her husband was not even a member of that club. Nevertheless, there were complications which led to demands for my resignation from the club, that I resign my commission in the Peshawar Lancers, a Guard regiment, you know. And now we get to the dreariest parcel of family history." He stopped short.

"Carry on," Garvin urged. "Carry on!"

"This goes back to the early eighteen hundreds and the first Earl of Sommerton, Archibald Turnour, T-U-R-N-O-U-R. We Turnours were of a collateral line. And when the earl then sitting in the House of Lords died without issue, I was next in line of succession."

"Lord Sommerton?"

"Not quite. The family council was unduly impressed by the prospect of having an earl sitting in the house. They informed me that in view of my scandalous record, drinking and whoring around, you know—and this latest scandal! Since the lady's husband was quite influential, the prudent thing, of course, was to let the title go to the next in line after me. Provided that I accepted a substantial cash honorarium and quit England forever and, in addition, that I bound myself, my heirs, and assignees, and so forth from ever spelling the surname T-U-R-N-O-U-R. So it is T-U-R-N-E-R. Now that that is settled, may I ask what you did; who and what you are?"

"In the battle of Kashgar, a few years ago, I was allegedly needlessly rough with the goddamn Marxists. Destroyed an armored division. Border incident, a triviality.

"I am temporarily released from exile. Normally, my duties as Admiral the Governor-General of Mars restrict me to that planet. I am Roderick David Garvin. Incognito. Marxist enemies."

"Ah . . . *the* Garvin, no doubt?"

The once almost earl stepped to a cabinet from which he took a bottle of Hutchinson's Invalid Fort, vintage 2052. He set out goblets. They drank.

"Do I address you as Admiral, General, Governor, or Excellency? When we have done discussing Egypt, you must give me pointers on destroying an armored division."

"Regarding address," Garvin said, "how about Bert and Rod, my lord? But for Christ's sweet sake, only in private!"

That agreed, they resumed viewing Garvin's taped show.

The field of dhurra led to words on dhurra cakes, porridge, and beer. "Since we're vegetarian, instead of feeding it to animals and eating them, we consume the grain ourselves. . . . And here's our cotton."

Garvin's voice again came from the speaker: "Damn me if this doesn't look like Martian improvement—"

"Quite right, Rod. Super-Egyptian, superlong fiber."

Garvin stopped the show when he came to women wearing broad-brimmed hats. Some walked down between rows of grayish-green poppy plants, slashing the unripened seed capsules. Others were scraping yesterday's dried gum from capsules.

"Papaver somniferum?"

"Quite right. During the wartime shortage of anesthetics, our crude opium did very well. Since it costs less than coffee and is subject to no restrictions, there is no crime in the occasional addict. With no prohibitions against it, there is no smartness in using the stuff. The few who do, well, they're regarded with benevolent contempt."

The terms of a lease of living quarters required less than the drinking time of a goblet of port.

"When my client comments, we'll need a bottle!" Garvin said. "But before I forget it, would you mind telling how you got so fascinated by ancient Egypt?"

"I devoted a number of years to archeological digs well up the Nile. The more I compared the cultures of antiquity with our science worship, the more I felt that technology had enslaved more than it had liberated. The late Dr. Brandon seems finally to have concluded that a century of supertechnology began as a dream and terminated as a nightmare!"

"That was Doc Brandon's view shortly before he died."

"The tomb and temple paintings," Bert resumed, "The colorful papyri gave me a respect, an admiration for the ancients. A true affection. Century and a half ago, that great Egyptologist, J. E. Manville Greene, wrote a delightful book on the ancient culture. His expression is so much more meaningful than my bumbling words.

"It's more the pictures than the written records that give one the feeling that theirs was a society of good humor, tolerance, inner harmony, and precious little of that competitiveness that makes the man with three speedboats feel inferior when he meets someone who has five. *My* Egypt has only one bit of competition: the masque, the girl who is to be Isis for a day. And very few are shaped for that honor. So few that there is no scramble!" He paused. "I hope you're not about to remind me of the poverty of all but the priests, the scribes, the nobles, and royalty."

"Right! The most dignified, the most serene, the really poised people I have ever seen were in a pipsqueak settlement of twenty or thirty Indians in the Mexican jungle, two thousand meters above sea level. They had something that few of our one-time high-living-standard folk ever have! I know what you mean."

"And I know what *you* mean!" Bert countered. "In Egypt, as well as in Old China, for instance, there was always the well-to-do person who encouraged and financed the talented lad. He'd become a scribe, and his grandchildren, friends of Pharaoh, or of the Son of Heaven. No wasted effort, no silly egalitarianism. The clod stayed the clod he was born."

Garvin reached for his recording gear. "The Warlords are working toward a Limited Democracy, doing away with the tyranny of the overrated 'common' man, who is quite too plentiful." He shouldered his pack. "If my client does not like my work, I'll suggest she dismiss me, and I'll head back to Mars, which I am stuck with!"

Chapter 20

ALL THAT KEPT his first view of Lani from being a cross between an opium dream and a politician's promise was truth: She did not look a day older than when Garvin had left her eighteen years ago, when she had refused to board his cruiser to go to Mars and safety.

Her hair was now black and curled to imitate the wig that the scribe's wife wore in the papyrus *Going Forth by Day*; her skin was tinted to accord with Local Egypt; and from toenails to eyebrows, there was not a wrinkle, not a droop, not a trace of crepe or sag. He realized finally that he had overrated, purely on technicalities, both Flora and Azadeh. Time had been gracious to each. Time had ignored Lani.

"If you'd only let me know, I'd have got shed of the makeup. These herb dyes are easy to take off. When we're used to each other again, I'll go back to local complexion."

Lani turned slowly in front of the three-leaf mirror. "When Mona told me about Doc's records, I wouldn't believe it, so I got these to check up. Most of us are experimental models. I mean, those who are not mass-cloned. How is she doing?"

"I phoned, but I've not seen her. There were nasty complications from the time Felix and I landed in Savannah. So, while the enemy trailed him to Nameless Island, I sneaked out here. Without being followed."

"They. The same people—I mean, new ones with the same old plans for me?"

"Right. But quite aside from security, you and I have a lot to get used to. For the moment, that'll keep. The minute I pulled up at the inn, I told the clerk to get me an appointment with the owner of the township and soon found out the name was Bertram Turner, not E. A. Wallis Budge. Your having had no problems here made it plain that I did not need my incognito, not in private. I'd cleared it with Mona and Number One General. My front is that I am making a survey for the Brandon Foundation and the Warlords. Actually, I am getting data for their state-of-the-nation estimate. Bert and I got along nicely. I'm off to a good start. He fixed me up with what I was looking for—a house well off the main stem and near the fringe of town."

"Idiot! You're in broad-minded Egypt, and I have lots of room right here. You're worried about drawing enemies to me?"

"With local hairdo and coloring, you're just another female Egyptian, only better stacked up and with the right kind of eyes to model Isis in a temple painting."

"Why don't you join the club?"

"If I have any manhunting to do, I'd be conspicuous the minute I got away from here. Meanwhile, I found a lot of Tokaija. Some dry, some medium, some five *put-tonos,* and a few bottles of Essencia."

"Essencia? Not really! We never had any in the cellars at Four Seasons Palace."

Lani was not marveling at the cost of the precious Tokaija essence. There was very little available; he had to elaborate. "Once I convinced him that I was the war criminal who nearly got a death sentence for destroying a Slivovitz division of armor, the fellow in that wine shop on Pont Neuf loosened up and let me have a couple of bottles of Essencia, provided I took a bundle of the regular Tokaija."

He did not tell Lani that he had injected into the wine the hormones devised by the Martian superscientists to make the Simianoidesses more pregnancy-prone. Although he could have opened the bottles and doctored the wine without risk of the wine's spoiling, he preferred a needle to penetrate tinfoil and stopper. He needed to keep the hormone truly secret from Lani, to eliminate the placebo potential.

"Meanwhile," Garvin resumed, "I am here at this crossroads spot, well, supposedly to collect gossip, traveler and trucker talk. Get opinions on the state of the nation. Not a poll. The minute you settle down to a routine of questions, you are slanting the answers. Just sit and listen, you get closer to facts, or what people think is true.

"Fact is, I am taking accumulated leave. I was getting chronic homesickness. Made a religion of sitting at my telescope, waiting for Earthrise. Azadeh saw through that right away. She was getting homesick. Mars and Gook Town had not been her home for many a year.

"The goddamn North Americans had spoiled things. So she is going to the Asteroid, where the folks are really her people. Naturally, each is going to get fed up with the old farm. I am tired, and I am retiring. Probably in France. And Azadeh may try it with us. Aljai's been back on the Asteroid and seems to be happy and where she belongs. We had a cozy life those six years."

Lani gave him time for a sigh before she broke the silence. "Marooned on the Asteroid and sitting on the palace roof, waiting for Mars to rise. Well, stopping in Bayonne to see Flora and meet your son—no better way of learning that we are getting older."

"All except you."

"Inside, I'm weary as you are. But this is our chance!"

"Chance for what? Just being here is enough. It's a peak!"

"Of course, it is the peak of all our years! All the more so if we look back, ages ago, to you and I meeting in the Mall of Megapolis Alpha."

"Jesus, woman! Thirty years ago."

"Or more. For fun and games, good for the soul, after

a battle like you and Flora had. We R and R girls saved many a marriage."

"Worked that way for me and Flora, though it was the craziest roundabout!"

"End: shanghaied to Martian observation domes, twenty kay-ems apart. You figured how to ride to my front door and fake geology reports to account for the distance on your bike. That was desperation and starvation!"

"Now I get it!" he cut in. "Alex called me from exile!"

"You thought you knew what would happen," Lani resumed. "I knew what had to take place when we had our farewell. But each was sure that we'd never again see each other."

Garvin drew a deep breath, then exhaled slowly. "With nowhere else to hide, you were a stowaway aboard the *Saturnienne*, with a crew of dopes planning mutiny. When we circled Saturn, and I married you and the Admiral, all looked grand—till mutiny on the Asteroid left you a widow and alive, thanks to the Gur Khan. And if his wives hadn't threatened to poison you, we'd still be marooned on that miniplanet—it is damn well our turn. A year or more. And who could ever have taken enough, sniffing, smoking, or with a needle, even to imagine we'd ever have this chance! See what I mean, just being here is the peak?"

Lani's kiss was fire and wonder and witchery.

"You mean every word of it, and every word means more to me!" She drew back and sighed. Levitation ended: Her feet came back to nicely polished tongue-and-groove floor. "Something you have to tell me," she said. "To make it really real."

"I'm not afraid of anything! Sound off."

"When we realized what we had, memories nearly drowned us. But you came back to have me permanently bleached, inspected, certified as the sure enough, the genuine, and only Lani Imperatrix, and talked into going to Mars as a glamour figure, a better way of being loyal to Alex than hiding until his dream came true."

There was a long silence.

"It is, isn't it?" she said finally.

"It is, Goddammit! And so?"

"Neville Ingerman betrayed an army and, in a left-handed way, caused Alexander's death. Bring me his head, and if the Warlords want me to, I'll go. To Mars, to hell, or stay right here on Earth."

Lani saw that he was doing some hard thinking. Coming nearer, she laid a hand on his arm. "I'm not holding out for an actual head. I'm not making a point of your doing the killing with your own hands. The simple hunt and kill is enough. Direct the pack, and the fact will make me say, 'Well done.'" She paused. "Rod, I saw what happened to one empress maker. Do not try any such crazy trick again."

Garvin grinned. "That poor son of a bitch was a dead man the moment he decided that I didn't have a chance.

"It is this way: Someone in Maritania, or in France, or both, briefed Marxists in Savannah. That was my hunch when I phoned Flora from Funchal, so I sent my son to Nameless Island, disappeared, went undercover, and had a talk with the senior Warlord.

"We are not sure it is Ingerman that is hunting me." After telling of the perfect housekeeper's disappearance one jump ahead of the Sûreté when Felix vanished, he concluded. "From Funchal, I phoned our ambassador in Paris. All in all, it is a sticky package. Begin to see why I have a separate house?"

"I'm not stampeding. I'll wear my makeup, and since the Egyptians are kindly, fun-loving people, maybe I'll be your assistant headlady. Relax while I get us a drink. This is our chance."

Chapter 21

THE BURMESE AND Malay fishermen of Nameless Island had no trouble with the primitive pirogues in which they set out whenever tide and weather were favorable; they went about their work in the matter-of-fact way of the Cajuns of Louisiana, who paddled similar primitive dugouts in the bayous and lakes of the flatlands. Catalina and Miguel had water and weather favoring them, but they were not Cajuns, nor Burmese or Malays. Tricks of the earthquake-deflected Gulf Stream drifted them off their course at times, but that was no problem; what gave them misery was plying the paddles. Between aches in the back, aches between the shoulders, and the relentless erosion of his palms, Miguel began to wish that someone had shot him to prevent his escape.

At times they rested, using their paddles only to prevent drifting off course.

Hour after cruel hour, lights here and there along the shore tantalized them.

"No, we are not going backwards," he assured Catalina. "And we don't drift enough to count. Those lights that don't move—they are the landmarks."

The moon was near the western horizon when they lurched ashore, floundering, stumbling from water to beach. Happily, this was a deserted stretch. Rocky outcroppings reassured Miguel, and hunks of coral and the fringe of scrub and palmetto made it clear that they had blundered into a desolate corner. Nevertheless, Miguel dragged the pirogue well into the brush, which would give them cover while they rested from their aches and weariness.

"Just in case," he explained, "she misses us and the boat and phones the mainland."

Wind and rising tide would cover their tracks in the sand. He blessed the island-grown opium, sprouted from Burmese seed, that had put the guard to sleep. The fugitives needed no soporific, but they did not oversleep. After a few hours, bedraggled and hobbling along with improvised canes, they dragged themselves through the brush and to the shore highway. Just another couple of tramps.

Well north of the fishing village where visitors and supplies for the island were picked up, they came to a similar settlement. His captors not having bothered to search him, Miguel had some currency: an advance against his pay as Number One Boy.

"That *putañero*," he grumbled whimsically. "Not even enough pay for my time in the tiger cage! And if I reported him to the Labor Relations Board, discrimination would block me." He chuckled, then shrugged and led the way to a fast-food spot.

Youth, freedom, and chow revived the fugitives, leaving only aches, blistered palms, and residual weariness to be ignored for the time being.

Miguel counted what remained of his cash. "Me, I am a stranger so far south," he said then. "Where do we go now?"

Catalina pointed to the bus stop. "Where else but to the nice people you used to work for?" And to spare a gentleman the embarrassment of discussing petty cash, Catalina dipped into her bra and produced a wad of well-worn but substantial bills. Her words had their origin in Miguel's improvisations regarding his employment along the riverfront: He claimed to have done odd jobs as well as working for a detective agency, also on assignment, doing things like tracing the stevedores and crew members who "accidentally" mismanaged the hoists that brought cargo from the holds of ships.

"Some things they sell to the pawnbrokers and little shops," he had explained. "Other things to waterfront girls, not for cash but, what you call it, take it out in trade. Nobody cares but the insurance company which picks up the check."

All this had a sound basis in fact: Catalina's shopping trips while the *Tiburón* was discharging cargo made the story convincing. And he did have actual employers other than Neville Ingerman. Finally a girl as charming as Catalina inspired him to look to their future away from riverfront business, maybe even to go far west, where many Orientals found a good life.

This girl was no siren: mestiza charm and the lingering bouquet of Seven Bells did most of the seduction as the Shore Line bus jounced, roared, fumed, and rattled along a neglected highway.

The rattletrap stopped at every crossroad and settlement to drop off or pick up mail and passengers. Nevertheless, and despite the bouncing, this was better than walking, though not much faster.

Being free of the shark-infested water that had kept them uneasy, apprehensive, and tense, Catalina was serene and stoical. Although the pirogue cruise had taken longer than Mona had reckoned, things were by no means off schedule. As the day and its weariness wore on and the sun was nearing the horizon, she knew it was time to speak her lines.

"What the chauffeur tell me, we get to Savannah before dark. With time for getting cleaned up, with resting. So you have quick wits and sparkle, no? Let us go to a hotel, the one I told you about. Not by the waterfront, which is mostly for sailors and river girls, but not too far away. Nice place. Not expensive. The *Tiburón* skipper, when he waits for teak brokers, he stays there with both of his wives. Good hotel, they do not despise Burmese or Filipinos or any other Orientals."

Miguel agreed, saying that the quicker he told his employer, the imaginary insurance company, that he had

made a mistake in taking the job, the more likely he
would be to collect some pay; the disaster had been no
fault of his, after all.

"No hurry. I am too tired. You are too tired. I am
nearly half dead. So are you. Too *machísimo*! Wait until
tomorrow."

When he figured that the doped sentry and the release
from the cage might in fact be a stage set for the "shot
while escaping" scenario, and Catalina an innocent pawn
in an island game, he had walked to the bamboo's cover,
like a Spanish grandee entitled to wear his hat in the
king's presence. Accordingly, he knew now that he was
not at all tired, though lovely Catalina surely must be
perishing. The meek, submissive Oriental woman knows
what she is doing, and in a silky way few occidental females ever learn.

When they reached the Shore Line terminal, Miguel
was ripe for further suggestions. It was a good idea, hu-
moring Catalina. When he got his pay, he would reim-
burse her.

Taxis cluttered the parking stretch. Catalina checked
Miguel before he could hail one. "When I buy cosmetics
and nice things, there is a girl who has a brother. He
does not belong to the union, so they do not let him get
in the parking line. Go this way, we find him, and she
will know I remember her."

Next time Catalina would get a discount, but the boss
would not know.

Harrigan, the driver, knew exactly where the Bristol
Inn was.

On arrival at the inn, Catalina told the driver to wait
just in case they had an errand to run. Then, at the desk,
she said, "You write the names in the book. I do not
write the English."

He wrote, "Mr. & Mrs. Miguel Rodriguez, City."

"Tomorrow," Catalina resumed, as she paid for the
room, "I go shopping for luggage and some clothes."

After going with Miguel to Harrigan's cab, she returned to the hotel desk. "These things I wear," she said
to the clerk with a grimace of disgust. "Feelthy! I cannot

stand it. A bath, yes, but putting myself in these things, no! Is there close by some shop that is not closed? Is it too late?"

Once he reassured the exquisite mestiza, she dashed for the first cab in the waiting line. "Take me to the bus station."

"Which one, lady? Shore Line or—"

"To that rattletrap, no! Golden Arrow Express, and shake out the lead." She tucked a five-pazor note in his hand. "This is not for the boss. I pay what the meter says."

The driver understood and performed accordingly.

Although Catalina was far from knowing why Miguel had been kept in a tiger's cage and then released, she did not like the flavor of the episode. Harrigan, brother of a riverfront shop girl, would remember where he had taken Miguel. If that was so important to Madame Broadtail, she could discuss it with him by phone.

Miguel undoubtedly was a charming young man. At least a portion of his background, as he had told her of it, was true. But spying on waterfront thieves and dealers in stolen goods was bad company.

Southbound on a main freeway, Catalina relaxed. She sighed and shook her head sadly. It would have been wonderful spending a few nights at that or some other hotel with Miguel, that most *simpático* young man. But romancing with someone who had to be caged like a tiger, that was bad business.

Chapter 22

INGERMAN AND DIANE did not bother to tell Miguel that they were taping the question and answer session. They prompted him at times when he groped and occasionally asked him to clarify an ambiguous reference. Except for such interruptions, it was Miguel's show, and he made the most of the opportunity. Wisely, he offered no excuses. There was no denying that the mission had been aborted before it was fairly started and that his only success had been, thanks to Catalina, his escape.

Being proud of such a girl, he gave her all credit.

Finally, Ingerman summed up the report. "Something went wrong. And the only people who questioned you were the Burmese fellow and his Chinese wife. She lived quite a few years in the barrio of Sampoloc."

"Just the Chinaman did the English speaking. The others don't speak it. Sometimes he talked to them in their language, and each time they gave me nasty looks, I gave him answers that don't mean anything." He grinned happily, wagging his head. "Because I don't know any facts! Don't know nothing, it is easy to play dumb. Comes natural, no?" Then, in a more serious mood, he resumed his tale. "The Chinaman said, 'You don't know what they have been talking to me? Then I tell you.' And he told me about a spy boat measuring how deep is the water, both sides of the island. And when the boat had trouble with the engine, some of the fishermen helped them to get the boat to the pier. All

144

very friendly, and then everybody's head is chopped off. Everybody thought the boat was lost in the hurricane that hit the coast next day."

"That was a bad storm," Ingerman commented.

"Before I work for you," Miguel countered, "I heard old men tell about a spy boat towed into Savannah. Boat all complete, only an explosion busted the propeller. But no crew. Nobody knows what happened. This was before I was born. But those fellows from the island are suspicious people. And I saw the parang, good as new, a fine chopper."

"I was not here at that time," Ingerman observed, "but I did hear about a boat and no crew. So you ended up in the cage?"

"That was when I said everybody was interested in the boy. Nobody watched for the Old Man. All the boy knew about was the teak, the elephants, and the girls. He didn't know nothing to tell."

"Tell us something interesting for a change," Diane cut in. "About your lovely Catalina. She sounds so romantic. Gets some home-grown opium in the village, dopes the guard, and away you went."

"Catalina is half Spanish. A mestiza. A ballerina in a dance hall near the U.S. Navy station. But she came to North America when the *insurrectos* made so much trouble. But she don't like Nameless Island. Is too old-fashioned. On the *Tiburón*, she told me it is out of date like any barrio in the wild Philippines."

"Fast work, eh?"

"No problem," Miguel answered. "I speak more English than she does. So I told her, 'If I do not like being Number One Boy for young Mr. Garvin, I'll get my pay and quit the job. And find something on the mainland. We quit this logging stuff and kitchen work.'"

Diane applauded. "You must have turned on the charm!"

Miguel shook his head. "Half Spanish, half Tagalog. What you call it...Eurasian? Yes. For Spanish, for American, for full-blooded Filipino, she is a Number

Two Girl, half wife. In this country, not the discrimination."

"You were smart getting an escape hatch before you had any reason to suspect danger. If some other operators had had that much foresight, they'd not have lost their heads." For a moment Ingerman relished his own grim humor. "But you can give us all some very vital information. You have been frank, no alibis, no excuses. Look back, see if you can recall what did go wrong. That girl and elephant-crazy lad could not have suspected you and told the boss lady something?"

Miguel sighed, frowned, and shook his head. "All my time in the cage I was asking myself that same question. Nobody asked me nothing about those Garvins. But when the Burmese English speaker asked me what part of the islands did I come from, I told him, the boondocks. And he ask, what you mean, *boon*docks? So I tell him that is what Americans say when they mean, way back of nowhere.

"Only this fellow tells me nobody from the islands ever talk that way. And before they are through with me and I am in the cage, I have learned the right way is *bon*docks, or it sounds maybe like *bun*docks. The Bontoc Igorote country in Luzon, where the young man has to chop off a head of someone in some other settlement and bring it to the girl he wants to marry. To prove he is a grown man, not a boy.

"The long-time-ago soldier learned the right way when he was in Luzon one or two enlistments. In other wars, things moved too fast, too much fighting, and nobody had time to learn from the Filipino people.

"So, into the tiger cage I go, to sweat until I talk."

"Boondocks," Ingerman said, as if to himself. "*Boonies* . . . sweet Jesus, that was a boner! Who'd ever imagined that an Americanism would be such a trouble-maker!"

Miguel brushed away the sweat that gleamed on his forehead.

"These people knew my story was all wrong, and they chop first and get facts later." He paused. "Fighting like a man with other men, that is one thing," he added defensively. "Sitting in a cage like an animal, waiting for the parang to lop off my head—that is something else."

"But you still have your head." Ingerman's voice was soft, almost whimsical, yet faintly unpleasant.

"Like I said," Miguel retorted triumphantly, "I told those *chingados* nothing. If they chopped off my head, how could I make some slip, maybe say something which help them do what they are trying to do?"

Ingerman's eyes narrowed, and then he brightened, chuckled. "Right you are! The five men on the boat talked their damned heads off!"

Although he did not say so aloud, Miguel was sure that he had won his case. Diane agreed.

"Miguel," she said. "I know your girl must be dead tired, and you look ready to fold. By now she must be stretched out in a hot tub, relaxed, and rested a bit. With the kind of enemies you've made, you oughtn't to leave her alone in that hotel. Oh, it's a good place, good enough, but that Nameless Island crowd knows the riverfront from way back before you were born. You two are both worn out from that escape." She turned to Ingerman. "Neville, darling, why don't you call a cab and get her out of the Bristol Inn?"

"Good idea," he agreed. "But she's just smart enough not to trust me any more than she'd trust you."

"No problem," Diane retorted. "Miguel's busted himself hurrying out here, not losing a minute. I'll mix him a drink, heat a can of soup, and give him a chance to clean up a bit before she gets here. And all she has to do is to get on the phone and talk to him, and she'll know you're all okay, that you really are the boss he hurried away to report to."

Ingerman regarded her with unfeigned approval. "Never thought of that."

Without waiting for a reply, Diane turned to Miguel. "Mike, while I'm fixing up a snack, you can be getting cleaned up a bit. Come on, I'll show you where."

When she returned from guiding him to the plumbing, Diane had a word with Ingerman. "If that girl is on the level—and she does sound pretty much all right—she really should not have been left alone as long as this. You're hunting old man Garvin, and my feeling is that his odd disappearance, after the only way we identified him was by my recognizing Felix, I'm wondering who is hunting whom. It might be you and me against a nasty pack of Warlords, and their intelligence gang, and all we have are undercover comrades."

"Madame, that is not sensational news. Brief me."

"This has to be ad lib, but you are good at that, considering how your improvising almost won that battle. If you have anything to tell me, I may not be able to give you an answer that is at all related to what you've said. You'd of course phone from the hotel, and your best chance would be while she is touching up her makeup. If there is anything confidential, and this is not a snow job —you Americans! You have the weirdest slang. Me savvey plentee. And I could never make sense of your weekly humor and whimsy magazines written in argot never taught in any school. We can't be literal-minded with her breathing down my neck and him auditing you."

By the time the cab arrived, a rejuvenated Miguel was sipping a martini before tackling soup and a sandwich.

When the cab arrived, Diane went with Ingerman to the door. Lowering her voice, she spoke in French. "If she is not there, I'll have to improvise. I think she's on the level, but—"

"*Bien entendu*," he said, cutting her short.

While Miguel was in the bathroom, cleaning up, Diane had cut the extension, just in case. Her brief lapse into her native language would not have attracted Miguel's attention. His story had rung true—but the people of Nameless Island had made too much of a point of *boondock versus bontoc*. Suppose he was not a native of the Philippines, as he had given Ingerman to believe? What could he have known that, revealed inadvertently or under pressure, could endanger them or their enterprise?

Diane poured coffee and a pony of Benedictine for Miguel.

"Of course, it seems forever!" she explained, setting out a pack of cigarettes.

When the phone rang, Miguel jerked back. The chair legs scraped. He settled back, got to his feet, then resumed his seat.

Diane answered the phone. "Traffic jam up! We thought you'd got lost," she told Ingerman, in a whimsical touch.

"She asked the clerk about shopping hours," Ingerman told her. "Needed some clean clothes, she was all ragged. But a cab driver took her to the Golden Arrow bus depot. Flew the coop. You and I are leaving town. Instantly."

"Oh, how lovely. Tell her to come to the phone and put her makeup on when she gets here. Mike's worn a track in the floor." She snarled the instrument cord, set it on the table, and beckoned.

"Mike, she'll put on the last touch of lipstick so you can kiss it off."

He lost a moment unsnarling the phone cord, fumbling in his eagerness. Back turned, he did not see Diane hitch up her skirt and unsheathe a stiletto, as dainty as it was deadly. One stroke with that silent weapon was all that was needed in the hands of an expert.

Chapter 23

RATHER THAN RISK a rental car, Ingerman and Diane put Savannah behind them as rapidly as express bus lines could hustle them to safety. They shacked up in cheap motels; they haggled about rates to give the appearance of having more time than money. The skimpy but presentable luggage suggested an illicit date, for which the name "Smith" was standard for the guest card. They always insisted on a room with television: not to mask honeymoon ecstasies but to get news reports essential to directing their general course.

The first night was misery.

With the TV turned low, the fugitives took turns sleeping and waiting for late broadcasts. The ensuing day of bus riding was devoted to pretending to catch up on lost sleep. The less they had to do with fellow passengers, the better. At times the "Smiths" zigzagged on impulse, but their general course was southwesterly.

Despite anxiety and increasing tension, they avoided discussion. Diane knew better than to point out that killing Miguel before he could be questioned had given them a head start. Ingerman shied away from suggesting that Catalina's hasty getaway indicated eagerness to get shed of the entire deal and return to the safety of Nameless Island, leaving Ingerman and Diane all the head start they needed, and without Miguel's death to magnify the importance of their enterprise. They had to avoid the clash that discussion would bring, but however wise they were in this respect, bottled up were pressure and tension nearing the danger point. If either blew a gasket, the other would detonate.

Each recognized the other as a potential menace.

The third evening, Ingerman snarled at Diane. "We're waiting for the other shoe to drop! You've been grand! How much of this are we good for?"

"Yes, the other shoe. It can't stay in orbit forever."

He grimaced wryly. "It's been forever, and we're still here. I'll hustle up some chow."

He had come to loathe the take-out food from Sandy's and from Ernie's and from Benny's, largely because eating had become loathsome. Next door to the sandwichery, he got a bottle of good sour mash whiskey and Red Rock Spring.

When he set the quick-energy ration on the dresser, he read Diane's glance. "You're right. We need this so goddamn badly that we can't risk it. Not yet."

The food would give them nothing but indigestion. They gulped the take-out orange juice.

"Eating on an empty stomach is bad, so they say," Diane commented.

Ingerman nodded. "Madame, you are durable."

"*A vous de même. En Américain*, you're another."

And then came the first newscast.

"...murder on the Savannah riverfront... unidentified Filipino...Hukbalahap vendetta suspected ...autopsy indicates victim was killed by stiletto thrust in back...death almost instantaneous...expert work ...tenants of the hastily vacated dwelling are sought for questioning...Mr. and Mrs. Norman Inglewood..."

The descriptions were based on a photo and confirmed by Alfred Hodgson, an employee of the Unique Answering Service. Latest flash: The deceased was non-union stevedore encroaching in union territory. "Local labor officials deny using court decision permitting crime and general terrorism in the furthering of the rights of organized labor..."

"So the heat is on the unions!" Ingerman reached for the bottle. "For once the government-legalized Mafia is doing our cause a real service! Instead of blaming us for their racketeering operations and conniving with management."

Diane thrust the bottle aside. He still was blinking perplexedly when she turned the TV up a few notches and peeled out of her dress.

"We need each other, and like nothing else!" she exclaimed.

Ever since they had met on Sainte Véronique, their lovemaking had been a routine on the level of deciding whether to start their day with café au lait or cocoa, or why not switch from Angostura bitters to Peychaud on their grapefruit.

This was a new Diane. And it was a new Ingerman who tore her slip to hip level.

When each was depleted and serene, Ingerman splashed dollops of sour mash into tumblers and ignored the mineral water. And now that the other shoe had dropped, the fugitives slept until well beyond checkout time.

At last Diane sat up and regarded the garment-littered room. "I don't know what would have happened if that broadcast had waited another hour. Nee-ville, what are you staring at?"

"The you I didn't know existed!"

Diane contrived to grab the bottle of mineral water without falling out of bed. Ingerman uncapped the bottle, and she poured the glasses full.

"Don't need lunch any more than we needed breakfast," he said. "Hang the 'Don't Disturb' card on the door. We couldn't eat now, not when we're so busy beginning to understand each other."

Toward sunset, when Diane did not feel like dressing, Ingerman went out for a fresh bag of lunch. His stride was brisk, his carriage alert and springy. He and Diane had renewed each other. When he returned to the motel, he saw that Diane's not wanting to go out for dinner was neither from weariness nor from letdown. Makeup and sparkle made it plain that looking forward to their next step left her neither time nor taste for wondering how the

Savannah operation should have been handled. That camera and its self-timer; a moment of whimsy, and now the enemy was looking for a man with mottled complexion and a quadroon with queen-size bra and opulent hips.

"We're going to keep moving along, but we're through running," he announced. He gave her a long look. "Bet you're bubbling over with ideas."

"And so I didn't bother with dressing?" she replied in fond mockery. "You've been figuring things out. Maybe in your sleep? *Dis donc*! Tell me, I've had too much suspense."

"Sending Miguel to Nameless Island went sour, and we don't know why. And we don't know how many enemies we made in getting rid of him. Fact is, we don't know really what we have left behind us."

"And so?"

"Those billboards along the road, the past twenty or thirty kilometers, they suggested a fresh start."

"You mean, on the right: ARE YOU BURDENED WITH SIN AND GUILT? And HAVE YOU MADE YOUR PEACE WITH GOD? And things about being saved?"

"We're getting into Stomper Land," he cut in. "And I felt pretty sour about their advice on being saved by anything but running far and fast. Finally it hit me. Those idiots, those fanatics who have just climbed down out of the trees, and are yapping about prayer in schools and no more evolution and teach creationism—they could help us and not even realize they were doing so."

"Nee-ville! What would our Comrade Komissar think? The very idea, exploiting religion instead of exterminating it! But how?"

"As long as we are not black, Asiatic, or Catholic, they'll bust their tails to convert and save us. Another thing in our favor: Sour mash does not gag us, and we don't even look Jewish." He drew a deep breath, then exhaled slowly. "But we have to have a visible means of support. Those fundamentalist fanatics are suspicious of retired people, I mean, strangers who happen to like the climate and want to settle down for a life of leisure. I'd be a nasty old man, and you are young and luscious enough to be nothing but immoral. One of them concubines, you know."

Diane frowned. "Do I have to be a barefooted, bedraggled, worn-out blonde? North American democracy is puzzling."

"As long as we are both gainfully employed, slaving away at something, it is okay to be brunette and beautiful, provided you don't wear flashy makeup on the sabbath or advertise female fascinations or dress better than the rural standard.

"It's a question of what kind of work we could do. A good many years ago, a nonsocially conscious friend used to say, 'I'll not work for another man, neither saint nor son of a bitch.' So he went nomadic, greasing windmills, dressing butcher's blocks, painting names on rural mailboxes. And he took pictures of rural school graduation classes and sometimes filmed weddings."

"I hate heights! When you mentioned windmills—"

"Whether you wore a skirt or jeans, you'd look immoral."

"The picture business is the thing," Diane declared. "Those whimsy shots of you and me wearing makeup— and look how it has fooled the enemy! It is our luck, a good sign. Yes, of course I know a little about cameras, and I was once a model when I was still too skinny to look like a woman. I worked a little in a studio." Seeing that he was about to object, she raised a peremptory hand. "Listen to me! All you do is stand around and look as if you know what I am doing. You do not have to know nothing. *Rien!*

"This city is large enough. I'll set secondhand cameras, also two or three albums of weddings and so forth, pictures we did not take. How else does a beginner get customers? I will talk the business while you are in the darkroom."

"Me processing and printing?"

"Of course not! Our work goes to the nearest city with a laboratory."

"I get it. We can leave the studio any time, part of our time, and if we lose money, no harm, just as long as we're working. Once we are saved and are Stompers in good standing, we'll get information. Like Harry Offendorf and I planned, and found Sister Zenia at one of the coed retreats. The abbot wore a robe, vestments or something. Chanted a litany instead of sticking to scripture. Burned incense. Graven images in the chapel. Meaning a crowd of goddamn heathens, bad as idol-worshiping you-know-whos. Stompers are out to convert or exterminate the likes of such. They know, and that is how we are going to be saved, mission accomplished."

"Accomplished?"

"Yes. The way it would have been when Harry traced the Sister Zenia, who must have been Lani, the Imperatrix. Yes, she disappeared, but not the way we had planned. Someone, somehow, helped one lone woman throw two able-bodied men from her cabin to the rim of the plateau and a drop of nearly a thousand meters. As far as the law could tell from the skeletons and from the cabin, there had been no struggle, no gunfire. The way Lani should have fared, but for someone who turned things inside out."

The plan included a serviceable but not too young secondhand car; and in addition to camera gear, they purchased an audiovisual outfit to get the sound effects of a camp meeting. As Ingerman put it, "Find out how experts sound when they're being saved, sanctified, or twice born. If I got the ecclesiastical drone of old times, I might become an evangelist. Who'd ever look for the likes of us in a fundamentalist area?"

"Nee-ville, there is only one thing that kept you from being a Komissar."

"Really?"

"You are not dumb enough to qualify. And before I forget it, let's find a salvage store. Secondhand clothes. Good things, but not too new. And luggage without initials on it—and let's decide on a name. I'm weary of being a Smith."

Chapter 24

GARVIN SET OUT from New Egypt riding a German motorcycle he had bought from a speculator who had guessed wrong and to his final pazor. After several spills and getting used to the performance of the race-bred engine, he toured nicely enough to General Kerwin's headquarters, First Army. That was where the Warlords kept liberal courts, bureaucrats, and legislators from working out their recipe for national suicide.

The bellow-scream of the cycle going uphill and around curves carried like a bugle call and was far more compelling.

"General, it sounds like Havelock's pipers raised to the n-plus-one power. Someone's coming to our rescue!"

"See who the crazy son of a bitch might be!"

Warlord followed aide-de-camp as Garvin swooped around the final curve and into the parking lot: There was sullen muttering, a backfire, then golden silence.

"Where the hell and damnation you been?" Kerwin exploded. "If you got my message, how'd you get here so soon? Looks like you've been in a road race!" He turned to the A.D.C. "Oscar, have someone take it to the shop and get fenders, paint job, and so forth. But don't touch the engine. It's too good already."

Garvin finally had a chance to explain himself. "No road race. Just my lousy cycling. Spent more time in space than on the highway. I was in a hurry. I have a message for you."

"Admiral Your Excellency the Governor-General, when you hear the one I have for you, it'll knock your— uh, knock you stiff! Or I'll buy drinks for the house."

"Speaking of getting knocked stiff, wait till I give you some news, and I mean *news*."

Suspense built up bilaterally as Garvin followed the Warlord back into the study, where an orderly was setting out drinks. General Kerwin's vocal vibrations had put human automation to work. The Imperial colors were saluted at retreat; twenty-one guns were fired on certain anniversaries; but there was one observance that depended solely on the status of the participants. Garvin and the General turned toward the hectare of plate-glass window and faced the red granite boulder gravestone to drink their respects to the Imperator and Eileen, Substitute Imperatrix. That done, Garvin snapped at his chance.

"Denny, I busted my tail to tell you that I made a deal with Lani. She finally told me to get her the head of Neville Ingerman. Whether on a silver platter or in a gunnysack, no matter. 'If the Warlords want me to, I'll go to Mars, to hell, or stay here on Terra,' she said. Now, let's hear your message before I go shopping for a double-bitted ax or a shiny new *kampilan*."

"Oscar," Kerwin said to his aide-de-camp. "Is the demonstration ready?"

"Yes, sir, and I'll round up the civilians before they go sight-seeing or start drinking."

"Denny, what the hell's all this?"

"You came to tell me you've gone Igorote, hunting Ingerman's head. My news for you is that he was in Savannah only a few days ago, to get your hide and tack it to the barn door in Slivovitz Land for a hundred thousand or whatever they call their skivvy-paper currency."

"You call that news? Why do you suppose I arrived incognito and wearing a beard? And what do you mean calling their money skivvy paper? The trillion pazors the Tri-Borough Bank up in Megapolis Alpha loaned Marxist satellites gave the Slivovitz the money they needed to stir up trouble in the Caribbean—when the loans default, your Parliament bails the bank out, and taxpayer-chumps pick up the check."

"Those goddamn bureaucrats," the Warlord grumbled.

Garvin grinned. "Their branch in Maritania was part of the money-laundering routine until I closed it."

"How?"

"The local vice-president-manager and entire staff were arrested for questioning."

"And shot while attempting to escape?"

Garvin nodded. "How'd you guess it? Do thou likewise. Now, you were telling me about Ingerman being in town."

"He was in Savannah, and in person. *And* with the doll your son was sleeping with to learn civilized speech ways and what it is like with a lady. The demonstration is to convince you that this is the real business, risking their highest-ranking American friend to spearhead the attack. Once I show you, you might not be so reckless. The fat boys in Slivovitz Land suspect you of having killed their next best American friend, Harry Offendorf, Minister of Something or Other."

"Denny, demonstrating that it's Ingerman here instead of Willie the Office Boy is nice work if you can get it."

"I have voice photographs that'll convince you."

Garvin yawned. "Duddell figured out how to graph sound waves back in 1897. Oscillograph. A bit of micro looking glass between two ribbons of phosphor bronze, all set in a strong magnetic field. Sound sets an electronic current varying in strength, and the mirror jiggles this way and that, which reflects a beam of light to a photographic film a couple meters away and makes a track that shows the wave form of the sound." He made a gesture of dismissal. "Oscillograph! Handy in ballistics. Petroleum prospecting and locating vibration in testing newly designed machinery."

"You space tramps never heard of photographing vocal waves."

"What are they good for?" Garvin retorted. "The courts don't accept them the way they do fingerprints."

Arrival in the security section enveloped them in the usual appalling jungle of chemical and electronic gear, computers, and scrambling and unscrambling machines. The Warlord stopped at what resembled a TV about thirty by fifty centimeters. In front of it and somewhat to one side was a pedestal with a mike and another with a control panel.

"It's all fired up, sir," a technician said to Kerwin.

"To convince you," the Warlord said, "I'll have them film your voice, and then you'll follow my argument. Say something to the mike."

"What'll I say? One, two three—testing?"

"How about the opener of your inaugural address to the Maritanians?"

"I followed old precedent and forgot what I'd promised them."

"I'll get a file copy, and then Oscar can read it, after you've been recorded."

"Reading a thing like that never sounds natural. I'll recite one of Doc Brandon's collection of old-timer poems."

"You remember any of them?"

"Aye, aye, sir. The one about Johnny came home one night." Garvin recited:

"Johnny came home the night before, drunk as drunk could be.
My own wife, my dear wife, my darling wife says he,
Whose hat is on the rack where my hat ought to be?"

As he spoke, a zigzagging line of peaks and valleys blossomed out bluish white on the fluorescent screen.

"Carry on from there," Kerwin said.

"Aye, aye, sir.

"You poor fool, you damn fool, you drunken fool says she

That's nobody's hat, it's a sugar bowl my mother gave to me."

"Jumping Jehovah! The damned thing's starting to fade."

A technician stepped from a doorway at the left of the oscillograph compartment, holding a sheaf of cross-ruled graph paper. These sheets he spread out on a table. "Sir, this one is the admiral's poem with the captain's lines," the technical sergeant explained. "The words are not the same, but they'd hardly ever be in an actual comparison. The rhythm of the poem hasn't changed, so the patterns of curvature are nearly identical, which makes good comparison of voice quality. If you strike a tuning fork and blow the same frequency on a clarinet, the wavelengths would be the same but the curves would look entirely different."

Kerwin cut in. "Rod, any argument?"

"Christ, no! But where's Ingerman come in?"

"Right here, Admiral," the technician answered.

Kerwin picked up the top sheet and read the next one, after which he explained, "The French Sûreté Générale —or is it Service de Sûreté? They had Diane Allzaneau's apartment on rue de Faures, in Bayonne, bugged for several months before you came to town. So we have her voice pattern, with your son's as an extra dividend.

"This sheet is from the answering service in Savannah engaged by Norman Inglewood. Diane phoned him to check the service.

"Allzaneau's bedroom sound track is interesting but not as useful as the dining room discussion of the difference between Grande Champagne cognac and Bois Ordinaires. That tape ties her to Norman Inglewood.

"And the Norman Inglewood sound track came from a tape of one of his long-ago orations on conciliating the Slivovitz crowd instead of letting so many of our flowers of the nation get shot up in battle.

"This wouldn't stand up in any court, especially not in ours, but it convinces me that Neville Ingerman was in Savannah until your son's etiquette teacher bailed out with him about two days before security closed in and found the empty coop. Well, not entirely vacated. There was your son's Number One Boy, Miguel. Stabbed to death with a stiletto. Very neat job. Whatever his story was about, Miguel's escape must have worried them."

He sketched out Catalina's account of the escape. "When they found out that she had checked out without bothering to take a shower, they were worried. When the hotel clerk said she had asked about shops where she could buy a change of clothes and then taxied hell-bent for the Golden Arrow bus depot, she gave them cause for worry, though they didn't until Ingerman came inquiring about her."

"Lucky she got out in a hurry."

"Smart girl, and Mona had told her to ask for a certain cab driver who parked well away from those having the hotel concession. He had made note of where he took Miguel. A lot of the wild-catting drivers don't bother."

After a frowning moment, Garvin beamed happily. "Devil on a life raft! With Ingerman and his Marxist buddies hunting me, I'm bound to nail him, and we'll get a lot of others. What's the bag limit?"

Chapter 25

A FEW DAYS after Mona phoned the Number One Warlord to tell him of Miguel Rodriguez's escape, the general called back and invited Felix Garvin to enlist in the First Army as a private first class.

"You understand," General Kerwin concluded, "that this is a matter of protective custody."

"Uh . . . who or what is going to be protected?"

"It is to keep you and various Nameless Island people from being observed and followed to find out where your father went after he left Savannah. Escaping from the island did not do Miguel Rodriguez much good. He was murdered soon after arrival in Savannah. Probably to keep him from talking when our security caught up with him. Your father is undertaking an undercover job and should not be interfered with.

"Wearing a uniform and being a member of the armed forces is the best way to keep you untraceable and not liable to be snatched as a hostage."

"Sir, you have just about made a deal, but would you mind giving me time to think it over, and I'll call you back tomorrow?"

Late that afternoon Mona said, "Now that we've had a tour of the island and you've met the elephant who can not understand any language but Hindi, you'd better take the general's offer. But first of all, and before absinthe hour and supper, Catalina would like to have a few words with you. In private."

While waiting in the guest house billiard room for his confidential talk with the girl whose spice-pounding on the deck of the *Tiburón* had originally interested him in teak-logging, Felix did a lot of speculating. When she finally appeared, he saw that her eyes, while not reddened, showed lingering traces of puffiness, and their expression was somber. She was not wearing a *piña* blouse. Her gleaming black hair was piled high and secured by a jade pin that looked amazingly like the haft of a child's toy dagger.

Then he recollected that Malays, male or female, had amazingly small hands. The deadly *kampilan*, which could shear a man from right shoulder to left hip, had an ebony grip little larger than the hand of an American who wears size eight or nine gloves. And a Filipino of the old school would ply the weapon with both hands.

"Felix, these are nice people, but nobody but the Boss Lady talks real English. I know the words, but I sound foreign as I look." She silenced him with a gesture. "I must learn the speaking. With the cassette recorder conversation lesson thing. I will be, what you call it, the camping follower, and when you are not doing the guard or the kitchen police, you will teach me when you hear the English from the book I read into the record thing. Then you say it right, and all day I practice."

"Catalina, the goddamn general—"

"The Boss Lady will talk to him."

"So I'll be your short-haired dictionary when I am not on duty. If she can fix it, you've got a deal."

The eyes were no longer somber; instead, they were triumphant, bordering on the magnificent. Felix knew that there was more than linguistics in this deal. That glow went far beyond him, and it was by no means related to spicery or a mattress upstairs.

"Catalina."

"Yes."

"You wanted us to be alone."

"Of course."

"There are three here."

Startled by his crisp tone, she glanced about. Deftly,

he plucked the jade from her hair. It was neither pin nor
stiletto: He had the haft of a thin two-edged dagger. It
would slip between ribs, but it would be at its best in
slashing the jugular.

He presented the weapon, jade toward her. "You, me,
and Death," he said.

Catalina slipped the blade into its hidden sheath.
"Felix, you do understand."

Hers was not a lover's kiss. It was the accolade be-
stowed by a Malay dedicated to death. Spanish blood
would not temper it.

And it was this Catalina who was with Felix when,
wearing the dress blue of First Army, he met with his
father, Mona, and Kerwin. There were five chairs in
front of the fireplace, but Lieutenant General Dennis
Kerwin faced the quartet he had convened. He had to
fight on foot. Each of them knew more than he or she
realized. Each was a bundle of conscious and immediately relevant memories of what had happened since the
Semiramis had been towed to her berth in Savannah.
Security had heaps of facts. What Dennis Kerwin,
Number One Warlord, wanted was what lurked in the
unconscious of each of the quartet. This was to be a
brainstorm session: no protocol, no rank, no seniority to
block freewheeling fancy, impulse, or notions. The most
inane comment, the giddiest quip, might evoke a response from another member of the group, and his or her
unconscious would disgorge a critical hint or clear direc-
tive.

"No matter how wild or cockeyed your notion seems,
sound off and save your thinking for later. Thinking is
grand, when it does not screw the living be-Jesus out of
things. Is that clear?"

Mona answered for the quartet. "Denny, you showed
us the voice curves that proved Ingerman is back in the
country with Flora Garvin's ex-housekeeper. We know
all about the cab drivers Security questioned, and the
hotel clerk Catalina told she was going shopping, and the
man who came to the hotel and wanted to see Catalina.

"And how Ingerman and Diane must have kept a getaway kit all packed, judging by the heap of laundry and stuff they left in the house, including an old handbag with a color photo and rent receipt and shopping tags, all dated a couple of days before the *Semiramis* docked in Savannah. I hope Security isn't as confused as we are!"

"Hold it!" Felix cut into her pause for breath. "Speaking of that photo and the man with the lead-gray complexion, and what the man at the phone answering service said about his looking like he'd had a lot of malaria shots. And the woman who probably was a quadroon. Well, she reminded me enough of Diane in spite of differences. And I just now remembered that back in Bayonne, Diane had a picture of the Old Man and Azadeh at some formal clambake in Maritania. Full uniform, decorations, and so forth. At the time, that set me wondering. I'd never heard of Garvin fan clubs."

The Warlord chuckled. "Neither has anyone else. Carry on!"

"Another thing I didn't think of at the Security briefing. Diane showed me a picture of a woman with hair the color of Mona's, only a bit more reddish. And her eyes were brown and longish, pretty dark."

General Kerwin grinned and wagged his head. "See what I mean? We're beginning to see Diane Allzaneau as picture-minded. That gives more meaning to the photo supposedly forgotten in the hurry of leaving that shack in Savannah. It is Diane with makeup to make her lips slightly full and to give her nostrils a slight flare, just enough to change her expression. And maybe a bit of padding about the hips.

"Now hear this. This is no drill! We are broadcasting the photo and its description to keep Ingerman and Dream Girl convinced that we are looking for people who never existed. More than ever, I'm convinced that the real Diane is very much picture-minded."

"What the hell good is that?" Garvin Senior demanded.

"It's like the unmad scientist who told you in Maritania that the explosion that worried you and smelled like rotten eggs might lead to a better rocket fuel or better vanilla extract. The method of 'pure science', re-member?"

Garvin remembered. "I reminded him that one false move, and most of Maritania would be blown way to hell and gone past the Asteroids. Anyway, a picture like the one Felix told me about on our way from France might help the Ingerman team pick Lani from among people she's hiding out with."

Catalina took the floor. "Admiral, they are looking for you. Oh, now I get it! They find her and know you will be seeing her, not so?"

"Their following Felix to get at me has everyone fooled," Garvin objected. "Denny, if Security had a brainstorm session, they'd remember that quite a few years ago Harry Offendorf, one of the Do-Gooder crowd, a Minister of something or other, came to see sister Zenia in a retreat, coed and semireligious. She vanished, and so did Offendorf and his chauffeur. But they finally found the bare bones of the men who came to talk business with the imitation nun who actually was Lani the Imperatrix. Someone pushed two Liberals over the edge and into a ravine a thousand meters deep."

"Where's that get us?" Felix countered.

"All the sound effects about assassins looking for me is manure," Garvin retorted. "The enemy thinks it is time to find and finish Lani before she shows up and glamorizes a nation that's been woman-ruled for the past century or more. Mother's Day was invented in North America. There are a dozen generals who could take over and govern Mars, and nobody would notice the difference." He made a sour grimace, then chuckled. "Not even the sons of bitches shot while resisting arrest."

"Admiral," Felix said then. "Not mentioning names, but if the story ever got published, there is a woman who would be internationally famous for beheading poachers and spies. Downgrading the sweat and gentle American woman is male-chauvinish."

Ignoring the quip, Mona pointed out that none of this

was catching Ingerman and the gentle female whose stiletto had settled Miguel Rodriguez.

Felix, who had slumped into a comfortable slouch while Mona defended female capacity for government, emerged from his trance. "Sir," he said. "Maybe it is relevant to tell you I remembered how I used to work in the pine forests of Dax, not far from Bayonne. That was when I was pretty young, but I noticed there was nothing but stupid lumberjacks, a lot of hot springs, and whores hanging around the hot tubs and bathhouses telling travelers what fun they could show them in a mud bath or hot spring. And that gave me the answer to Madame—uh, Mona."

"Private Garvin," the Warlord answered. "Forestry in an area as immoral as Dax might be amusing, but is it relevant?"

"General, give me permission to get back into civilian clothes and fix me up with papers to prove I am a civil service bureaucrat making a survey or study or something about ships' stores in the turpentine forests north of Pens—"

"Pensacola. Garvin, are you interested in turpentine or etymology?"

"Etymology?" Felix asked. "You mean the origin of words?"

"Quite right. And having spent a long life so near the border of Spain, you must have a smattering of Spanish. Hence, Pensacola—*pensar*, to think, ponder, cogitate; and *cola*, as in *besa mi cola*."

Felix parried that one. "Sir, you'd better ask the Admiral; he spent quite a while in that area. What I had in mind was the Reverend Galen Thatcher. My dad had quite a talk with him about the Stompers and their feud with the Testifiers and how they wanted to save all the sinners before the Lord destroys the nation with a real dose of bombing. Lani moved from one sort of religious retreat. Well, she'd probably find another."

Garvin the Governor-General pounced to his feet. "I used to wonder about the derivation of Pensacola myself, but for a wonder, I think what you really had in mind might be to make friends with Stompers and get the lowdown on all the retreats in the country. They think everyone but them is damned and in need of being saved."

"Well, if I got into a state of grace," Felix replied, "I might learn about groups that the Stompers think are particularly in need of salvation, and that could lead to gossip tying in with Lani."

Old Man Garvin turned to the Warlord. "General, this brainstorm business works. I bet until this meeting neither my son nor I have ever thought of being evangelists. But I still don't see how that would nail Ingerman."

Catalina emerged from dark revery. "So many things Miguel told me that night, paddling the pirogue and riding the bus. He was not the Marxist you think. His people were Hukbalahaps. Farmers who wanted land and freedom. No Socialist silliness. No atheism, no craziness to make the world a Marxist religion. Ingerman and his girl, they will join some idiot church." She groped, fumbled a moment. "Like Felix wears the army uniform. He gets lost in the crowd, all looking alike. Marxist fanatics with other fanatics."

"Keno!" the Warlord exclaimed. "Felix, see supply and draw whatever gear you need. I'll give you an order right after we've had dinner in my quarters."

Rod Garvin, however, had the closing line. "Denny, I have to get back to my post and duties, such as reading an order that arrived while I was on the road. Just give me an okay to communications, for me to phone Flora that our son is an evangelist. And to avoid domestic clashes, I ought to phone Azadeh."

"Write your own ticket, Rod, phone hell and the Asteroid if you want, but for Christ's sweet sake, be careful with that cycle, riding in the dark."

Chapter 26

"GENERAL KERWIN MUST have forgotten I had Maintenance fit my cycle with infrared sensor gear," Garvin remarked to Felix on the way to Communications. "Riding at night is a lot safer than going by daylight."

"Things as sticky as all that?"

"For me, no. For Egypt, it could be. And before I forget it, your job has more possibilities than you suspect."

"Such as?"

"With good headwork plus a liberal luck ration, and getting along with the Reverend Galen Thatcher, you may speed things up a lot. Even get the key to the situation."

"You might brief me a bit. Back in Bayonne, priests are harmless bastards you're polite with but don't pay any attention to. These Alleluia Stompers sound like they're not quite used to wearing shoes."

"Why not let the preacher speak for himself? He was so reasonable, it amazed me when I dealt with him, and he seemed to be the type that improved with age. You won't miss your teak-logging. Catalina is going with you."

"Hell she will!"

"Hell she won't! Mona nudged me into a corner and whispered a thing or two while the party was breaking up. If Catalina hadn't had that brainstorm notion, Mona would have gotten you the ship stores assignment anyway. But the general's getting the notion made it all the better. Knowing the Stompers the way she does, Mona figured that if you went alone, too many men and women would be watching you too closely. That goes for any stranger in that country. But showing up with Catalina, coming from Pensacola—she'd pass as a refugee from Cuba. Men with wives or daughters wouldn't be so wary of a stranger who came with a woman.

"Now that that is settled, let's phone your mother and get eaten out for not calling her sooner. For hell's sweet sake, stick to teak-logging and don't blab out anything about Miguel getting killed or that jewel of a housekeeper having done the job. Ship stores is okay, but skip Tagalog language lessons."

In order to avoid slips, Felix told Flora that he had a dinner date at the Warlord's quarters and had to hustle along, then left the talking to his father. This left Garvin free to dispose of the standard questions and answers and get down to telling Flora what he had worked out.

"Near as I can figure Bayonne time, you could get to Biarritz before I arranged for a whack at the new three-dee conference hookup with Mars."

"Conference?"

"Sure enough. The new Lunar, Martian, and Asteroidal network we've been developing. We can include Azadeh. Whoever is talking, the other two can see and hear. Might find out what would happen if all three start talking at once. Anyway, while Azadeh is getting all prettied up, you and I can have a few words to ourselves."

"What has been going on? Another promotion?"

"Christ, no! But things are shaping up. Sorry, that's top secret, have to skip details. Well, my retirement plans depend on what you and Azadeh cook up—such as if Felix should go spacing, he could see you and Aunt Azadeh when you and I are in Maritania. And when we are in France, that'd be routine, and maybe our wandering daughter—Camille, remember?—might find a spare day or two for us in Bayonne.

"Now I'll call the Asteroid to get the me-and-Azadeh son away from polo ponies and his inspector of something or other job long enough to spend more time in Maritania, seeing his mother and the rest of the old folks."

Garvin had figured things nicely. By the time Inter-Terra Luna Mars & Asteroidal Communications—ITLMAC—arranged the conference connection, Flora was in Biarritz, where the Aga Khans, camel jockey sultans, cannibal kings from Dahomey, and upper-bracket Marxist officials who found their native lands insufferably dreary assembled to keep in touch with the Solar System's business.

Once in the communications booth, Flora unleashed the sable coat that covered her from ankles to jade ear pendants.

Eternally Flora, she was not wearing the see-more blouse he had suggested. As far as the screen revealed, she wore the welcome-home sleeping gown she had designed to celebrate his arrival in Bayonne. Here she was, Mademoiselle Bayonne, giving him an exclusive view such as she had never, in her days as the world-famous Sudzo Girl, given the detergent-buying continents. With lights and makeup, she could get back on TV in a twinkle.

She needed no theme song. A look at what was awaiting his retirement to southern France was sufficient.

Having lived dangerously, Garvin recognized peril. What she said was as immaterial as what she displayed. This was also the woman who, hating space, had headed for Mars to face a dozen camera teams and to wish him bon voyage in circling Saturn. And when he'd convinced her that the cruise had been rigged to be a one-way trip to liquidate a political pest, she had revealed her ultimate self, her innermost self, and for the first time in their stormy marriage there had been a night of truth. After a flare of fury, of pure hatred for her cousin Alexander, who had sent Rod on that one-way trip, she had realized why Garvin was without anger: because he was too fascinated by her and by his chance to outplay Alexander and the Consortium. He would win. He would be an even greater nuisance—and thus prevail.

Rod and Flora: each understanding the other for the first time.

Yang and yin: Neither can ever conquer the other.

"Madame, your trans-Atlantic image would make the Sphinx of Egypt drool and the Great Stone Face blow his brains out. Let me see how Azadeh comes in and how she sounds."

Since thought exceeds the velocity of light, he had time to wonder how Azadeh was going to cope with Flora. They had always gotten along so perfectly.

And then the screen cleared and blossomed anew: Here in the Warlord's communication system, and in Biarritz, the First Lady of Mars faced her conference partners.

The Governor-General's palace in Maritania contained one of the pilot stations of ITLMAC. Azadeh could easily and without causing eyebrows to lift step dripping wet from her shower and stroll casually to the Governor-General's viewing booth.

"You two chatter away until I touch up my makeup," she said.

When she appeared again on the two Terrestrial screens, she wore the same flirtation veil and high-necked brocade gown that she had worn years ago when waiting with her father at Maritania Spaceport for Garvin to finish his breakfast with Flora, whose last-minute arrival had deprived Garvin and Azadeh of a shared breakfast and honeymoon's final moments. Accordingly, Flora had her night of truth, and so, in her own way, did Azadeh.

ITLMAC worked perfectly.

Each speaker saw his or her audience, lenses zooming to include group listeners. Capacitors stored vibrations when speakers cut in on each other. People insist on being people, and scientists go fruit and nuts offsetting this trait.

Finally Garvin got his chance. "While you young

ladies are arranging my fate when I retire, I'll get on another circuit and have a word with Alub Arslan and see whether he can persuade our son to get away from the Asteroid long enough to spend more time with his mother, whether it is in Maritania or in Basses Pyrénées, France."

Garvin had outwitted mutiny en route to Saturn, but he was not so reckless as to predict success in setting yin against yin. Lao Tzu, Chuang Tzu, and Master Ko Hung had dropped profound words on the matter. However, the ultimate judgment could come only from the test of experience.

"Nice thing about scientists," Garvin mused as he pushed buttons. "They *know* everything, but the tangle-footed bastards never *do* anything. They leave that to dumb sons of bitches like me."

And then Alub Arslan, Number One prince among the Khans who ruled the Asteroid, faced Garvin on the screen.

The "Valiant Lion," nicknamed "Extravagant" by his friend, the skipper of the *Saturnienne*, which had been destroyed to protect that miniplanet from North American culture, had changed little, thanks to the planetoid's serene life-style.

That lordly beaked nose, of course, could not change; and though he was quite a few years older than Garvin, his face remained smooth, scarcely lined. The beard was now silver-gray, with white promising an early takeover. And that the prince spoke English suggested that Lani, his wife for several years, had softened his bias against Terrestrians as a race.

"Before I forget it," Garvin began, "either Flora or Azadeh told me about your son's death, and both send their regrets. And I am good and damn sorry, too. With Lani in armor plate seclusion, she's not heard the news."

Alub Arslan sighed. "Some of your splatter-assed, loudmouthed Americans rake me over the coals for being nondemocratic, but those God-double-damned knot-heads can't understand that my so called Asiatic-style tyranny is a pile of crap! Lani was one of the best,

but with palace intrigues, I had to get her off the Asteroid to save her life."

"Hey, wait a second! Lani was teaching you English,
but that was not her vocabulary!"

The Gur Khan blinked. "Oh, *that*? As a space admiral's widow, she was a model of High Propriety. So was
my Americanese until a young Dutchman, who'd gotten
so puking fed up with the Terrestrial madhouse that he
took to space tramping, showed up. From here, he
teamed up with a prospecting party. Asteroidal explora-
tion, you know. He admitted that my English was correct
but that it sounded like I'd learned it from a sweet little
old lady who'd spent her life in a nunnery."

"I never met him," Garvin put in. "But my son did.
And he is now introducing Dutch-Americanese in the
mint julep belt. But my condolences about your son."

"Thanks, Rod, and the same to Azadeh and Flora. I
miss that boy. I was thinking of abdicating and letting
him run the show. Well, you blew a perfectly good
cruiser to protect this asteroid from American culture,
and look how it turned out. Me speaking your frigging
language. Well, the foreigners are not all the human gar-
bage that your mutinous crew was."

"It was a grand life-style." Garvin sighed. "If it had
not been for Azadeh, and getting Lani out of a nasty fix,
I'd still be here. Well, I have to get back on the conference circuit. If you see Aljai, give her my love and say
I'd phone but I heard she's married. She was one of the
best!"

"That's no problem. She's in town now, with her husband. While I'm having her paged, the priest of the Starfaring Goddess wants a few words with you. Ever since
you and Aljai shot two mutineers and stopped them from
looting the temple, he thinks you're the greatest. Also,
the prime minister wants a word with you. While you're
gabbing with them, Aljai will have time to put on her
makeup and the Guard troop will turn out. She'll have an
escort."

The line was busy until the roll of saddle drums and

the tremendous peal of gongs deafened Garvin. The woman who materialized on the screen was indeed Aljai.

When destroying the *Saturnienne* to settle the mutineers had made Garvin a public benefactor, the grateful Gur Khan had given him a cozy little palace, with Aljai as permanent concubine. Never a glamour girl, Aljai was the one to take along when hell bubbled over. She wore a silver lamé gown, one of Flora's favorites from her Sudzo detergent career. Her tall coiffure was an extension of the gown's Burmese motif. And behind her an attendant, one of the guard, held a double-decked gilt parasol.

"Kee-rist!" Garvin blinked, gaping. "Married nobility?"

"My father went up one deck," she explained, "and I inherited his rank when he died."

"Your husband?"

"He's a farmer."

"He must be a good man, the way you're decked out!"

Aljai laughed softly. "This is the costume for appearing at the Gur Khan's court. When we heard all the farmers in North America were revolting for more subsidies, Alub Arslan made it clear that there'd be a tax revolt, and why not make this the official court regalia for farmers' wives. Everyone's happy."

Garvin frowned. "And they pay for the gowns?"

Aljai shrugged. "Between democracy and socialism, you North Americans are more than half crazy. Rod, it's an idiot's game, and you're worn-out weary. Get out of it."

"I am, and when my special-duty job is wound up, I am retiring."

"You and the Warlords and the rest of who's running the country ought to move in with us and learn the art of running a planet or part of one. Dump all that academic muck that swamped your onetime North American common sense. Behead the intellectuals—well, there's more to it than that, but that's a good place to start."

"You've not changed a bit!"

"It's my makeup. Remember?"

"I was thinking of the way you and I quelled a riot. The survivors really amounted to something. But there was something that went beyond your gunnery backing mine that night."

"There was?"

He nodded. "Such as, whenever Mars rose between dark and late bedtime, I'd be sitting on the roof watching that big red blob, and thinking of Azadeh and our son, and asking myself if I'd gone too far in protecting the Asteroid. And when Mars-watching was over, you never made me regret what had promised from the start to be a life sentence."

"That was my makeup."

"There was one time when sunrise caught us off guard," he told her. "And you were more beautiful than ever, with no makeup."

"You talk the weirdest nonsense!"

"An intellectual female would have smashed the binoculars over my head, and remained as frozen as outer space. All we need back on Terra is that mystic blend of honey and a double-fitted ax, and we'd have something like what you people have had for ages and ages. And patience, common sense."

Chapter 27

BACK IN EGYPT Township, Garvin poured Madeira for himself and Tokaija for Lani so they'd have an appetite for brunch.

"Too bad," he quipped, "that you don't have leak-proof, gold-plated slippers so I could drink champagne out of one or both."

"So *that* is all the romance you can cook up! Wait till I pout and sulk till you fill the bathtub with Paul Masson Brut."

"Jesus, woman! I never could drink that much. Not even if you laced it with Demerara rum."

"Knothead! I meant for me to bathe in."

"That would make it taste a lot better, but even so, skip the soap or I'll not take a drop!"

However, and despite all the whimsy, life in Egypt Township offered more than a honeymoon to cap the years and the quirks of destiny that had kept them separated yet linked ever closer. There was the Right Honorable, the Almost Earl of Sommerton. When they were not drinking Bertram's Invalid Port, he was hoisting the Rainwater Madeira that Garvin had moved to Lani's house along with the Tokaija.

Bertram's yarns, they suspected, were disguised autobiography. However much his Egypt gave him, he had few if any other companions capable of relishing the whimsical and humorous. His repertoire included stories such as the one about a lieutenant of the Peshawar

Lancers who faced a general courtmartial and the certainty of dismissal from the service for chasing a Kashmiri *nautch* girl down the hall of a very proper hotel in London, when between them the unhappy couple wore not even the tiniest fig leaf. The charge began, "In that he did appear in public, in violation of her Majesty's regulations governing officers' dress in public..." The specifications that followed were spectacular and explicit. The lieutenant beat the rap, and on a technicality.

With comparable starters, the Almost Lord Sommerton would settle down to proving that Isis, Osiris, and Horus were the original Christian Trinity, which dated back to 4000 B.C., and that the cult of the Virgin Mother was of equal antiquity. He claimed that the sooner the Stompers ceased bawling and bellowing, the sooner they could lay claim to human intelligence.

"Symbolism apparently is beyond the scope of literal-minded fundamentalists," he summed up. "Their descent from the trees does suggest that Darwin was literally correct."

Bertram seriously considered Garvin's studies during the long interlude of exile to Maritania: a project devoted to the reconstruction of classical Egyptian speech. "You're quite reasonable," he affirmed. "Coptic Christian ritual and liturgy originated when that language was still the vernacular of Egypt regardless of the official Latin or Greek.

"Coptic, a Greek corruption of the word meaning 'Egypt,' is a cousin of Ethiopic, Aramaic, Himyaritic, Hebraic, Arabic, and the rest of the family. Arabic by its nature could swamp Coptic, whereas the alien Greek and Latin could not. The Moslem conquest of the seventh century did what the Ptolemies and the Romans could not do. Your approach, using tapes of Coptic liturgy, the only survival of the language in these past three centuries, was scientifically right."

"Scientific, but no thanks to me! I got the tapes from a group of scholars. Aside from Azadeh, my Martian wife, life in Maritania was a dreary mess, stupid as space in general! Silly bastard Terrestrians ought to learn to get along on Earth before they pollute space. Anyway, the routine was audio tapes, comparing modern and classical Greek, Coptic and current Arabic. The only scientific linguistics I ever tried was when I met Azadeh. Her Martian-Gook speech wasn't awfully far from Uighur Turki, a bit of which I picked up while I was freighting irrigation gear in Chinese Turkistan."

"Even so, you're quite a scholar," Bertram declared.

"Scholar, my ass! I had a long-haired dictionary."

In one of these sessions, Bertram clarified the matter of the acquittal of the nude lieutenant and the Kashmiri dancing girl. "Quite simple, you know. The regulations provide that an officer engaged in a sport may appear in whatever dress is appropriate to such a sport. Manifestly, the case had to be dismissed."

"You've led an interesting life, Lord Sommerton," Lani remarked. "We were speaking—remember?—of Coptic liturgy last time we met."

"Madame, something more important has been engrossing me," Bertram admitted. "I've been groping my way toward the subject. The people of this township, especially the female segment, virtually demand that you be Isis in the forthcoming pageant."

"Sweet Jesus, Bertram!" Garvin cut in. "She came here for seclusion, privacy."

The Imperatrix became stately. "Would it not be appropriate if this committee of War Criminal and Remittance Man gave me a chance?"

"Quite right, madame," Bertram said. "It is this way: You have won the gratitude of the past seventeen Isises. Each declares she would never have had a chance if you had appeared and made them look like hags."

"With your slick talk, how could any Kashmiri girl ever have run out on you?"

Bertram blinked and gulped. "Despite your isolation, local women have had many glimpses of you. The new girl, you know. They were the first to perceive that you don't look a day older than you did when you first arrived."

Although Lani did not raise her voice, the onetime

Empress of North America took command. "Bertram, it is awfully sweet of the girls, but I must decline. My excuse is one they are bound to accept."

"What might that be?"

"The Isis-Osiris Pageant is keyed to the vernal equinox, is it not?"

"Quite properly so. Always has been, since time immemorial."

"You couldn't possibly postpone it?"

"Impossible. A fertility ritual is keyed to spring."

Lani made a gesture with both palms, from a bit below bra level to somewhat below the navel. "Not showing yet, but I am totally pregnant, and by the equinox I'd be quite impossible. Virgin goddesses have been giving birth for millennium after millennium, but never in pageant, painting, or papyrus has one ever looked pregnant."

Bertram bowed his head. "Madame, your predecessors will understand all too well. Every one of them has found motherhood a dreary and a repetitive ordeal."

He got to his feet, snatched the bottle, and poured dollops. "Madame, I dedicate these glasses to safe delivery. Sir, I trust I am not out of order in congratulating you?"

Lani answered for Garvin. "Thanks to hormones developed by the Consortium of Maritanian Scientists, a cooperative project was not required. Parthenogenesis was established before history began."

Once Bertram, with hat, stick, and gloves, had departed, Lani turned on Garvin. "What are *you* looking so dumped on about? You and Bertram will be innocent bystanders, outswilling each other with gin and bitters. 'Gin pahits,' I think you call them. Singapore, you know."

"Darling, I promised you Ingerman's head."

"Oh, *that*?" Her smile was wonder, witchery and affection quite new. "I was just in a romantic mood. Giddy lovers, you know."

"You mean you're backing down on your deal."

"Your Eminence, hasn't it ever occurred to you that whatever happens to Ingerman and his damned head, as soon as Labor Day is past and I am all okay to travel, I am busting my tail to get to Maritania and settle down to being a mother and Empress Dowager?"

She meant it.

He had hoped for this. What a blessing that he had nothing now to do but get Neville Ingerman's head, and throw it to the guard dogs at Alexander's grave.

"I'll tell the Number One Warlord to land the fastest and deadliest cruiser in the fleet, right here, upstream, beyond the ridge and the papyrus lagoon," he said. "I knew you'd be sensible! Alexander doesn't need any avenging. Alexander's great triumph will be the North American Empire, with Mars the capital, and the Asteroid a voluntary, happy outpost of the Empire."

Chapter 28

AFTER AN INDOCTRINATION course that included getting used to their new identities—Fred and Catherine Gruber—Felix heard First Army Security's summing up:

"You are going into the Jump Off Fiery Gizzard Salvation Gulch area. The people are neither funny nor dumb, except for their religion. They are quite friendly and hospitable unless they suspect you of being a snooper, as in the days when revenue officers looking for illicit whiskey stills would disappear.

"A warden who cracks down on 'foreigners' for taking game or fish out of season lives long and happily among those nice, old-fashioned people. But if he is mysteriously missing, you can bet it was because he arrested a native for some violation.

"You may suspect immorality among these God-fearing people, and may be right, but remember, *that* is in the family. You can take that qualification figuratively, or if your mind is low and sufficiently evil, you can take it literally. But you are foreigners, so your camper's all-purpose room has a framed 'God Bless Our Home' and also a marriage certificate, backdated so it won't look like a twelve-gauge Browning automatic deal." He paused impressively.

"Is that clear?"

"Major, it is so clear, it is dismaying," Felix said. "May I make a suggestion?"

"You may, but first let me add an unpleasant fact before I forget it. In that region, any woman who is not, repeat, not blond, blue eyed, Anglo Saxon, and Protestant is likely to be suspected of immorality if she makes even the slightest slip. Now, that question, Mr. Gruber?"

"Sir, purely in the interests of not bitching things up before we start, Catherine and I ought to work out a plausible background and get used to having each other around the house. Some spot where we can get a lot of convincing local color while we are outgrowing that just-married syndrome. That date is too far back but could be made believable with intensive practice, like in Saint Augustine—I mean the one in Florida."

"Why that town?"

"It's been Spanish-flavored for more than six centuries, and with so much historic stuff you can pick up so many easy-to-remember landmarks that we'd convince even a dumb native. And there are not many Saint Augustine natives. Small town, and lots of tourists. I've been studying the poop sheets when we weren't getting our briefings."

All that Felix had improvised was true, but his inspiration came from the prospect of a G.I. honeymoon and the chance to take some pictures that would make a few of his French Army buddies wish they were dead. Security swallowed the package.

In Saint Augustine, Fred and Catherine had nothing to do but ride around in the horse-drawn *calesas*, purely tourist bait, to see Fort San Marcos and its Spanish cannon, its moat and drawbridges and asymmetric arches long forgotten by modern architects. They saw the oldest house in North America and the narrowest street; they crossed the Bridge of Lions to Anastasia Island; they learned that Zoraida's Palace, with mosaic facade and *mashrabiyeh* windows, had been a fashionable gambling house, a brothel, and a museum of antique Persian rugs, though they never saw a trace of gambler, bawd, or Oriental carpets. The slave market, where neither black nor white had for several centuries been sold at auction, was monopolized by senior citizens whose most violent exercise was playing checkers. The most entertaining, however, was the fourth and final position of the Fountain of Youth, like each of the first three the genuine and original position of the one discovered in A.D. 1513 by Ponce de Leon.

Presently, Felix got around to noticing that Mrs. Gruber wore a tiny golden crucifix. "Honey, those security meatheads should have warned you! It's okay to wear it here, but not where we're going. Mind taking it off and keeping it strictly out of sight?"

"No problem at all! When Magellan discovered us and our islands, we killed him, but with gunpowder and steel armor they won and got even by saddling us with their religion. Naturally, a lot of us believed it, though quite a few pretended to buy it while quietly staying pagan. Like the Bontoc Igorotes and the Ifugaos."

"Ifugaos?" He frowned. "I read about them. Terraced rice fields in the steepest mountains. And leaf-gold, thin little strips like jackknife blades. Seems odd, no gold rush ever developed."

"Not so odd, not really." The Spanish grandee among her ancestors took charge; a grandee was one who was entitled to wear his hat in the presence of the king. "Some day, I may have to tell you why."

If Catalina had been a man and there had been a king of Spain in that neighborhood, she would have borrowed a hat and donned it. She went stately in a way that would give ordinary royalty a definitive lesson in the regal freeze-out. It was not her voice, it was her momentary presence that made her words mean "None of your business until I get around to it."

The supreme politeness: The thought was put across without any words, and so without discourtesy.

By the time they had put the turpentine-processing plants of Pensacola behind them, living in a camper had gotten each used to the other; and when Mrs. Gruber commented on the committee of clowns that had designed their home on wheels, Felix knew that his G.I. bride was living her role. In this, he relied on the Old Man's doctrines; a man with three wives surely knew what he was talking about.

Catalina was not suggesting that the camper should be refitted. "The *cabrón* who figured this thing should live in it the rest of his life!" was all she said.

Finding the city hall of Jump Off was easy: Although the Confederate flag would not be flying, two cannons were displayed, twelve-pounders captured in the battle of Jump Off Ridge, February 15, 1864. Felix had scarcely parked the camper when a square-rigged man wearing a gray herringbone suit came out of the city hall. Barely clear of the captured guns, he raised his black felt hat.

"Good evening." As in other corners of this region, any hour past three of the afternoon was evening. "Mr. Gruber, Mrs. Gruber. Glad to see you. Naturally, we've been expecting you."

"Thank you so much," Catalina answered. "I'm sure you are the Honorable Cyrus Buford."

"People have been mighty friendly," Felix said. "Nobody's set the dogs on us, but for the mayor to greet us personally—after all, bureaucrats are not so awfully popular."

"You and Miz Gruber are the first ones we ever heard of that admitted they could not tell a slash pine from a scrub oak."

"As a matter of fact, I still can't," Catalina chipped in. "My examination was just for routine clerical work."

Inquiry about Reverend Mr. Thatcher drew a counterquery. "Him that used to preach at the United Christian Disciples?"

"Fouled up again!" Felix exclaimed. "I never say things right!"

The mayor cut a chew. "They used to be the Alleluia Evangelical Disciples, which folks called the Stompers, and a pack of no good knotheads, the Lord's Testifiers. When they declared peace, neither would work under the other one's name, so they settled on a new one, like I done told you. And once they had made peace between them—well, sort of—Brother Galen got busy with more and more healing and doing a lot of good. He listens to people talking out their griefs, but some figure he ain't sanctified like he used to be."

"If he talks to lots of people, maybe he could understand me better than a lot of the folks. You been doing better'n most."

"Maybe if you chawed tobacco, you'd speak plainer."

"Could be, but I might get puking sick when I talk to someone."

"Just practice when you're talking to yourself," the mayor advised. "Ain't no one going to be humiliated thataway."

Felix had not decided whether the natives of Jump Off used microwave, heliograph, or pine woods telegraphy, when a lean, tallish man stepped from a neat white cottage nestled among sizable oaks. Though he walked quite erect and carried himself well, his deliberation suggested that he lacked the energy to move in accord with the heartiness of his greeting. It wasn't that he looked so old: More likely, outright weariness was slowing him down.

"I'm sure you're Fred Gruber, the turpentine expert." His voice held good fellowship, with not a trace of mockery. "I'm Galen Thatcher," he added. "Mrs. Gruber, I am proud to meet you."

"Reverend Thatcher," Felix said. "The mayor told me you live in a house that is painted instead of whitewashed. Or do I call you Doctor?"

"I'm Brother Galen, and I am a sort of country doctor. Served in the medical corps during the war. Not as an M.D., just as a hospital orderly, but I learned from doing odd jobs, and later, I studied whilst I was still preaching."

The eyes were keen and level, dark blue and kindly in the deeply lined, lean face. The man looked and sounded pretty much the way the folk of towns southeast of Jump Off had described him.

"So we are Brother Fred and Sister Catherine."

Dangerous character, this medical person. Something about him had almost made the imposter call himself Brother Felix. Thatcher's straightforwardness, his built-in honesty, could be contagious. Happily, Felix had prepared his pitch to include nothing but the truth, as far as the scope of his mission permitted.

It took Brother Galen little effort to persuade Brother and Sister Gruber to have a bite to eat.

"Rest your camper while my bike is resting. Nothing much in the larder except fried tomatoes and odds and ends."

"You mean real fried *green* tomatoes?"

"There'll be other odds and ends. I didn't get around to saying I've been a widower, past couple years, and doing more circuit-riding practicing medicine then preaching. Come on in. I like to get news of what people are doing and saying. If you forgot where you're going and what you're going to do when you get there, just limit your gossip to others along your way."

As Felix had anticipated, the fried green tomatoes had plenty of company: farm-cured ham, grits, biscuits, and gravy.

"These preserved peaches," Felix finally found a chance to say, "are larruping."

"They've not been ruined by irrigation."

"Remind me of apricots the way we fix them in France."

That led to explaining his Americanese, and naturally enough, he got to evangelists.

"'Brother Galen, when you're not too tired, maybe you would tell us about revivals and camp meetings, things like that."

"Am I to understand that you are interested in being saved?"

"No, sir, not a bit. It is something like this: I've been raised in France all my life. But when I was born, I was recorded with the North American Imperial Consul General, or maybe it was the ambassador. My mother and my father are both American citizens, which makes me one, only I don't know how to act like one."

"Mmmm...I begin to get your point. But it is not as clear as it might be." He chuckled. "Naturally, I'd be puzzled. Never been in France."

"Well, in France everyone is routine religious, like

saying *monsieur* instead of mister. Which used to mean
something like 'my lord,' like in England, only in France
it doesn't mean much, if anything. Now, in this country,
some people are in a 'state of grace,' and others seem to
be 'sanctified' or 'born again,' and a lot of people say
things like you just did, about being saved. In France,
you get christened, and you go to mass, whatever that is,
or you do not go."

"It is as simple as all that?" Brother Galen began to
find this talk stimulating.

Felix frowned. "Uh... well, they confess things,
sometimes."

"Sounds as if you never got religion in France."

"Jesus, Brother! They're all *Catholics*."

"That is the most confusing theology I've ever heard
in a long lifetime! Tell me more, please."

"Well, I have heard talk about revivals and mass bap-
tisms, and it makes me feel as ignorant as a bump on a
log. I was so dumb that when I heard of Jump Off
Church, I thought it was a new way of being a Baptist,
and I felt like a fool, even though nobody mocked me.

"Folks out this way are always talking about religion,
and in France you never bothered to talk about it, no
more than you made a point of saying you drank wine.
Nobody but a pure fool drinks water except it's from a
special spring and he's got some kind of a disease. In
emergencies, if you're awfully thirsty and there is nothing but water, you add enough brandy to make it potable.
Anyway, you are an ordained preacher and working as a
doctor—you'd be too busy to explain things, but you
might tell me where someone makes a full-time job of
preaching and has nothing else to do. Someone told me
about an evangelist at Fiery Gizzard. Different people
told me different ways to get there and got me all confused."

"Brother Fred, I have rested up enough from my medical circuit riding, and your problem has got me interested."

"This evangelist I heard people talking about has got
you wondering how he got so popular. Some tell me he is

a sort of miracle man. A sinner, a wine bibber, lusting after dissolute and immoral women all his life. Instead of going to confession, he got a revelation, and it seems he's preaching like a prairie fire."

Brother Galen sighed. "Every man has his own approach. With what little I learned in the medical corps, I knew I could do more good trying to heal perishable bodies than to save souls, which are immortal and are bound to survive."

"Brother Galen, did I understand you to say you'd fire up your bike and guide me to Fiery Gizzard instead of me going far as Rising Star and then following the signs along the road, the ones reading, 'Are you burdened with sin and guilt?' and 'Have you made peace with your maker?'"

"I meant exactly that, Brother Fred. This evangelist may be starting with more dedication than I did."

"One more thing." Felix looked worried. "Some of the turpentine people seem to get religion every time an evangelist appears. If I go, do I have to be saved? I'd feel like a fool, not knowing how to go about it."

Despite his considerable experience, Reverend Galen Thatcher, self-made M.D., unlicensed to practice, faced a new problem. After a long pause, he answered, "Fred, eat a couple more of those fried pies. You, too, Sister Catherine."

"I won't," Catalina countered. "Not unless you have camper brunch or supper with us and get us better acquainted with this part of the country."

Chapter 29

THE NEVILLE INGERMANS, now established as the Inglewoods, were doing well enough to be convincing as a couple operating a portrait studio. Furthermore, because there was no other photographer in Rising Star, they had the virtue of not competing with local talent.

The men who, with their families, had quit Rising Star in the early 1800s to settle in Texas had been a single-minded lot. At sunrise each took a cap-and-ball six-shooter from under the pillow and holstered it. Then he downed a dollop of whiskey, cut a chaw of tobacco, and made up his mind for the day. Those who had not quit Rising Star were really fixed in their opinions. Their only concession to changing times had been that a man might go about without a belted handgun and not feel stark naked.

Although the truce between rival sects of fundamentalists had resulted in the organization of the local Church of United Christian Disciples, there remained a congregation of more than one-third of the original Alleluia Evangelical Church, also known as the Stompers. Also, there was a group of uncompromising members of the Church of the Lord's Testifiers.

"No matter which we join," Ingerman said to Diane in the privacy of their whitewashed cottage a couple of blocks from the main street, "we'd have two groups *agin* us. Only way of avoiding trouble is to contribute to each group while you and I are getting calluses on our knees, praying for divine guidance."

In due course, and after sufficient coaching by Diane, he filmed a wedding using the audiovisual gear. Diane took care of arranging the drape of skirts of bride and maids of honor, the bridal veil, and floral arrangements. Tactfully, she ignored male members of the cast.

Feminine sensitivity enabled Diane, without eavesdropping, to know how she rated with the ladies of Rising Star, and these appraisals she translated into the local vernacular:

"...she sure keeps an eye on that old coot..."

"...I'd not trust her alone, not even with an Egyptian mummy, not if it was a man..."

"...she must be one of them harlots! Funny he'd buy that shotgun when he don't never go a-hunting..."

Meanwhile, Mistah Inglewood got points for chawing tobacco, and when he got a spring-operated dingus from the big city, the thing that flung little earthenware saucers whizzing, he'd bust each one with his shotgun. Damn fool business, wasting shells when he could be getting game for the table. There was debate as to whether shooting clay pigeons was a boast or a fair warning.

Now that the Inglewoods were doing nicely, Diane let the word get around that weddings and barbecues were not the only things they could film for projection at the local movie house.

"And what's this Egypt business people are getting more and more upset about? From what I've heard in the short time we've lived here, it's always been a den of iniquity, but a lot of you Rising Star folks sound like something new has come up."

Diane's fair question got interesting answers, and these she boiled down for Ingerman to digest: "Them Egyptians are getting worse and worse all the time. Ain't stopping with worshiping graven images and gods with the heads of animals. They used to have a springtime festival about how Osiris gets murdered by his wife's lovers, and he's cut up in seventeen pieces and scattered

all along the Nile, and when she comes home and hears
about it, she goes stark mad and hunts all the pieces and
sews them together, and brings him back to life with
spells and stuff. Well, that's heathenish, but it served
him right, she being his born sister. Worse than the Jukes
and the Kallikaks—they at least didn't *pretend* they was
married in their sinful doing."

"So far, this is old stuff," Ingerman cut in.

"Nee-ville, darling, if it weren't for me, you'd never
know what Rising Star is thinking. Seems the media have
discovered the Land of Egypt, and they call the spring
festival the North American Oberammergau that's going
to be world-famous, outshining the original one. Which
is fraudulent. There is not—pardon me, there ain't no
crucifixion, which'd just be blasphemous. It's getting to
be indecent: They're calling it the Passion Play of Ancient Egypt. As if there ain't enough immorality already,
Isis cohabitating with her own brother, how much lower
can they get?"

"They can't be all that dumb!"

"Oh, can't they?" Diane retorted. "Look at the idiotic
things people recite and actually believe on Sundays.
Scholars, scientists, big businessmen. As you say it in
Américaine, the smartest believers are nuts and fruit
every Sunday for an hour or so. Do quit interrupting me,
si'l vous plâit! None of these people have ever gone to
Egypt to see goddesses wearing skintight sheath dresses
so thin that a ninety-year-old drooling fellow with cata-
racts could see all the points of interest."

"Probably female Rising Star influence."

"Whose else? Well, everyone thinks it'd be great if
someone got movies of all the fornicating in the streets
and such like, just to prove what a public nuisance Egypt
is."

"Every pornography fighter has a marvelous collection of *feelthy* pictures imported from Paris or Cairo.
That is standard equipment. To keep crusader zeal fired
up."

"And that festival is just what we need. I nearly
laughed out loud when someone asked me if my husband

would allow me to undertake anything as risky as min-
gling with a crowd of fanatic Egyptians."

"From all I've been able to gather, the Egyptians are a
pack of farmers. Hardworking and almost as good at
agriculture as Mennonites or Amish."

"You've still not told me what we have to gain," he
countered. "Suspense is overwhelming."

She ignored his mockery. "In spite of the truce between Stompers and Testifiers, there are two congrega-
tions of hardworking, uncompromising fanatics. Even if
there is not a bit of sex on the courthouse steps at high
noon, or not even any really spectacular female expo-
sure or phallic symbols like they used to parade in
Egypt, the things that standard tourists never see when
they make the museum rounds in Original Egypt, a pack
of crazies, even a handful, could start a red-eyed mob
racing to tear New Egypt apart. Almost like a democracy: The group intelligence sinks to the level of the low-
est members."

Ingerman brightened. "Keno! Under cover of a mob
attack, we could complete our job, and when Garvin and
Lani turn up missing, Rising Star, or Egypt, or both, will
smell hell, and we'll be on our way."

Now that she had him hooked, Diane knew that it was
time for the explicit answers she had refrained from demanding.

"Nee-ville, my dear, do not count your bridges before
they are hatched. You and I do not even *know* that Garvin or Lani is in Egypt. You gave me some circumstan-
tial evidence, yes. Very reasonable inferences, yes. But
if we waste Rising Star, you and I are blown up by our
own booby trap! We'd have to start all over again. If we
could.

"I knifed Miguel. For what seemed a sound reason, a
real necessity, at the time. This put you in bad with
whatever friends you had in Savannah and who knows
where else. You've never blamed me for it. Whether I
was right or wrong, it limited us badly. We are downright
lucky in finding Rising Star. I don't want to waste this
place. It is not too late to back out on the filming by

saying you won't let me go to Egypt. Now it's your move."

There was a long silence. "I did not cut you off short," he said finally, "but I did give you a skimpy answer the only time we even touched on that subject, seriously, I mean. I still can't—meaning, will not—mention names, but a close friend from way back gave me dates and facts. Right after Sister Zenia vanished from that coed Christian retreat, the Brandon Foundation, which for years has been Mona Smith, changed fiscal agents and cut the retreat to a modest endowment trust.

"At the same time, the Foundation had the new fiscal agent make payments to Egypt, in an amount greater than the old agent had been paying the retreat.

"The giveaway is this: These changes were made before the bare bones of my old friend, Harry Offendorf, were discovered, along with ditto bones of a half-ass criminal who settled labor union problems, and you know how. Being Harry's bodyguard was a promotion to respectability! Sister Zenia had to be the hidden Imperatrix. We planned that caper. We could not have been mistaken. Nobody but Garvin could have killed two men, stripped the bodies, and dumped them into a ravine a thousand meters deep—with not a shot fired nor any blood spilled."

"Took you a long time to act on it."

"Took the news a long time to get to me. About one-third of the really big bankers in North America have been lending enormous sums to Marxist countries, and when the loan goes sour, the taxpayers bail the bank out. It's one of our ways of sinking North America. An intricate process of 'laundering' money included a branch bank in Maritania, but a penny-ante vice-president made a trifling error. As Governor-General of Mars, Garvin arranged for him to vanish, mysteriously.

"A big-name banker in Megapolis Alpha committed suicide, so the story goes. The Warlords are learning things from Garvin and his Martian security system. Giving aid and comfort to anyone suspected of being a

Marxist is suicide for anyone who makes a tiny slip or is caught with his pants down and suspected of illicit deals.

"If I am wrong in this, it is my fault, not yours. And you were right in the Miguel matter, right in principle, according to the book. From here on, *chérie*, your mistakes, if any, are mine. It's your turn to get down to facts. Just how do you figure we are going to profit by your filming?"

"There'll be media operators there; the pageant is becoming well known. Box the—no, *case* the joint. It is the *damnedest* language that you people speak! I'll have views of the town, bird's-eye shots from the ridge overlooking the joining of the rivers. Of course, I studied maps when I had a chance!"

"Mmmm . . . sounds good, no matter what happens. But I should be with you for this reconnaissance."

"Nee-ville, don't be so *machísimo*! You proved your nerve, your quick thinking, when Alexander kept a three-star general from shooting you to death. You snitched an order form from his office, wrote a forged order, and no fault of yours that General Kuropatkin lost his army instead of destroying Alexander's. The pageant is becoming so popular, so newsworthy, that some veteran media man might be there and recognize you. Which would be a disaster. Until the Rising Star mob wrecks the town, you simply must stay out of sight! You need it for cover. You still are too famous to work without a mob screen!"

Ingerman knew that she was right.

"One thing more," she resumed, "and then when you say *tais toi*, I'll hush and mix us a drink. But first, hear me out!"

Voice and eyes nailed him to the barn door.

"Do what you want about Garvin, but no one and nothing must harm Lani. We need her. You and I and our Comrade Komissar, back in Sainte Véronique, we were idiots. Simpletons drugged senseless by ideology as silly as the religion of the Stompers! Worse, in fact. Here we are, fugitives wanted for murder, and from Savannah to this front door no one has asked for I.D. cards, not at motel, not at hotel, not anywhere. And all the way, people in the poorest farming counties living better than anyone in any Marxist land. Two centuries after the revolution, as poor as ever. They used to export wheat, now they buy it from American traitors. They have to because their ideology doesn't work.

"These Rising Star hillbillies live better than anyone but the highest Marxist officials.

"Listen to me! How do you say it, this is no drill! I'm not mocking you. I had my first suspicions when I saw the Marxist fat boys, the elite—they had twenty-room apartments except for those who had personal palaces. They could drive nothing short of a Mercedes long as an opium dream. Back home they drank imported wines and gourmet delicacies, but life in their paradise was so mortally dull and dreary that they escaped for the luxuries of Biarritz, the joy of living.

"I saw that, but like a fool believer, it took me too long to see the self-evident. Running from Savannah and living here woke me up. Don't look so dazed! Your ideologies are as silly as the religion of these apple knockers!"

She had to pause for breath.

"How does Lani fit into your plan?" he asked then. He was fighting not to understand.

"Your labor leaders have millions of serfs, and they own the best legislators that money can buy. But they are playboys compared to the real, the great racketeers, of Marxism. Break out of your sugar candy Easter egg, it's hatching time! Forget your Garvin vendetta and help me get Lani out of trouble when the Stompers tear this town apart. This woman-ruled nation needs an Imperatrix, someone to worship, glamorize. She must be twice my age, but lights and makeup will take care of that. Her son by the Number One prince of the Asteroid was killed playing polo. She's too old to produce another. She'll be grateful to us and rely on us to help her in a job that will wear her to a frazzle. You'll be the brains of the outfit. Once you get that idiotic ideology out of your system, your experience with government will be valuable. With the security system Garvin built up for Mars, which makes it the actual center of the Solar System, we'll all be safe, and Garvin will be tired, retired, and happy in Bayonne."

Ingerman was groping. The sweat gleaming on his forehead must have been near the freezing point. Diane knew that it was time to let up on the pressure.

"Nee-ville, darling! While I am mixing us a drink, we both need a touch of lightness and whimsy. Eighteen centuries ago, a party girl by the name of Theodora quit spreading her legs for one of the host's noble guests. She talked Justinian, Emperor of Byzantium, into passing a law making it legal for him to marry a whore. And she was the real ruler of the East Roman Empire. What a Solar System we'll have.

"Two ex-whores are bound to be better than poor, lonely Theodora, ruling an empire single-handed."

Chapter 30

BEFORE THE PAGEANT—the Passion Play of Osiris and Isis—began, there would be a parade through Egypt Town, and it would feature an unpregnant goddess. Lani, however, had to make an appearance. Slowly, she pivoted before her once-flattering friend and now overcandid three-leaf mirror.

"Mmmm...silhouette not too bad, but falling out in favor of Susie Haskins was the smart move."

To the very last, Garvin had been declaring that she was just right. The idiot actually meant it. Normally, he could from a distance of a country kilometer spot it if a female ankle was a single millimeter oversized.

Pure stubbornness, Lani thought. Or vision failing. Or he's in love. Could be a blend. Accordingly, she would not contradict him flatly. If she had worn a skintight, slinky sheath, like Isis and her sister, Nepthys, she might have convinced him, but that would have been too cruel. Even with her selection of dress, there was a shade too much emphasis on fertility and not enough on elegance. So she wore a long, frail tunic, gilded sandals, and an overdrape such as Ani's wife wore at the opener of *The Book of Coming Forth by Day*. Her own hair,.dyed jet-black, simulated tight curls that reached over her shoulders to a shade below breast level.

Few of the unpregnant wenches of Egypt, shopping at the new supermarket, were as seductively shaped.

Garvin accepted her reservations. "Okay, darling.

Suppose we skip all this pussy-oriented religious crap and stay home and sit on the roof. There may be some space phenomena."

"You've been holding out on me?"

"Hell's fire, no. Just a hunch. But you said you might walk pregnant, even if you didn't show, like I said you didn't."

"It's this way," Lani explained. "Susie would think I was snubbing her because she is taking my place, so I really ought to be on the street long enough for her to see I am applauding. And with a better man than she'd ever find even in an opium dream."

"You goddesses are a touchy lot," he said, falling for her line.

"Admiral Garvin, goddesses are women, first and for keeps."

"You spoiled my lines. I was going to say women are goddesses except when they are contrary bitches and hellions." He cocked his head. "Let's get going. The pageant's firing up."

From a distance, drums were thumping. Flutes wailed. Trumpets bawled and brayed. The jangle of sistra told Lani that the women were busy. She pounced, a neat move, though short of her usual agility, and snatched the sistrum from her dresser.

That ancient instrument was something like a hand mirror with the glass knocked out, leaving only handle and frame. The oval vacancy was barred by five wavy strands of heavy wire, on each of which were metal washers whose perforations permitted them to slide right and left freely, yet retarded so that no matter how you shook the sistrum, the *tinkle-jingle-jangle* was never the same: Apparent monotony was the mask hiding incessant variation.

Lani flicked the instrument. "It works. Let's go."

Although the sun was still well over the horizon, the Egyptians carried torches. Quite a few women, especially those with attractive legs, wore frail tunics that were pierced by slanting light.

"That combination of belly dance, cakewalk, and

tittie-wobble does things for sistrum jangling," Garvin remarked.

Many were wearing classic Egyptian dress modeled after temple paintings and papyrus scrolls as pumped out by the job press for export to Real Egypt's tourists. Others settled for calico house dresses or slacks. Come as you are was the slogan. Only a few male purists wore classic Egyptian costume.

Egyptians thumped drums, clashed cymbals, tootled pipes and flutes and kept two-meter-long horns bawling and braying.

The goddess sat on a throne. To her right and her left, half a dozen ladies of honor danced along, each shaking a sistrum. Each wore the finest frail linen, and each kept it swirling, along with breast-length curls, natural or wig. And each intoned a Coptic liturgical chant, a Christian variant for a Johnny-come-lately faith that followed the fading of a tradition five thousand years old or older.

Because of the crowd, stakes had been planted, each fitted with rings through which red rope was drawn to keep a lane clear for the procession. The remainder of the broad thoroughfare was for spectator standing room, except where flatbed trucks were parked on both sides in staggered intervals of about twenty meters. These vehicles gave the media the elevation their craft required.

Egyptians gods, goddesses, mortals, each meticulously costumed to match the originals in *The Book of Coming Forth by Day*, hawked their wares as they wormed through the thickening crowd:

"Genuine reconstituted antique *skay-rabs* from the tombs of the Pharaohs!"

"Ice cold dhurra beer for Egyptian thirst!"

"Masque programs for the show in the temple! Get the names, get the story on real *papie-ree-us*. With picture writing in *heer-ey-oh-glyphics*!"

Egyptians and outsiders bellied up against the ropes. A few had cameras. Most were too happy to bother with pictures.

From the trucks, or racing to the next station, professionals were busy with still cameras fitted with telephotos; some had zoom lenses. Agile AV operators, shoulder packs making them look like dancing hunchbacks, raced to get head-on, then broadside, shots and bounded to the next spot. They had covered many a riot or disaster: This, their first whack at Egypt, was fun for the media.

Having seen his share of parades, ceremonies, and official functions, Garvin could identify much of the equipment the media used—if not the make, at least its range and purpose. As Governor-General he often had cocktail hours at the palace for the media. It was important to recognize odd-looking gear, which might be a disguised weapon and not a picture taker.

As Garvin and Lani neared the spectator area, the Egyptian majority parted to make way for the woman who had declined the role of Isis. Despite her pregnancy, her shape and carriage remained elegant. After all these years, she still showed no noticeable lines or chin sag. In any medieval Christian country, she would have been burned as a witch.

Then, with a start, Garvin sensed that he had been on camera. A good-looking woman, getting ready for a head-on shot of the approaching goddess, was belatedly shifting a long lens for a close-up of a distant subject. Neither Garvin nor Lani was sufficiently different from other Egyptians to rate a shot. The sensing that had often warned Garvin that the other fellow would go for his gun had worked. Maybe Lani's outstanding good looks had invited the grab shot; habit made him see trouble where none lurked.

And now the enthroned goddess, with a thirty-meter gap between her palanquin and the musicians who led the procession, came into view. Her canopied throne was carried by a dozen of the sturdiest wenches on each side. Despite the transparency of their handcrafted linen lace, they were not stealing the show from the hour's goddess.

"Proud as a goddamn queen," Garvin said to Lani. "Shaped like a mattress, but for a stand-in, not a bit bad."

As goddess for an evening, the avatar was too imperial to be the essence of femaleness. Nothing jiggled, not even the sistrum. In ritual posture, she held the *crux ansata*, the key of life, which ever was without beginning or end.

Her headgear was the horns of Hathor, another aspect of Isis: a lunar crescent in which the solar disc, the life-giving Sun, was cradled. Without form, life had no expression. And the Moon was the womb in which material form was conceived. Each day, a newborn Sun emerged from darkness, coming from the eternal virgin. Garvin had always known these things, but the Christian Coptic liturgy made sense of it all for the first time.

Two thousand years of literal-mindedness had buried the self-evident.

A moment of silence made way for the sistrum jangle at his side. Lani waved. "Susie, you're marvelous!" she called.

Although the divine head did not turn, the carefully made up Egyptian eyes shifted. Her lips shaped and re-shaped, as if she had spoken.

Lani took Garvin's arm. "Let's go. I've had it, and she got it."

"'Imperial Highness, any danger of being raped or robbed if you went home alone?"

"Not in a crowd like this. Not even in California. Got a date with that camera girl?"

"So you saw her?"

"Before you did!"

"I was too busy looking at you."

"Oh, what a liar! You were trying to find out if you could stare through Isis's gown and see her navel!"

"I'm going to film some of the filmers. See if Security recognizes any new media bastards."

"Meaning I'll perish of thirst or else get paralyzed nipping just another drop of Tokaija every minute I wonder when you'll be bored enough by the masque to break away."

"They can stuff their Passion Play. I'm not wasting a minute of our Last Chance Honey-Year! I'll loop around to my headquarters, pick up the AV outfit, and head for the back of the temple. Habeeb will do the rest."

Once clear of parade spectators, Garvin lost no time. Habeeb, the temple designer and caretaker, had accompanied Bertram Turner from Egypt to assist in founding the colony in North America. That elderly fellow's name suggested that he was a Moslem. This, however, was protective coloring for a Copt of ancient lineage. His fellow Copts assumed he was a Christian, a harmless error that he never corrected. Once he had gained confidence in his patron and in Garvin, he corrected their justifiable belief that he was secretly one who followed the religion of antique Egypt. "A free man has no belief," Habeeb told them. "He has only tentative acceptance, and these change according to a circumstance and his increasing insights and depth of vision."

Garvin found a station behind the players, with the camera people facing him. He bagged the sitting ducks quite handily, then hurried to Lani's door, two blocks from the main street, and up to the roof.

The flat roof, the least esthetic style of construction, offered unique blessedness. It was good to sit elevated as if on one's own miniature mountain. With a breast-high parapet and no other dwelling higher, there was coolness and privacy. Dwarfed potted trees and potted shrubs, pieces of lawn furniture, and a canopied corner combined to make a microworld.

Lani had never decided which she preferred, making love in bed or on the roof. With lounge and cushions and that deep-napped Khotan rug, the difference was a matter of mood rather than comfort.

The little refrigerator was far more in play than the TV, though the latter did sometimes offer news. If after Labor Day she could not talk Garvin into returning as Governor-General of Mars, she might at least get him to devote a few months to reorganizing Eileen's staff and getting them shaped up for the real Imperatrix. In this, she could count on Azadeh as an ally.

There was nothing wrong with Flora, who, as Number One Wife, had gotten along marvelously with

Azadeh and Aljai. During her years as a supposed widow, Flora had been no virgin; her premarital daughter by Alexander made that plain, and rumor had it that Flora had slept her way to Mars with the late fabulous Doc Brandon.

Flora simply hated Mars, and she seemed to have a purely social bias against whores, in spite of the number of those who had, and those who had not, abandoned professional or recreational practice on reaching legitimate imperial rank.

Flora would never object to Mona, Lani cogitated. My very dearest and most loyal female friend, Madame Broadtail. Never a wife and mother, and I've been both. Some women are incomprehensible ... better ship the surplus hormone-loaded Tokaija to Mona. Being a mother seems to do something, though it is a pest!

And then, closer to the stars, the once and future empress stretched out on the adjustable "drunken lord," a modern variant of the classic Chinese chaise longue. She could hear the chanting downtown, made more effective by distance.

"It does something," Lani said while Garvin probed the little refrigerator. "You studied Coptic, as you told Bertram, but neither one of us can understand what they are saying, no more than a bunch of occidental Buddhists chanting a sutra in Pali or Chinese or Japanese have the foggiest idea of what they are saying when they follow the mimeographed poop sheet. Somehow it makes this idiotic little colony really real."

"We'll never forget this dizzy little colony. They're happy as though they had good sense. Bertram isn't off his trolley, the way I used to think he was." He set the chilled Tokaija and Sercial on the end table.

"It sets me wondering," Lani remarked, "whether it was the hormones or the local atmosphere that made me an unwed mother."

Later, when the masque was over and the Egyptians were busy with domestic fertility rites, there was a whirr of planes.

"Are we going to be bombed?" she asked. "Not that I care, but—"

"This is the phenomenon I mentioned. The crop dusters are killing an imaginary papyrus plague. Remember?"

"Of course! I was just mind-wandering."

"Festival night was the best time. Nobody'll pay attention to a bit of extra noise. They dust cotton, why not something else?"

She laughed softly. "For Egyptians, fertility is fun. For those poor Stompers, the idea makes them feel guilty."

And then naval smoke screen blotted the stars.

"Where's the cruiser?" Lani finally asked.

"You'll see nothing until directional jets fire to change her course or slack her descent. Now, relax and feel important. Cruiser and crew will be sitting behind the ridge, except for the watch that gets ground leave to swill dhurra beer and talk the local girls into fertility drill. Waiting until your labor day plus n, when you feel like traveling Marsward."

"Make it n plus two and see what happens without hormones."

They drank to that.

Chapter 31

THE ONCE REVEREND Galen Thatcher sopped up
the final smudge of sauce from his plate. "Miz Catherine,
you have mastered the art of converting groceries into
the most savory delicacies I've ever tasted."

"It's only the condiments I picked up in Tampa and
Pensacola, and driving to the big town every week to
stock up the freezer."

"Let's have no more back talk! Fred, if you folks
want to attend a real old-fashioned revival and hear the
new evangelist, here is your chance. It's in Fiery Gizzard, not far from here." He chuckled. "Being saved is
not mandatory!"

A new evangelist! That left Felix on the verge of buck
fever. This might justify his hunch. He gulped, then
steadied his voice to reply. "Sounds mighty interesting!
And this is a good time, seeing how the folks of Jump Off
have forgiven us for not being twelfth-generation pioneer
stock."

Thatcher sighed. "We are too clannish and intolerant
and have a built-in resentment and fear of government,
which last is easy to understand." His lean, deeply lined
face brightened. "Even these isolated settlements are far
and a handful of centuries better than the Old Country,
when a Christian in danger of being cremated alive by
fellow Christians had to ride hard and fast and find safety
with Suleiman the Magnificent, Sultan of the Terrible
Turks. And that's my basic reason for turning from

preaching to healing. Intolerance. We have progressed a lot but still have a long way to go. But as soon as you folks can break away from your records and reports and what your message recorder stores up for you during the day, I'll fire up my bike and lead the way tomorrow." He paused and made a wry grimace. "Unless I get an emergency call by radio. Home or bike, I'm on call."

On the next day, as they followed Thatcher, Felix said to Catalina, "I told him that you and I are worried about the radical Stomper element going hog wild, so you ought to stay at the wheel, parked for a fast getaway. I heard they're going to have a movie of the iniquities of Egypt."

"Oh, I hate to miss that. I love iniquities."

"Honey, I am taping the voice of the new evangelist, and if someone gets suspicious or fanatical—"

"Tape his voice? In case he's Ingerman?"

"Well, he just might be."

Catalina became her own sweet self. "I'll be ready to roll!"

By the time Felix and Thatcher came to the chairs and benches, gas tubes suspended from trees cast a brilliant light on the gathering crowd. A theater-size screen was at the left of the platform that awaited committee and evangelist.

"Where do we sit?"

"Once the crowd shapes up, we'll sit well to the back and get outside seats," Brother Galen answered.

"You've got special reasons?"

"You must have heard things about how some revivalists affect emotional crowds."

"I heard people get emotional. If someone didn't want to be saved, he might be lynched."

Thatcher sighed. "It's been a good twenty years since a general rating a three-phoenix flag camped with his escort right outside of Jump Off. I was conducting a make-peace revival between Stompers and Testifiers."

"Three-phoenix? Must have been General Kerwin."

Thatcher shook his head. "Name eludes me for the moment. But I remember him, right friendly, plain, and straightforward. Given to profane cursing and swearing in languages I'd never before heard spoken. Like he had fought in wars all over the world."

"He curse you?"

"No, he didn't. Generals usually do not roar, shout, bellow, snarl, or bark, and very few of them strut."

"You don't seem to despise generals like most Americans do."

"If it weren't for good generals, we'd be a slave nation speaking German, Japanese, Russian, or almost anything but Americanese. The one whose name I can't recall gave me my start. I was preaching against the heathens of Egypt to give the Stompers and Testifiers someone new to hate instead of each other. Well, when the Stompers got to stomping and going glassy-eyed and hypnotized, he got ready to leave, but he took time to say, 'Reverend, you are for peace and amity, but you stirred up nothing but hate and war and riot.' Now I remember. He was the Governor-General of Mars, Roderick David Garvin, and he said, 'Reverend, you have a tiger by the tail. Beat it half to death and let go while you are big enough and it is still too groggy to eat you.'"

"You took his advice?"

"I started with folk medicine we all knew about. We planted opium poppies and dissolved the crude gum in corn whiskey. Good anesthetic during wartime shortages. If we could not save a patient, he died feeling no pain."

"This meeting here. You mean it's going crazy? Or likely to?"

"Can't say. Sitting in back is better than getting caught in a crowd or a stampede."

Then the P.A. opened up, and Felix saw the speaker up on the poop deck. The man did not jibe with the description Felix had heard at First Army Security. Nevertheless, he got a standing ovation. Whoever he was, he was not second team.

"Halleluia . . . God bless you, Brother . . ."

Finally the crowd piped down, and he began:

"Brothers and sisters, the Blessing of the Lord be on you. Before the sermon I am going to show you the wickedness from Egypt come to inject poison into the veins of our nation."

Felix and his mentor had back row seats at the outside. Darkness and the widely spaced poplars offered a tactful exit.

The lights blinked out. A projector brought a blob of color to the screen. It solidified and pulled into focus, showing weird human figures, some with the heads of jackal, jackass, lion, or crocodile. One had the long-billed head of the ibis, and another the short deadly beak of the falcon. There was a female monster with the head and horns of a cow and a shapely woman who masqueraded as a lioness, snarling for strife and war and fire.

The male figures wore the Egyptian kilt; the females wore sheath gowns, clinging and taut.

A man wearing a tall mitre, the double crown of Egypt, faced a woman whose headdress was a crescent in which a disc was cradled.

The speaker filled every ear. "These are the monsters worshiped in Egypt, that center of iniquity. The male human is Osiris, the man they say became a god. The female is Isis, the sister of Osiris. Their son, Horus, is not yet born. That bit of incest is reserved for later."

There was a pause. "He's got them hooked," Felix whispered.

"At the risk of his life," the evangelist continued, "the dedicated proprietor of the Lone Star Studio filmed this blasphemy. When you do not hear my voice, which was dubbed in later, there will be chanting in Coptic, based on the liturgy of the early Egyptian Christians. The sacred words of divine worship are warped to honor Isis, the virgin mother of Horus, the rising sun."

Osiris now faced a woman of brown complexion. Unlike the goddesses, she wore a transparent flowing robe. Her headgear and wig suggested high status, although far short of Isis, the sister-wife. Two men stood by dressed in medium-length kilts. One had a secretary's pen and tablet. the other had a cord that he held as he would a tapeline.

The woman gestured and chanted.

The man with the tape set to work as a tailor, measuring Osiris for a close-fitting garment. The scribe wrote when the other spoke. The evangelist cut in:

"Aso, Queen of Ethiopia, a guest at the Egyptian court, is planning his death, and he does not suspect her. Aso pretends that the measurements are made to tailor a robe of honor for Osiris when he returns from a tour of foreign kingdoms, each of which he will instruct in Egyptian culture."

The scene changed to a spacious court at one side of which was a row of papyrus such as fringed the river. A breeze stirred the triangular blossom-fan of each stalk. To the far left was a small temple whose columns were decorated with hieroglyphics. The camera zoomed in on the group that came from the temple. Two figures emerged to stand in front of the chorus: Osiris and Isis.

He chanted a line.

She answered.

The chorus took up the liturgy. Osiris removed the crescent and disc from his consort's head and handed it to an attendant. He set his double crown in place of the queenly headgear. Having appointed his sister-wife to rule the land during his absence, Osiris stepped to a sedan chair, and eight bearers took him away.

The following scene showed jackal-headed Set, the envious brother of Osiris, the tawny beautiful Ethiopian queen, the tailor, and the scribe. The conspirators, however, had not met to cut cloth. A crew of craftsmen had a log on which they set to work, carving and shaping and trimming. Chanting, they plied chisel and graver, adz and plane.

As the chant subsided, the craftsmen drew aside the slabs they had pretended to carve and inscribe, revealing a coffer, gilded and inscribed in hieroglyphs. The lid was similarly adorned.

The evangelist raised his voice. "Exquisite! Very like

a coffin and a perfect fit for Osiris, the man who is to become a god."

The scene changed to show a banquet table and seventy-two guests, the great lords of Egypt.

Bearers carried the regal sedan chair to the banquet room.

Osiris stepped out. Dancing girls, food and drink servers, and musicians took their stations and set to work when the monarch was at his place. Once they pantomimed service and entertainment, they stepped aside to become the chorus, changing the lines from early Christian to pagan Egyptian.

The Ethiopian queen came on stage and hailed Osiris.

The preacher translated; "Lord of the Two Kingdoms, your royal consort is detained, and in her place, I welcome you. Brother Set will present the surprise, provided you prove that it is for you and no one else. Not a robe of honor but a beautiful coffer."

Each guest pantomimed trying to fit himself into the coffer. Only Osiris succeeded. He probably stretched himself out when the conspirators slapped the lid into place and nailed it down, airtight and watertight.

This was the first mummy case in history.

Bearers seized it and hustled it through the papyrus to the imaginary Nile beyond.

"Now I hear distant music!" the evangelist announced.

Sistra jangled. Drums blasted the ears, and cymbals clashed. A new scene filled the screen:

Eight bearers carried the returning queen, but she came as Isis the Goddess.

What Felix knew about Egypt and its culture he had summed up when he told the Old Man that he preferred to learn about teak-logging, Burmese girls, and the meaningful things of life. More to this than I imagined, he told himself. A fool answer I gave the Old Man.

And then Felix got a jolt that yanked him from his cogitation. On the screen he saw the Old Man, with a tawny, black-haired girl who walked as if she might be pregnant. When a few paces brought the couple closer to the camera and almost abreast of the advancing goddess, the woman fluttered her hand in greeting. Though the goddess moved her head only a millimeter, the almond-shaped Egyptian eyes shifted and her lips almost parted. She had seen the gesture of applause, and heard whatever the pregnant girl had said.

And then Dad was off camera, along with the brunette lovely who Felix suspected was carrying his half sibling.

"The Queen of Egypt has become the Goddess of Magic," the preacher announced. "Anyone who wants to learn how she coped with the brother-in-law who made her a widow may come back for the second installment, which will be presented next week."

The revivalist broke the long pause. "While we are singing 'Bringing in the Sheaves,' whoever is not in a state of grace may withdraw until after Holy Communion is served."

"Time to get out! Right now," Brother Galen said.

They did so.

Having the doctor-preacher's taillight to follow gave Felix a chance to be thoroughly disturbed by the sight of the Old Man and the pregnant brunette. Instead of finding Ingerman-Inglewood, it began to look as if the enemy had found the senior Garvin. If Brother Galen had recognized him, having so heartily approved of him would incline the preacher to discuss his appearance in Egypt, and in all innocence.

Felix and Catalina were gladdened by the sight of the parsonage. Once indoors, Doctor Galen prescribed sour mash that had been aged in a small keg, well charred. "How'd you like the show?" he asked.

"The folks watching it were being readied up for a sermon that would build them up to lynching mob mood. Good people in a lot of ways, but all their lives feeling guilty about things and fearing hell's fire and damnation," Felix observed. "That Ethiopian queen, good-looking girl and two shades darker than the Egyptians, shining up to Osiris. History repeating itself. And then there was that Isis. The Lord punished her, and so she is a widow, coming home to bad news. Nice people peeping down into hell and feeling good because they went to heaven by hating the bad ones."

"Fred, you are nearer right than you ought to be."

"This virgin goddess mother business, not to mention whacking away at incest, is a grand way of stirring up trouble. After all, it seems to be an old American custom, if you can believe the newspapers. So the wicked Egyptians take a beating." Felix gave his mentor a challenging look.

"You've not lost much time getting to know your legally native land. Maybe you don't realize that most religions, including our own standard ones, are symbolic. They should not be taken literally, but that is exactly what many do, particularly these fundamentalists, who do not stop to realize that in translating a scripture from a language the translator had not spoken from childhood, there are bound to be mistakes. Did the ravens feed Elijah in the wilderness, or did the nomads? A misplaced fly speck would make the difference. Couple of centuries ago, the King of Great Britain visited this country. The newspapers said that 'the king ate two hot dogs.' Well, that made sense. But if that were translated into a foreign language two thousand years from now! Rather puzzling.

"When you are dealing with symbols and myths, you get into far worse confusion. Particularly with our people. Our culture is literal-minded. The curse of the west."

Felix frowned. "Literal-minded?"

"Isis is material, tangible nature. Osiris is the life principle of nature. It is helpless, unless, until it has form. And form is useless until there is life in it.

"Isis wore a crescent supporting a disc. Moon, darkness, is her symbol, the womb of form. Every day she gives birth to the sun, the Life, immortality. Osiris is the solar principle. Sun and Moon. Spirit and form. Call them brother and sister. Neither is ever born out of anything. Each always was an expression of *one*, never a part or half. Of course, Isis is a virgin. Who or what could touch her? She gives birth to what always was.

Truth, but put into words, you get nonsense and confusion.

"The Chinese speak of yang and yin, the polar opposites of *one* cosmos."

"That's a skull-cracking business," Felix admitted after a long silence. "Takes a lot of pondering. But for starters, the happy Egyptians don't seem as crazy as they did."

"Here's the next step," Thatcher resumed. "They murder Osiris. When Isis recovers the body, Set tears it into many pieces and scatters them all over the land. Isis assembles the fragments, and by her magic Osiris is revived, and he becomes king of the underworld; he judges and revives the dead. He is the promise of life everlasting.

"Get a hint now? Why the Copts—the Egyptians—took so readily to the Christian faith? It was old-time business to them."

"I'll be damned!"

"More yet. Set, a sort of devil, scattered fragments of Osiris, and life principle, all over the Earth. Isis—Nature—received the fragments of spirit, and life took form. Resurrection of what never was dead. A bit of life flipped into every furrow, and from it the always-was is reborn into the supposedly new. A fertility cult? Sure. But with imagination, you see it refers to all living things. Strike out the words, get it directly, and you'll know. The ancient Egyptians were too smart to intellectualize. And what little truth we have—we are logical and literal-minded; we destroy it."

Felix got up. "Brother Galen, there was a message from headquarters. Got to go to a conference. I'm so wide awake with what you've said that I could not sleep. So we have to ride."

"Take a couple of fried pies to eat on the way."

Once on their way, Felix said, "I'll have red ants all over me till Security checks the voice curves I got this evening."

Chapter 32

COLONEL EMBERG HAD risen from buck private to aide-de-camp of the Number One Warlord because of his knack of liquidating critical situations before others present realized that things were getting sticky. Red-headed as always, and amiable whatever the problem might be, he sat at the work table with Major Barlow of First Army Intelligence and local Security. The problem was Private Felix Garvin, also known as Fred Gruber, on whom the major's somewhat-pop-eyes had for some while been fixed. Felix was not being as revelatory, as candid as he should be. To blat it right out and suggest that the son of Admiral Roderick David Garvin was covering something or someone was not the approach, but Intelligence and Security had to look for trouble at the first awareness of unease or wondering.

What made it worse was that Felix had been quite handy with surmises and suggestions in the matter of Miguel Rodriguez's death. It was time for Colonel Emberg to take over, and he did so.

"Garvin, your reports on Operation Turpentine are interesting but singularly devoid of an opinion, inference, or recommendations."

Amiability got a forthright answer. "Sir, my orders were to report what I saw and heard." Felix's glance shifted enough to indicate Major Barlow but not sufficiently to make it personal and his words disrespectful. "Opinions and the rest not being mentioned, I left them to professionals instead of getting myself hooked for a bad guess when it was not my duty to make any guesses or surmises."

Emberg kept a military straight face, but his glance at Intelligence meant, "What'd I tell you?"

Barlow made a slightly sour but good-humored grimace. "Garvin, you dished out some worthwhile opinions at the brainstorm session, and some that didn't work out. And no one ate you out for errors."

"Sir, that time I was obeying orders, not poking my chin out."

The Warlord's A.D.C. spoke. "General Kerwin directs me to get your hunches, notions, guesses, and inferences. If Intelligence fouls up in evaluating your guesses, that is their responsibility. Short of willfully and knowingly submitting false information, your mistakes are their hard luck, and their hard luck finally is General Kerwin's, for having such fumbling incompetents. Is that clear?"

"Yes, sir. I have it taped by the minirecorder in my pocket." He paused, then resumed most solemnly. "It would have been disrespectful if I had asked to have that statement in writing."

Emberg drew a deep breath, and exhaled slowly. "Garvin, you remind me of the time I flung a mess cup of hot coffee at a trespasser instead of shooting him or his dog. Your father had published the order, and I did not have a tape recorder, but he nevertheless recommended me for promotion to private first class. And he let me keep the trespasser's nine-millimeter automatic pistol. You, too, have good prospects if you stay in the armed forces. Now, for Christ's sweet sake, keep General Kerwin happy! He's tough and cranky, but he won battles."

"Garvin," the major cut in. "Where's your official wife? We tried to get in touch with her, but no luck."

"She left early, and I fixed my own breakfast. She set out on a shopping trip so she'd have something decent to wear in case she had to come to headquarters to answer questions about the report. She did all the typing from our field notes. And figured maybe I might not be able to answer all questions, her English and my handwriting not being standard Americanese."

Emberg found this more amusing than did Major Barlow. "In the preliminary report, she stated that she had nothing to add, of her own account. When do you suppose she'll be home from shopping?"

"Her being a civil service employee with a lot of back pay to spend, there is no telling."

"Colonel," Major Barlow said. "Is he violating an article of war, or does he rate a decoration?" After a pause, he added, "Garvin, have your fun but get down to business when I show you the pictures your father sent from Egypt Township."

Emberg changed the subject. "Your reports were a worthwhile survey as far as the natives are concerned. You were going about things in the right way. Nothing is too trivial, and nothing is irrelevant. The man in the field can't be expected to know how trifles fit into the broad picture that Security has. But your hunches, notions, and surmises are part of that microview, provided you offer them for what they are."

The Security and Intelligence officer followed Emberg's lead. "Things became interesting about the time you met Thatcher at Jump Off, and his attitude at the revival at Fiery Gizzard rates more than the bald statement that you took his advice and bailed out. Was it seeing your father's image on the screen? Or was it the evangelist saying that while the congregation sang 'Bringing in the Sheaves,' anyone not in a state of grace could get out before Holy Communion was served, or whatever you do when bread and wine is dished out."

"Felix," Emberg put in. "Major Barlow is right on the beam. Call this a brainstorm session and spread your wings."

"Well, with all this harping on iniquity and incest, you'd figure they never heard of the Jukes and the Kallikak families. But nasty business when those Egyptians celebrate the Isis and Osiris capers. Things were getting tense, and I got uneasy.

"We hadn't seen any of the snake-handlers in our

travels, but we read about two fanatics getting sanctified and handling moccasins or rattlers and getting bitten. No doctor allowed to treat those crazy coots. It was God's punishment for them not being in the state of grace they claimed to be. My orders were not to be a hero or a snake-charmer, and I was ready to haul ass out when Brother Thatcher figured things were getting hot. I was a stranger, and I didn't know how to act sanctified, and I had a recorder to get the preacher's voice curve. Damn glad I had a good excuse for leaving." He paused.

"This is interesting. Carry on."

Felix resumed. "And the show was cut in half, maybe into thirds. Like a TV soap opera. Continued next week, in another spot. The real fanatics would go to Rising Star and then the town beyond. Each place scooping up the most all-out sanctified. At each stand the concentration gets stronger, till there is a red-eyed mob, dead set on taking Egypt apart. It wasn't too clear how that tied in with finding out if Ingerman was mixed up with the Stompers, but that's the way I felt watching the show.

"The camera operator got lots of spectators watching the parade, but my Old Man got a long flash, so he'd be recognized, or maybe the girl that was young enough looking to be a daughter of the hideout Imperatrix."

"Felix, we're still listening."

"Well, my feeling is that Rising Star is the hot spot."

"You needn't be too concerned about your father and the pregnant girl. We have troops and checkpoints stationed."

"Until my old man leaves Egypt?"

"Are we telling you, or are you telling us?"

"Your saying things at times," Felix retorted, "could touch off rememberings of what I'd forgotten. Just as my mention of Rising Star made me recall that I'd not gotten around to saying that the preacher thanked the Rising Star Portrait Studio for filming the masque and parade. If he hadn't spoken the words, I'd never have thought of looking for a credit line on the film. Nobody ever does."

"There was quite a bit of media coverage of the doings in Egypt," Major Barlow observed.

"Sir, that's different! TV is on the air and then it's dead stuff. These people have their own film; they can tote it from one settlement to the other, whacking away and stirring up indignation and trouble.

"And now I remember how I was guessing to Catalina that a newcomer in Rising Star being able to set up a business and make a go of it so soon was news in country where strangers are shot on suspicion of being Internal Revenue men. And come to think of it, first thing I heard of Rising Star was in a turpentine-belt newspaper, mentioning the new studio. This was about two weeks after we talked about Miguel's death."

"These trifles do add up," Barlow conceded.

"Another thing," Felix added. "I've just about blown my front. Being friendly with Brother Galen was a big help, but it made Operation Turpentine too conspicuous. A new Watson's Liniment salesman would be better. The old one retired. Catalina got that while she was prowling and shopping and gabbling with the women. That Watson deals in more than the aches and pains department. Spices, flavoring extracts, and such like. And swamp root for people too holy to drink whiskey. That tonic is hundred-proof sour mash with herbs and prune juice to flavor it.

"Major, I don't mean to be insubordinate, but how about that sound track I submitted?"

"Very positively not the voice of Ingerman."

"Sir, before I forget it, this pictures business—the couple that killed Miguel were photo-minded."

Barlow raised his hand. "Hold it! Here is where you come in." He dipped an envelope from his briefcase and took out half a dozen color photos, nine-by-twelve-centimeter prints, crisp and sharp. "Ever see her?"

"That's my mother's jewel of a housekeeper."

"Your father saw this young woman filming him, so he sent the pregnant girl home and got to work filming just about everyone the media had sent to cover the event."

Emberg picked it up. "Diane Allzaneau was spying in
Egypt and got the image of your father and the Imperatrix. Most likely her purpose was to fix their images on
as many Stomper minds, fanatic and sane in a way,
against the day when there is to be a mob attack on
Egypt. With at least two non-Egyptian casualties. But
the laugh is on them."

"How come?"

"Ingerman, using the Stompers, is looking for the
Governor-General of Mars and an Empress Dowager
circa sixty years old and quite broad amidships. Ingerman is on the job, and if he does not run that studio, he
knows who does. More than Ingerman may be involved,
according to Major Barlow. Intelligence and Security are
to go into this very quietly and find out who is behind
Ingerman.

"And how far up in our government it begins, was
General Kerwin's view. There was a lot more to your
report than you realized, and that we had to extract it
without even a local anesthetic is simply part of the business.

"Your father was playing a hunch. That your play-
mate, Diane, had leveled a camera on him touched off
the idea that if he filmed the media people, we might
recognize some friends of troublemaking Liberals, the
enemy's old reliable friends, still working at us, never
stopping. You and Catalina did very well."

"Now that she and I have our back pay, what is my
status and what is hers?"

"General Kerwin has not directed it, but he believes
that you should return to regular duty, garrison and permitted to sleep off-post.

"As for Catalina, she is ex-civil service and never was
under armed forces jurisdiction. Where and with whom
you spend your off-duty time is of no interest except to
the young lady herself. You are an American citizen over
eighteen, and your mother could not prevent your enter-
ing the military service as a career. Catalina is equally
independent.

"You and Catalina are to get certificates of merit, and now that you have clarified your report, you may hustle to your quarters and let Catalina model her day's shopping."

According to the book, "Dismissed!" would have sufficed, but the red-headed colonel had ways all his own.

Chapter 33

AS HE HOOFED it toward the mobile-homes park to tell Catalina how Operation Turpentine had won applause from the Warlord's aide-de-camp, Felix's cogitating took on a promilitary flavor:

Sure the army screws things up at times, but when they do things right, they do it in a big way. Now, when those slimy politicians and bureaucrats cook up a do-gooding operation and get a lot of votes from the suckers they have sweet-talked, they are bound to foul up. The only perfect score they get is when they dream up a king-size screwing, and it works with high precision . . ."

Developing the basics of political science lasted until he got to the camper and saw the motorcycle chain locked to the vehicle. The bike, one of the hundred-cubic-centimeter gadabout and shopping jobs, was secure against bolt cutters. Smart girl, Catalina. The only things not secure were the panniers, port and starboard. When she shopped, she went all out. At the wheel of the camper, she drove skillfully and well—but on a bike Felix had no time for a shudder.

The boarding port snapped open.

"Oh, I thought you'd never come home! I was pacing the floor, with red ants crawling all over me."

He was aboard with the port closed behind him before he had a chance to comment on the cycle. Catalina's dress was distracting, and so was she.

"Pacing the floor—" he exclaimed. "Goddammit,

darling, you didn't wear that almost-down-to-the-ankles thing home from shopping, not riding that bike!"

"Of course, I had to change into this before I could start pacing! But you ought to see what I wore home on the bike."

If all those empty cartons were any indication, she must have looted half a dozen shops. Clothes were scattered all over the small all-purpose room, which tended to be cramped even at its best.

"I just had to see what I'd bought and decide what I'd wear first," she explained, reading his roving glance. "Operation Turpentine was awfully interesting, but I simply could not wear anything nice!"

He eyed the see-more fabric and structure of the dress. "If you had, it'd not have lasted long. The women would have torn it off to keep the men from raping you, and me from emptying a three-eighty magazine into them and not stopping the mob."

"But it's not a see-more, not really. I'm wearing a slip and things. And it isn't so extreme, it's simply not the unisex things that so many of these wenches wear because, well, slacks do disguise unfortunate legs."

"You look like the Queen of Sheba dressed up for her first date with King Solomon."

Felix forgot all about the light cycle until after supper and a few drinks.

"That bike? I bought it with my back pay, of course. And what for? To tend to household business while you are doing 'parade rest,' 'mark time,' 'at ease,' and 'pass in review.'"

Before Felix could remind her that there were such things as fatigue details and practice marches when the rolling kitchens got lost and the drinking water reeked of chlorine strong enough to bleach imperial blue to snow white in three minutes, Catalina had convinced him that she did wear a slip and things beneath the seductive gown.

Well before Catalina had modeled half the day's purchases, Felix felt like a bigamist. He had set out with a sweet, serious-minded girl who was never too tired, a comfortably ardent companion, and here he was, sitting and blinking from seeing familiar territory become a realm of wonder.

"Christ on a life raft," he said to himself as they finally tumbled into bed for keeps. "Who'd ever imagine that two women could be put into one package and no bulges anywhere! And all with the same equipment."

When Felix awakened, it was long after reveille. But that did not worry him. Being on special duty, he had privileges. He might, as a matter of group discipline, be restricted to quarters for a couple of weekends and perhaps nicked one-third of a month's pay, but that was all. His military career would not suffer.

And then Felix realized that he was alone. There was a note pinned to the vacant pillow beside him:

> *Querido Mío.* If I am not able to come back, give my new things to some nice girl who could wear them and make you think of me. I am doing like the Igorot headhunters when they go to take a head. They eat no meat, drink no spirits, and make love with nobody. Not until I have taken the head of someone I do not name. It is the old religion of the primitives, when they are to go silently and invisible. In the Bontoc country, only men take heads to prove to the women that their men are manly and worthy of respect. With American women trying to be imitation men, it is not improper for me. Your father is a headhunter, and so are you. So I do not compete for a hundred thousand pazors. For me, this is one time only. Not a career. It is for honor, like your father hunting the enemy. I love you, and you will be greater than your father.

It was signed with a lipstick kiss.
Felix read it a second time.
"I might have known it. I might have known. Serious-

minded girl and touchy Malay honor. And that cut-stab
hairpin."

He had a good guess as to her destination. And Felix
knew that any attempt to help Catalina would be
insulting.

Chapter 34

WHEN GALEN THATCHER parked his cycle in Garvin's patio, he was ready to fall apart. Weaving his way to a leather upholstered chair in the ground floor living room, he plopped himself into its depths. "Before I had a chance to ride to Egypt and tell you that I saw your image on a movie screen at a Stomper hate revival in Fiery Gizzard—you and a very good-looking young woman watching the Isis parade—I had to give a pack of midwives some emergency assistance and then serve as deputy coroner in Rising Star."

Garvin sat bolt upright, then relaxed and poured his guest a shot of Demerara rum. "Brother Galen, First Army Security told me about my being a screen star, but this other deal—was the coroner killed in a shoot-out, or was he just drunk or absent without leave?"

"I'm so used to emergencies, I didn't ask any questions. Too tired most of the time. Murder in Rising Star. Wife of the fellow who opened a photographic studio there not so long ago."

"What'd the man say?"

"Nothing. Seems he was out of town. His wife's throat was slashed by an assailant apparently standing behind her, making a drawing cut—" He gestured. "Jugular. Quick and fatal. Seems she had no chance to defend herself. There was a book of sample photos, individual and family poses, portrait and wedding stuff, lying on the floor. She must have turned to get it for her customer,

and that was the last of her. She probably was dead
when the killer ran a stiletto hilt deep into her
back. The weapon came from the victim's garter-
sheath."

Garvin got up and fished a pack of photos from a desk
drawer. He handed them to Thatcher. "This the
woman?"

"It is. Good God, man! I hate to bring you bad news."

Garvin grimaced. "Not so damn bad. Rather good."

Thatcher blinked. "Well, when a couple of Army
checkpoints halted me on my way here, I quit worrying
about you, but that Egyptian girl looked so pregnant in
the movie, I didn't know if I'd get here in time."

"Thanks, Brother Galen, but the local midwives did
nicely." Garvin drew a deep breath, then exhaled a long
sigh. "It would be a kindness if you stayed around the
house. She is leaving in a few hours. I will not be going
with her. Unfinished business. The no longer pregnant
brunette is the long-missing Imperatrix. She is at last
cutting loose from the past and emerging to become part
of the present."

"Even an empress gives her *neo natus* priority over
sentiment."

Garvin made a gesture that included not only the cluttered living room but the entire ground floor. "It is all
yours. It would be dismal business coming back to an
empty house."

"Don't I know! I've been doing so a couple of years
now."

Garvin eyed his visitor. "In case you need a sleeping
pill, and none in your black bag, dissolve gum opium in
Demerara rum," he said with heavy-footed irony.
"They're in the refrigerator."

"So you've been insomniac?"

Garvin shook his head. "Practicing medicine without
a license. I've mixed paregoric for the Imperatrix."

"My respects to the Empress. Say to her, for me,
'*Ave, imperatrix dea, ora pro nobis*. No matter how
fouled up my homemade Latin is, it'll work. Since before
history began, mankind has worshiped virgin mothers.

Take off with a trail of exhaust flame, heading Marsward, and from this colony, she'll be a new one, an avatar of Isis."

"You think so?"

"Americans are the world's most credulous believers."

As Garvin stepped into the midafternoon glow, he marveled that Thatcher and the Warlords had expressed a comparable view. Democracy, limited or unlimited, had let them down; the public needed a goddess.

The street was jammed with Egyptians, mostly in carnival costume, but quite a few were dressed for work. Whether mourning for Osiris was offset by his resurrection and the birth of Horus, Lani's son, life was a pageant, a masque. The next season would bring them a new Isis, none the worse for new face and figure. Happiness and their hustling bodies swept Garvin along until good luck poured him into Lani's doorway.

Half a dozen ladies-in-waiting, each fitted with skintight sheath gowns and headgear that made each a minor goddess, welcomed Garvin. With Lani's departure, he'd be someone else's Osiris.

"When'll she be done dressing?" he asked.

"We got tired of waiting, so she's all prettied up for the parade, and your son is sleeping."

One mischievous wench said in a stage whisper, "She can take off her headgear, but be careful with her hairdo and makeup."

Though purely teasing, Egypt's mind rarely got far from the center of creation.

An open litter, its columns, throne, and canopy agleam with mosaic silver, waited in the ground-level reception room. Garvin went up a flight of stairs to the boudoir, beyond which he got a glimpse of Lani's bedroom.

Lani's towering headdress with solar disc reposing in the crescent moon reminded Garvin of a myth other than the daily birth of the Rising Sun. Each year the sun lay dead three days, after which came the resurrection, the unconquered sun, ever victorious, stepping from the tomb and moving northward, inviting life to rule again, life without end. And before the dawn of history, white men who had known this had built Stonehenge on Salisbury Plain, and red men of Mesa Verde had known of the rising from the dead after three days in the tomb.

No wonder Brother Galen had finally awakened.

Lani, sitting in her Egyptianesque chair fashioned of teak from Mona's island, reassured Garvin. Seeing became something close to believing and made Galen's notion and the Warlord's hope at least for the moment seem nearer to reality than to an opium dream.

Isis looked at Garvin. Seeing his wonder, she, too, believed.

There was a timeless moment as each regarded the other.

Then Isis was again a woman.

When Garvin's awareness returned to the world of time and space, he brought with him a shred of knowledge, an understanding of what "collective unconscious" meant.

For a moment he wondered how long it had taken the ladies-in-waiting to withdraw and close the door.

Garvin gulped, blinked, and swallowed. He groped for words. "Now we don't know what it was we knew, but we'll never forget that we knew *something*."

"Mind if I stay crowned and dressed?"

"An imperatrix, no problem. But Isis—" He made a gesture of futility.

"I made time for leave-taking," Isis said.

"Tomorrow, each will be sorry."

Lani sighed. "They say you won't even walk alongside the litter carrying us to the *Asteroidienne*."

"No more than I could wear an Osiris mitre and sit with you. Somewhere, sometime in Egypt, we became one, but I didn't know it until I saw you as Isis. We spent our lives thinking we were two."

"Same for you and Azadeh. You and Flora; you and Aljai."

He nodded. "Meeting Isis made them really real.

Knowledge came too late. Too late for all. Especially you and me."

Lani laughed softly, a caress without contact: total understanding, happy and rueful and grateful.

"We're still higher than kites. At that rate, where and what were we moments or ages ago? It's beyond all the idiotic fanciful things you ever told me, long ago. We can't stay this way long. No humans could."

"Before our feet touch floor," Garvin said very slowly, "I'll go all-out wild. While it's real, I'll say it. So we can remember what we meant and won't laugh it off."

"Tell me. While you can."

"You were Isis during that silence when we could not speak."

"You mean, an *avatara*, borrowing my body?"

"Something happened. Put it into words, make a damn lie of truth. You were you, and you were Isis. Don't try to explain fourth or fifth dimension. Put into words, it is as crazy as anything the Stompers believe."

"Maybe theirs is real to them. They're wired up differently, so they have a different reality."

"Madame, that's gospel. Thatcher saw through it. He never wanted us exterminated. We still don't want to exterminate them. Different wiring diagram."

There was a long pause. Finally Lani spoke.

"You've had a handful of years with each of your wives. Azadeh wouldn't mind my being an ex-hooker, but Flora would. When you've had a good vacation in Bayonne, with Flora never wearing the Sudzo panties that made her famous from Paris to Khatmandu to Timbuktu, come to Mars to be the power behind the throne, helping a harassed imperatrix.

"Any half-ass astrologer knows that women are moon-ruled," Lani added, "changeable as lunar phases. Skip the nonsense that someone has prescribed for female humans, which the silly bitches have been gullible enough to buy, really or self-deceptively."

"Madame, that's too important to laugh off or snap at."

"Bring a case of Tokaija. I'm leaving quite a bit here for Mona, just in case she gets notions. Being a mother is all she has skipped so far. Oh, I settled Inspector Morgan with a geologist's hammer, but I never supervised a quintuple beheading of spies."

"I have unfinished business, so I should not promise. Still and all—"

"Roderick David Garvin, there is something I have not told you. Did it occur to you that while you saw me as real Isis, I could only see you as real Osiris?"

"For Christ's sweet sake!"

"It had to be true for both or false for each."

"One more like that, and vigorous young men will arrive, wearing white jackets and smiling soothingly as they lock us up in separate cells."

Lani flowed out of her Egyptian chair and took his arm. "We've got to knock this off! I fed your third begotten son just a nip of that paregoric to make sure he'd not squall and bitch up my departure. Normally, he is being tittie-fed, but not in public, hence emergency formula. So, have your *au revoir* look. He is quite an improvement on the puckered red horror that made you feel sorry for anyone squeezing through a narrow gateway."

They had a look at the Divine Horus.

"*Au revoir*, you said? I promised Flora I'd be back, and maybe Azadeh would join us, for awhile, in spite of hating Terrestrians. I know what it is like with an empress. With a goddess, well, I'll bust my tail to find out.

"So, muss up your hair a bit, and our good-bye kiss will smudge your makeup enough so the ladies-in-waiting won't be too scandalized by a neglected goddess. Leavetakings are pure hell, and I've made a career of them. I do not want to be in the crowd going with you to the *Asteroidienne*. I'm going home to watch the audiovisual coverage and the stock shots. I'll be sitting on the roof.

"Galen Thatcher is at the house, ready to fold. A good

doctor takes more of a beating than a combat soldier, I'd say. I knew I'd be in a dark mood when I left you, so I made a point of making him stay."

Garvin turned to the stairs leading to the ground floor. When Lani jangled the sistrum to let the ladies-in-waiting know that she was ready to have her makeup retouched, he knew again that one never is inured to loneliness.

Chapter 35

THE RECEDING SOUNDS of Egypt on the hoof baited Garvin from emotional anesthesia. As the procession moved out of town and upstream toward the ridge, silence closed in on the loneliest man in Egypt. Quiet and lifelessness made him tiptoe into his own house. When he heard a stirring, a cough, and a muttering, he recalled Thatcher. Since he and his visitor were living, it must be the town that was dead.

The doctor was buried in a deep chair, his long legs stretched out. A book that had slipped from sleep-relaxed fingers lay on the floor near his black bag. Tiptoeing, Garvin took the twelve-power binoculars from the coat-rack and cat-footed his way out of dusk and up into the brightness of the roof. The ruddy light made the dwarfed umbrella trees a strikingly brilliant bluish green. They cast shadows far longer than themselves, reaching close to those which lined the opposite parapet.

Leveling the binoculars, he saw that the point of ruddy silver was the canopy of Lani's litter, bobbing with the trotting gait of the bearers. The shell of the *Asteroidienne* gleamed like a cylindrical mirror.

The canopy shifted southward and vanished in rounding the shoulder of the ridge. The trees had been cut down to give a clear view of the cruiser, which no longer needed concealment. An elevator would whisk Lani to the bridge to join the skipper.

The TV was still on army signal corps wavelength. He

snapped on the switch to be sure he would miss nothing. Crackling static mocked him.

"Have fun," he retorted.

This reminder of the outside completed his return to something approaching normal awareness. Belatedly, he sensed that he was not alone and realized that too much of him remained with Isis. Letting go of the binoculars, he twisted and fired at the shape that emerged from the shadow of the umbrella trees. Fire flashed from the gloom, and the blasts were a single prolonged sound. A numbing jolt made him lurch, stumble, recover, and plop into the deck chair instead of to the tarred gravel of the roof. During that instant he glimpsed his assailant, doubling up. The man still had his arm partly extended. He had fired as in target practice. But for the bungling of inexperience, he would have hit Garvin dead-center, drilling him from back to front. Instead, Garvin's 11.2 had given him a belly buster.

The gunner crumpled. His automatic slid out of reach.

Garvin wondered who would be the first to feel pain.

Give the assassin enough time and he would pray for a second bullet to terminate his misery.

Garvin had survived quite a few gunshot wounds. For the moment he knew only that he had to outlive and outwit the wounded enemy: Neville Ingerman, whose head he had promised Lani.

A nice coronation gift, but the timing was not right.

Gut shot. Miserable business.

Garvin was remembering the Security report and the description given by the telephone answering service. Ingerman had used makeup to establish a false coloring and a deceptive expression. But now he had resumed his natural color. Worn, weary, and haggard, he was recognizable only by one who had often encountered him face-to-face before Alexander's death.

Neville Ingerman, hunting an elderly imperatrix, broad-beamed and looking her age, had not recognized the filmed image of his intended victim. Garvin, the supposedly reliable stalking horse, had found a new dream girl. For lack of better game, Ingerman had evidently

decided to settle for a mere Governor-General. How well
he had planned! He had even caught Garvin off guard.
And of the very few who had even approximated such
fine fortune, Ingerman, lying there on the deck, had lived
longer than any of his predecessors.

Had Ingerman devoted more time to small-arms training and less to social programs and ideals, he would have
killed Garvin.

All this flashed through Garvin's mind, and as he realized that his wound was more serious than he had at first
realized, his resolution solidified. With one shot he could
kill Ingerman—but Rod Garvin demanded more.

He could not risk quitting his chair. He might collapse
and be unable to rise. There was work ahead of him:
cruel, bitter, calculating, and infinitely more difficult
than killing Harry Offendorf, who, like Ingerman, had
thought he had a sure thing.

Then he heard footfalls *clump-clumping*, the footfalls
of one drunk, drugged, or half asleep. Garvin twisted his
head far as he could, and the 11.2 shifted to throw a slug
where Garvin's eye focused.

"Don't shoot! It's me! What's going on?" Galen
Thatcher was getting into the show.

"Grab that gun! This is better'n the second coming of
Christ! I don't want to kill this bastard too soon!"

"Sounded like two shots. Rod, you're hurt."

"The hell I am!"

Thatcher's fatigue-numbed wits got into gear. He
snatched the nine-millimeter automatic and pocketed it.
Then he recalled that he was a healer and that he had a
black bag down on the ground floor.

"That poor devil is in bad shape. Where were you
hit?"

"Just a graze. I'm a case of shock, letting him almost
drill me through the back. And him almost making it.
Tend to him first."

"You're a true Christian."

"Christian, my ass! I want this pig fucker to talk with
a witness hearing him. Get going."

"With that wound, we've got to get him to what

passes for the Egyptian Hospital. I can't treat him here.
Abdominal wound. Nasty business. You're badly shaken
up. I've got to get busy."

"You will treat him the way I tell you."

"Rod, I am not licensed to practice surgery, but I do
live up to the oath."

"Galen, you can't win on that one. I can't hurt you,
but I can and I will kill that son of a bitch the first move
you make to do anything I tell you not to. Is that clear?"

In the ruddy light, Ingerman's face was bluish gray.
Sweat gleamed in little beads on forehead and wrists;
each drop, a tiny lens, glowed red in the low sun. Ingerman muttered something.

"If you want his dying statement, I'll have to get to
work immediately," Thatcher said. "Do you have one
tiny scrap of humanity?"

"Get my bottle of Demerara rum from the refrigerator." Garvin lowered his voice. "I need a drink. I
wrenched my back. That twist—it hurts like hell. And
get that ball of raw opium. Set the stuff on this table
where I can reach it."

When Thatcher was well on his way, Garvin addressed Ingerman. "You are hurting plenty. Play ball and
I might let him give you a break."

"That pest house of a hospital. Shove it."

The man had guts, but this was no time for chivalry or
decency.

"You are Neville Ingerman."

"I am not."

"'Norman Inglewood' who paid a phone answering
service when I came to town had no reason to kill me.
Neville Ingerman had plenty. Your buddy, Harry Offendorf, went hunting for Lani the Empress. He found me,
and I finished him and his chauffeur.

"I have done as much for you, but you'll not have it
as easy as they had it."

"Horse shit."

"You saw me in the fiesta movie someone filmed in
this town. You may have done the camera work. You

were not interested in me. Lani was your game. You missed her. I'm second choice.

"You gave me no chance. I do give you a chance. An easy out or begging for a bullet that I will not plop into you."

There was no rebuttal. Garvin did not like the sound of the man's breathing. Moment by moment it became ever more urgent to make the correct decision in outwitting Ingerman. And when Thatcher returned, Garvin was still groping for answers.

He ignored the rum and opium ball that Thatcher set on the table. Garvin was soaked with icy sweat. What sustained him was knowing that however bad his own pains were, the enemy's were worse. He sensed that but for Ingerman's fortitude, the difficult would become impossible.

"Miguel said he was from the Philippines," Garvin resumed. He faked whimsy, which may have cost more power than it was worth. "Smart lad, but when he said 'boondocks' like an American, my son saw the fraud, and Miguel confessed. You were awfully smart in so many ways but not bright enough to fire from the hip when I had my back to you for a perfect shot. You stretched your arm like on a target range, and here you are, gut shot.

"You bunglers, you idealists, can't even shoot a man in the back and do it right."

"Rod, for Christ's sake," Thatcher cut in. "Let me give him a shot of morphia. You'd make an Apache envious!"

"It's his choice, if he dies without admitting his identity. And by the way, Galen, what a patient says is not confidential, not when treason is involved. How many thousand deaths did your caper cost us when you sold an army to the Marxist liberators, Ingerman?"

Ingerman only mumbled.

A far-off roar and hiss and thunder strengthened Garvin. He straightened and used his sleeve to wipe sweat from his forehead.

"Lani, Empress of North America, is on her way to

Mars. The *Asteroidienne* is taking off. For the first time in your life, tell the truth, and with a witness to prove that you're able."

The gleaming shell rose deliberately, enthroned on her exhaust blast. Garvin glanced at his watch. "On schedule and to a hair."

Not far from the parapet, the TV came to life.

Colonel Emberg announced, "Lani, widow of Alexander Imperator, is emerging from years of seclusion and now accepts the homage of North America, of Mars, and even of the Gur Khan, Paramount Prince of the only known inhabited asteroid of our Solar System.

"Inhabitants of three worlds, it is my privilege to invite you to salute the ever-youthful empress, former fourth wife of the Gur Khan, the avatar of Isis, the latest of history's many virgin mothers."

The *Asteroidienne* was now well above the rimrock and accelerating. Her shell reflected a sun too low for flatland illumination.

Colonel Emberg was cut off, and Lani filled the screen. She no longer wore the skintight gown of Egyptian temple and tomb painting. Instead, her original coronation dress made her a glamour figure, North American style, but her black wig was topped by the tall headgear of Isis, crescent moon cradling the solar disc. Floodlights blasted from cruel angles but could pick no flaw in her throat or chin line. First the sonorous Coptic chanting could be heard, and then, in clear Americanese: "Isis Avatara bids farewell to the Township of Egypt and to the people who welcomed her for a full twenty dangerous years."

Ladies-in-waiting removed the headdress of the goddess. Others removed the wig of black curls, exposing tawny copper hair; and finally, two set on her head the silver hood and kingfisher feather-trimmed crown of the Imperium, from which trailed long jade pendants with moonstone studs.

A bearer carrying the nine-stage imperial parasol stepped behind Lani.

A nursemaid then brought on stage Lani's blinking son, Horus.

A bearer followed with the nine-yak-tail standard.

Lani spoke. "Good-bye, Egypt, and I am as sorry to say this as I am happy to add that since Alexander can rest in peace at last, it is wonderful to greet North America, Mars, and the Asteroidal folk. I hope to serve the three worlds until Limited Democracy elects my successor.

"Whenever that time comes, I am ready to step aside. I am a lot older and much more tired than I look. The Warlords will rule the empire while I am engrossed in my newborn son's getting acquainted with life.

"I'm unable even to try to live up to what my friends of the Township of Egypt have said of me. As so-called Avatara of Isis, I am at least the dozenth Virgin Mother of history.

"Sri Krishna, a Unitarian minister assured me—and he was a great scholar—had *two* virgin mothers. Gautama, the wisest and only fully enlightened man in recorded history, is said to have been miraculously conceived and born."

"Galen," Garvin said. "Cut the switch."

The doctor did so.

Garvin addressed Ingerman. "Why didn't you murder her when you had all the chance you needed? I'm a cheap second choice."

"That was a teenager with eyes like Lani's."

"The voice was hers. You often heard it. As empress, she never showed her face publicly, not below the eyes, that you recall."

"She sent a double to Mars," Ingerman was still defiant, but the fire was dimming.

"Neville, you and I have hated each other from the first. For a beginner, you've done me more damage than the dozen experts I have killed. I'm playing straight with you. That woman is the imperatrix. Lani is one of Doc Brandon's genetic experiments, and hormones account for pregnancy at her age.

"You hated Doc Brandon, but his work reached from the grave to sink you.

"I'm hurting, and damn it, man! Give yourself a chance. Give me a break. You are the only man to give Garvin a serious wound and live to know what he had done."

"I . . . am . . . Neville Ingerman."

"Galen, do what you can. Morphia. The works. All. Get people on their way home from the Ascension of Isis."

"You need help."

"I was pretending to be a fellow sufferer. Get him on his way and give him his chance."

Garvin stirred a fragment of gum opium into a dollop of Demerara rum.

"Too bad I'm unable to be a stretcher bearer," Garvin added when Egyptians came to get the patient.

"You capitalist, you imperialistic son of a bitch," Ingerman retorted. "Thanks—and I'll outlive you yet."

Garvin watched the Egyptians give Galen a hand. Now that the tension was over, the doctor became a zombie. Army surgeons had learned to move as automatons and do well. Thatcher had only zeal, dedication, and not the experience he required. And when, among the Egyptians, Garvin saw a medical corps sergeant, he had a happy moment.

"Joke's on Ingerman!"

He broke off another bit of sun-dried poppy juice and crumbled it into the rum. He stirred with his finger. Soon it would dissolve.

Chapter 36

GARVIN COULD HAVE gone with Ingerman to the Army field hospital that had been included in Colonel Emberg's protective cordon. He recognized but rejected the opportunity that appeared with the medical corps sergeant. Wearing Ingerman down to confession had left Garvin depleted.

He wanted to be alone. Overpowering Ingerman and controlling Thatcher had been too much. And now, thanks to homemade tincture of opium, he knew that he had been right.

Telling Thatcher and the enemy that his wound was only a graze had not been far from the truth. Happily, each had believed him.

"Glad I didn't let him needle me with morphine. Couldn't be sitting here, digesting what's happened. Soon be Marsrise. While Ingerman's enjoying scrambled tripe."

Leaning way over and reaching out with his revolver, he flicked the TV switch.

Lani was saying, "*Please*! Let's have no more of this Isis nonsense! I don't know why I let an AV crew hound me all the way to where I'm going."

"But your picture image did perform a miracle, Divine—uh, Madame Is—uh, Imperatrix."

"If anything happened, it was hysteria. Is that clear?"

"But it is a miracle. The Gur Khan believes that being part of the Empire will be good for the Asteroid, when for so many years he shied away from American influence—"

A consortium of warlords intruded. These Garvin ignored.

"The more Lani denies she is a goddess, the more they're going to insist she always was one," Garvin commented. He took another nip of the rum. "If religion is the opium of the people, there's a spot for everyone between Taoism and Stomperism. Marxism doesn't count."

Now that he felt so much better, what had started as the darkest, stickiest day of a crowded life was turning out just right.

"Got everything but a good long rest, and I'll have that soon. No matter how lousy a soap opera is, you've got to sit till you see how it turns out."

Seeing his life as an entirety, Garvin realized with a jolt and a thrill that an old established story had been reversed and had become new:

From the hour of their meeting until the final moments of leave-taking, he and Lani had believed him to have been the catalyst whose quirks of fortune had boosted her from deluxe call girl to *avatara* of a goddess to miraculously become dowager empress of three worlds.

"*Me*, shaping *her* career? Pure distilled horse crap! From the start, Lani was shaping mine. She was the catalyst that never changed, no matter what she set a-bubbling!

"If it had not been for Lani, I would have been a space tramp who married Alexander's cousin because she thought she was knocked up but wasn't. I'd have been grounded for life, works manager of spaceways shops. If it hadn't been for Lani, I'd never have met Azadeh, never become a war hero, never Governor-General of Mars, never known what it'd be like with an Empress—or with an *avatara*! I'd never have amounted to a madman's shout down a dry well!

"Hail, Divine Isis! Don't bother praying for me. I have had it, and it's a double dip."

It was now fully dark. Screen and speaker were dead.

Egypt must be at home, too contented communing with each other to think of Osiris and Isis. Although Garvin felt no pain, he splashed rum into the glass and fumbled crumbs of opium into it.

"Tired ... Godawful weary ... living those years over again."

What kept him awake was the rising of Mars, up and over the rim. It was the same old Mars of his boyhood days, but much larger and redder than ever before. Mars, where after six passionate and battling years he and Flora found their first Night of Truth, after which they could never wholly break the bond. Mars, where he and Azadeh had lived, each only for the other, and happily, until homesickness, temporarily, as they had reckoned, had parted them.

"Mars, where I'll retire if Azadeh doesn't want to divide her time between there and Bayonne."

So many expanding images, all coalescing in that ever-expanding red disc. Being good and goddamn weary, Garvin yawned and knew that it was time for a long rest, after which he would awaken to see how Eck & Ag had developed.

Epilogue

THE BURMESE VILLAGERS of Nameless Island found nothing as fascinating as their festivals, the dance-and-drama pwe, and temple ceremonies in honor of Buddhas, Arhats, and, of course, the 700 million forest devils who had to be kept in an amiable mood. None of these activities required Mona's supervision, and Mona and Felix Garvin needed no assistance in their study of more scientific approaches to teak-logging. Accordingly, they ignored the lookie-squawkie box until Felix remembered that the Number One Warlord had sent him to survey the situation and ascertain whether Norman Inglewood or other foreign agents had been snooping on or offshore of the island.

Felix phoned using his code name, Fred Gruber, which got him directly to General Kerwin. "Sir, as a matter of form I am reporting that, thus far, there is nothing to report."

"Well done! These goddamn bureaucrats use five hundred typed pages to tell me a lot less. Come to the mainland at once, with Mona Smith if she is at liberty to leave, and be prepared to take government transportation from my headquarters to interview Galen Thatcher, thence to Egypt for a talk with Bertram Turner and others, at will. Forget this Gruber crap. That problem is solved for keeps."

With this order executed, Felix and Mona returned to the island. There, with emotions under control and facts marshaled, he phoned his mother to inform her that she was a widow. He quickly learned that she had been aware of the fact long before he had; Flora did not know whether to flay her son for gross neglect or to go into hysteria. She did both. Finally summing up by declaring that Felix was as thoroughly self-centered and heartless as his father ever had been, she heard the blend of fact and surmise.

Mona listened on an extension, making notes on matters that must not be skipped. These she fed him, a scrap at a time.

"...I'm still in the forestry business. Making a survey."

"How to make turpentine out of teak juice?"

He ignored Mommie's sarcasm. "Just logging. And I have been out of touch."

"*That* is what is so abominably abominable! Staying out of touch when you might have known that those horrible Egyptians would let someone assassinate him while he was getting Lani off to Mars, where she belongs. Divine Lani! Virgin Mother, no less!"

Thoroughly irritated by a skinning when he craved sympathy, he snapped, "If you got the news before I did, tell me if there's anything left to say."

"I've had nothing but smoke screen censorship," Flora retorted, "which is why your thoughtlessness is so outrageous."

Felix gave Mommie Galen Thatcher's facts and inferences and Colonel Emberg's report, as well as a statement by the Right Honorable, the Almost Earl of Sommerton.

"He was sitting there on the roof of his house, with Demerara rum laced with locally grown opium. He had gotten a grazing wound, turning edgewise just about when he would have been hit squarely and killed if he'd not been warned by instinct."

Felix gave Thatcher's blow-by-blow account of how the Old Man had pretended he was no more than scratched, thus breaking the enemy's heart.

"But why didn't he go to the hospital when Ingerman did?"

"Nobody knows. They found him sitting there, looking as happy as a spotted-ass ape. General Kerwin would not allow an autopsy. I do know Dad distrusted doctors. They'll prolong your life when you'd rather die in peace."

"Oh."

"You've guessed?"

"Tell me."

"That edgewise shot might have damaged the spine. He plopped into a chair and would not risk getting out of it. Suppose he believed he might end paralyzed. So he had more rum and opium.

"Maybe an accidental overdose, trying to fool friend and enemy. And here is one of General Kerwin's guesses: People trying to shoot him by surprise never lived to make it. But this time he was caught off guard. Knew he was slipping. Time to quit."

"But *why* no autopsy? It's the law!"

"In a limited democracy, law is kept in its place by common sense. Dad was a war hero. Why give surviving enemies a treat? Rum and opium. Suspicion of suicide? He nailed the final important traitor. His widow or widows are likely to get the hundred-thousand-pazor reward on Ingerman's head. Lani will see to *that*."

She managed not to say, "Oh, that's nice." She said, "Then Ingerman is dead?"

Felix laughed. "His identity was a death sentence. They patched him up, fed him a humane shot of painkiller, and hanged him at Alexander's grave. The Liberals could never get used to the end of the great idealistic days, when you could shoot a president and instead of being cut down by a bodyguard, you were taken alive, proved insane, and turned loose."

There was a long pause. "Are you coming home to finish school?"

"Sure am. Dad told me about the Chinese widow with three sons. One at Oxford. One at Cambridge. The third one, not really a half-wit but subcaliber for that family, she sent him to a big-name university in North America, where he'd feel more at home.

"But once I get a bit more schooling, I'm going back to North America. That's where I belong."

"When could I expect you?"

"I can't say, not yet. I am packing up the Old Man's things, and there is a case or so of Tokaija that Lani left for Mona. I know she'd split it with you."

"Let her drink every drop, and then you hurry home."

ABOUT THE AUTHOR

E. HOFFMANN PRICE (1898–present) soldiered in the Philippines and France during World War I. At war's end he was appointed to the United States Military Academy, where he entered intercollegiate pistol and fencing competition. He was graduated in 1923 and commissioned in the Coast Artillery Corps. His first fiction sale was March 1924, to *Droll Stories*. By 1932, he was writing full time—fantasy, adventure, westerns, detective. When the pulps folded, he earned grog, gasoline, and groceries by holding two jobs and by filming weddings and practicing astrology in his spare time. Thanks to his incessant motoring, he met and made enduring friendships with Farnsworth Wright, Hugh Rankin, Otis Adelbert Kline, Lovecraft, Howard, W. K. Mashburn, Clark Ashton Smith, Edmond Hamilton, Seabury Quinn, Jack Williamson, Robert Spencer Carr, Leigh Brackett, C. L. Moore, and a comparable number in the nonfantasy fields.

Since early 1965, Price has been known in San Francisco's Chinatown as Tao Fa, the *dharma* name conferred by Venerable Yen Pei of Singapore, and he is mentioned in prayers every new moon and full moon in two Taoist-Buddhist temples. As a gourmet, he cooks shark fin soup, sautées *bêche-de-mer* with black mushrooms, and steams "tea-smoked" duck. He declares that in addition to silk, gunpowder, and the magnetic compass, beautiful women were invented in China. Doubters are invited to meet him at dawn, on horse or afoot, with sword or pistol.